THE CONSTANT IMAGE

A season's love affair—there seemed little possibility of harm in it. Indeed Harriet Piers, young, pretty and American, spending the winter by invitation in Milan, intended it to be no more than an episode, perfect by its very transience, in the winter's brilliant social round. So did Carlo Dalverio.

But neither reckoned on the strength their passion for each other would acquire. And Harriet had not calculated the power of an old and sophisticated society to enforce the rights of family against the lawless claims of love.

Two traditions, two civilizations, meet in a conflict which demands of the lovers far greater fortitude and understanding than they could ever have imagined would be required of them.

THE CONSTANT IMAGE

MARCIA DAVENPORT

A New Portway Book

CHIVERS PRESS
BATH

First published 1960
by
Collins
This edition published
by
Chivers Press
by arrangement with the author
at the request of
The London & Home Counties Branch
of
The Library Association
1987

ISBN 0 86220 574 3

British Library Cataloguing in Publication Data

Davenport, Marcia
  The constant image.
  I. Title
  813'.52[F]   PS3507.A66515

  ISBN 0–86220–574–3

Printed and bound in Great Britain by
Redwood Burn Ltd, Trowbridge, Wiltshire

Alla cara amica
NELLA
con affetto e riconoscenza

For such as I am all true lovers are,
Unstaid and skittish in all motions else
Save in the constant image of the creature
That is belov'd.   TWELFTH NIGHT

One

THE LAST moment before the house went dark was pure enchantment. All had been splendour and brilliance, laughter and gossip, amidst the loveliest colours of festivity, white and gold and scarlet. The solemn, classic *maschere*, black-clad and white-gloved, with their silver chains of office, were showing the last comers to their places; then the lights went slowly down, changing the mood of the audience as they faded. Attention was turning from beautiful heads and shoulders, smiling faces, jewels, marvellous gowns and gloves, precious furs thrown back on the white-and-gold chairs, with chatter and eager scrutiny running like an electric charge round and round the tiers of boxes, up and down between boxes and stalls. The murmuring and rustling faded with the lights until at the moment of extreme beauty, the last lights gleaming softly in the red silken depths of the boxes, with all the rest perfectly dark and the audience perfectly silent, magic was wrought before a note was played.

Harriet Piers loved this moment keenly. To her it was still new, but one could see La Scala a thousand times, she thought; feel it, rather, for that was its true effect, and never be less moved. It brought always the same sharp sense of a missed breath, the impulse to name the moment with some word drawn from all one's experience of beauty. But the word eluded her. She sat very still in her corner of Lydia Marchisi's box, her hands crossed in her lap, only her eyes

9

slowly circling the house. They did not pause at the Dalverio box a short way along the tier to her right. Both parties had gaily exchanged bows on taking their places. That is enough for now, she thought, there are three intermissions coming, I don't know yet about those. She knew that Carlo Dalverio, standing in the dark back of his wife's box, was looking at her. He had a way of looking at a woman as suggestive as a touch of the fingers, and since meeting the Dalveri a few weeks ago Harriet Piers had been at pains to seem unaware of this look when he turned it upon her. But whether he knew it or not he had touched her imagination, which informed her of his glance upon her shoulders, her arms, the nape of her neck, trailing a faint chill of pleasure overlaid by doubt; a prudent doubt, a poised one, but nacre nonetheless, a cold, pearly enclosure for the fragile thing inside. She knew this even while she really preferred not to know it; she sat thinking, perhaps I know too much, for I know too that Pina Dalverio is also looking at me, which she can do without turning her head. And she would not do that without a reason. She feels, she senses or suspects something; but what has she been given to suspect?

Nothing; Harriet Piers reminded herself that a bit of play was part and parcel of everybody's life here, a game played by well-defined rules. Her looks and her manner belied her inexperience of this, she had never played at it, but she had seen and heard enough to resolve that she must seem to be skilled if she should be challenged to a match. Nobody wants to be clumsy and a bore; she wanted to enjoy her stay here, she also wanted no trouble. This, if it came her way, she would have to play like certain other games where the best approach was cool assurance, even bluff, which could carry a reasonably clever person through the early rounds while he was privately taking lessons and studying the book.

She watched the conductor threading his way between the woodwinds and fiddles and stepping up to his place, she joined in the polite spatter of applause; she thought, in the last instant before his poised hands brought out the crashing chords which part the curtains on *Otello*, they all say that Carlo Dalverio flirts with everyone, that it means nothing, it is a bubble like those always bobbing about in the air here. How much better must his wife know it than I! She's been married to him for a dozen years.

She wanted to pay attention to the opera free of these distractions; the chorus was thrilling, the scene a masterpiece, the terror of the storm really believable, the voices superlative. Milano had vibrated with anticipation of this newly-mounted *Otello* on which the Scala had lavished its best, and now on Santo Stefano the gala audience settled down to listen with the concentration of real *intenditori*. For a fortnight past no influence or money could have procured a seat for the sold-out house. Harriet Piers had wanted very much to be here and was overjoyed when Lydia Marchisi invited her; even the oldest friendship would not take such an invitation for granted. Her gown was as spectacular as the other creations around her, her hair as beautifully done, her jewels as fine if not so bold and lavish as those of her neighbours, and on leaving her flat she had laughed as Angela held her white mink jacket for her.

"What a lovely fur!" said the maid with shining eyes, touching it gently.

"Yes," said Harriet Piers. "I thought so last year when I bought it in New York. But it will look like rabbit compared with lots of other furs to-night."

This was true and it amused and pleased her. She had been here long enough to taste the savour of Milanese life, but not long enough to become critical of it. She might come to that one day if she should remain here, but she had no plans to stay; no real plans at all. It was enough to be spending the winter here, mostly because of the rare luck that a friend of Lydia Marchisi's was going to Buenos Aires for five months and had suggested that Harriet Piers take her charming flat, complete with Angela, since she seemed to enjoy Milano so much. It had come about so pleasantly and casually that the absence of any real purpose in it was irrelevant. Harriet Piers was enjoying her stay immensely, delighting in the easy hospitality and friendliness of the people she met, thrilled with the music, proud of her progress in Italian, revelling in the lovely clothes, the delicious food, the impromptu way in which meetings and gatherings came about; one found oneself with gay groups at luncheon or cocktails or late suppers after the opera almost without knowing how. But she had not reckoned with the kind of tiny playing-with-fire which almost any meeting with any charming man might ignite; if a bachelor had chanced to strike this tinder Harriet Piers would have responded with carefree enthusiasm.

As it was, she believed that Pina Dalverio had taken alarm, and taken alarm when—she searched her own mind—she hasn't reason to do. But she is jealous. This was a thing to be sensed exactly as one smelt the faintest wisp of smoke; and jealousy was something that Harriet Piers did know all about. Jealousy had buffeted her own youthful marriage and harried it, tempestuous and undisciplined, to its end a year ago. She imagined that there was nothing she could understand more keenly than another woman's jealousy, and she of all people had the least desire to arouse it. Of course, she knew, each woman's breaking point in this respect may differ. For a time she made an effort to put this out of mind and do justice to the music she had so wanted to hear. She was disturbed suddenly by the coincidence that all this should touch her while she was listening to *Otello*. One needn't carry imagery that far! But she did not lightly dismiss the awareness that this was a world very different from her own, and that jealousy as a detonator might precipitate very different results.

The Iago was magnificent. He was well into the drinking-song, the tempo was full of drive, the scene of excitement; his chromatic scales slid like icicles down her spine, and Harriet Piers was lost at last.

Carlo Dalverio usually stood through most of the performance. He was a man of intense, driving physical energy which only escaped manifestation as restlessness because it was controlled by so much disciplined grace. It was less trying for him to stand, lightly balanced, arms folded, than to sit on one of the narrow lateral benches in the back of the box, scrupulously reconstructed in their original form like everything else in the theatre. He would not have changed them, nor the obstructive but beautiful partitions between the boxes, designed for the subtle privacies of the eighteenth century; nor the ladies' chairs, placed as much to display their occupants as to command the stage; he would have changed nothing, and like everybody else in Milano he was as proud of the miraculous reconstruction as they had all been of the original. He had been standing at the opera all his life, first in his mother's box and now in his wife's. The chairs and stools were always occupied. Pina would have felt denuded in a half-empty box, and when the opera was some cacophonous modern work which guests were not eager to hear, there was an inexhaustible supply of relatives who were happy to come. He liked it so, he was used to it, he and Pina had lived all their lives among crowds of family.

He stood looking over the heads of his wife, of the Contessa Bettoncini from Vicenza with her daughter Maria Chiara, and of Pina's dearest friend, Riri Minghetti, a widow who bored him to tears. Back of them were crowded the Conte Bettoncini, Carlo's friend Gigi Santangelo from Torino, and a young man invited for Maria Chiara. There were two more here than even Pina usually attempted, but it was a gala and nobody minded. They were so crowded, in fact, that Carlo Dalverio laughed silently because there was barely room to turn one's head and nobody would glance at him to observe that he stood with his eyes fixed on Harriet Piers.

He saw her face in profile as she sat watching the stage. He studied her head, small and classically shaped, with its cap of dark, shining hair cut close, lying in well-shaped tendrils against the nape of her neck. He liked women to be extremely chic, no new mode was too extreme to entertain him; but he was amused and admiring that this pretty American had calmly resisted what she called the eggbeater school of hair-dressing and battled it out with the best coiffeur in Milano to keep her distinctive head exactly as it was. She had a mind of her own, they all had; some of the evidences of their wilfulness and independence were in fact irritating. Slightly as he knew her, he had not failed to notice certain of these signs in her. But other things mattered more; she was original, different, refreshing; whatever she was doing here all alone, and it was a strange thing for a woman to do, she had sufficient money and style to do it with flair, and friends enough to keep her charmingly on the scene.

The real question about her, though, was too challenging for a man to ignore. Why was she really here? In Dalverio's view there could be but one answer and if it existed, its identity must be known to someone among his intimates, for in Milano such a thing did not remain a secret. Yet nobody had the answer; Dalverio had not been alone in seeking it; and from every aspect he had concluded that the almost impossible must be true. So if nobody had yet claimed the benefit of this delightful creature's presence, and before somebody else does, he thought, why might it not as well be me? He had been moving subtly towards this aim in the course of meetings amidst his friends and Pina's, at his own house, at the Marchisi, at cocktails and impromptu parties in the evening. As far as he knew, Pina liked Harriet Piers and so did the other women who had met her—or so they all would until they had reason not to. But three days ago was the first time that he had dropped in alone at her flat for a drink at seven o'clock.

" Oh," she exclaimed, when he appeared. " I thought you said you and Pina were coming by on your way to dinner."

" So I did. I was telephoning from my office." He stood for a moment looking down at her. She was seated on a low tufted divan with one foot tucked under her. She had a most intriguing face, saucy and animated, the strong chin softened by a tender, sensitive mouth; and those beautiful American teeth! Her nose was straight and short, her forehead wider than one saw in Italian beauties, and her eyes he thought wonderful—pale grey thickly fringed with lashes darker than her hair, deep-set under level, black brows. These arched with amusement, or was it mischief, when he said, " I hope you haven't telephoned Pina meanwhile? "

" I thought of it."

" A pious idea. Of course it would have been a disaster."

" Really? Would she mind? "

" Hah!" He went to pour her the whisky and soda she had indicated and returned with a glass also for himself.

" I thought you only drank vermouth or bitter," she said.

" At midday. We are taking to all your American habits as fast as we can."

" Including the bad ones. I've never heard such trash as the stuff on the radio here. I'm always trying to find some good music."

" Don't tell me. It isn't the music you're staying in Milano for? I couldn't bear it. Oh, those girls who come to study singing, those drears yearning around La Scala."

" Thank you. Of course, that's just why I'm here."

" Yes, I did think so, you've every qualification. Including the bad skin and the spectacles."

" Now, Carlo, that's cruel. Just because there are a few like that——"

" Very well, then, why are you here? "

She smiled; she had a radiant smile. " Because I like it. I'm having a perfectly wonderful time."

" But where? With whom? When? "

" Well, right now, for example, with you."

" If you like to play with me——"

" Of course I like to play. But perhaps I don't know all the rules."

" One learns them quickly."

" Or else." They laughed.

" It is very unusual, just the same," he said. " Pretty

Americans and English like to stay in Rome. Venice. Florence, probably." He made a sarcastic face. " But here? I don't even see why you came in the first place. Ugly, bustling, bourgeois Milano. Full of industry and commerce. Not the real Italy, my dear, none of the——"

" *Dolce far niente,*" she chanted. " Architecture and atmosphere and fascinating men with nothing to do but make love."

" The book, complete. *Allora?* "

" I came to visit Lydia who is my oldest friend. We were babies together, at school together, came out together, we were never apart until the year she married Sandro and came here and I've scarcely seen her since. So when I could come——"

" When you were free to, you mean? "

" I came. I was with them at the Lake in September and October and then I came here with her for a bit. Then it happened about this flat and I decided I'd like nothing better for the winter. I didn't want to overstay my welcome. Sandro might have got bored."

" Eh? " He looked at her sidelong.

" Oh, nonsense. Can't you people ever think of anything else? Lydia's my dearest friend, I just told you."

He threw back his head and shouted with laughter.

" Very well," she said, resigned. " I had a frantic flirt with my best friend's husband so she threw me out."

" It happens all the time."

" I suppose it does. But Lydia is American and——"

" No! " He leaned forward, his brown eyes wide with derision. " You mean to say that human nature is altogether different in America? And I've noticed nothing ever happens to people's marriages there . . ."

B

" Well, nothing is going to happen to Lydia's here. It's a good one, the best I ever saw."

He was careful not to let her know he had heard the banter go out of her voice, and something wistful come in.

" Lydia is a very good wife," he said seriously. " Is Sandro faithful to her? "

" How should I know? Lydia wouldn't talk about it if he weren't. You said yourself, she's a good wife."

" A good Italian wife, what's more." He wagged a finger in the air. " That is not so easy for an American."

" A lot of us are married to a lot of you."

" And it is either very good, or impossible, don't you think? "

" I don't know enough to think," she said demurely.

He changed the subject. To-morrow was Christmas Eve, and he asked her how she was spending it. He had rather hoped that Pina might think to invite Harriet Piers on Christmas afternoon, or at some convivial point, but Pina on holidays was wholly immersed in family. He had already decided better not suggest anything himself.

"Oh, Lydia's asked me, of course," said Harriet. " They're even going to the Duomo to-morrow night instead of to their own church, so that 1 can see the midnight Mass there; and I'm to spend Christmas Day with them. I really do worry lest Sandro get fed up with me. And they've asked me to La Scala the next day—I think it's too much. But they're such darlings, so cosy and hospitable."

" Sandro is doing you no favours, my dear. If it's true that he's resisted temptation, then he thinks of you as a sister of Lydia's just some more family, of which he has the usual supply. But I've known Sandro all my life," he said doubtfully, " and——"

"You haven't known me, though." Her clear eyes sparkled, a fresh and charming oddity, he thought, with such dark hair. Her hair and her pale brunette skin, her strong eyebrows, could easily have been Italian and they gave him a sense of ease, they mitigated the feeling of entire strangeness; but those eyes, light in colour and deep in mood, witty but inscrutable, yet innocent; those strange eyes might be the key to he did not know what. Ah, well! He rose and sat down lightly on the divan beside her. "I hope to change that," he said, and laid his fine brown hand along her shoulders. Her neck was cool and creamy, the short curled ends of her hair unexpectedly crisp; his fingers played with them for an instant; then his other hand lifted her face to his and he kissed her with a quick sense of surprise. Any new venture has its own novel flavour but he had never before sensed this curious freshness, a quality of delicacy or fragrance which he knew to be essential; it was she herself, nothing which came from scent or art or artifice. She was not eager, her mood was tentative, but she did not draw away. He spread his hands across her neck and down her shoulders, drawing her closer for another kiss, holding her for a moment with strength and lightness, careful not to unleash real passion, the time for which might be quite far away. A clock struck eight.

"*Dio!*" he said, springing up, "I've stayed too long." She rose to see him out, laughing. "Why are you amused?" he asked, taking his overcoat from the cupboard in the gaily painted entrance hall. He stood waiting for her answer.

"It's too silly," she murmured. "No real reason."

"Yes, there is," he said. He put a finger under her chin. "You are thinking, 'This is how he usually spends this time of day'—or something of the sort. Is that not so?"

She laughed again. " You are going to be late."

" Dreadful. At my mother-in-law's, too. Shall I come again? "

" I should like it," she said. " But——"

" I know."

" I like your wife very much. She's been charming to me. I like everything here." She might as well have asked him outright not to spoil it all.

" One needn't be clumsy," he said.

" One isn't planning to be. Or planning anything at all."

" But I will come sometimes. After——" He waved at a heap of packages in Christmas wrappings, her gifts for Lydia and her children. " We will see you on the twenty-sixth." He kissed her hand and hurried away.

Towards the end of the first act, the love scene that he admired as much for Boito's inspired adaptation of Shakespeare as for Verdi's most thrilling erotic music, he put his attention on the stage. It was a good performance, all the brouhaha of recent weeks was justified. Perhaps the old folk were right; they had been saying that their memories of Toscanini and Tamagno, Maurel and Pantaleoni, would diminish the best that this present production could attain. If so, Dalverio saw this as reason to enjoy whatever one could in the world as one found it. He was too young to have known the great days, and so better able to stay in step with these times. Pina was different, she had been born in a family fanatical about music, the Verocchi who had been pillars and patrons of La Scala even since its inception. Her mother could—*purtroppo*, did!—recount and linger over every name, every detail, every anecdote of the casts and the happenings of forty and fifty years ago. She and her husband had been off on a chain of reminiscences about *Otello* when he hurried in, late for dinner, the other evening; and Pina, he saw at once, had not been listening, but wondering where he was. There were certain patterns which long habit had designed for such occasions, and both followed them automatically, but with caution. His greeting to her was skilfully modulated. If it were too casual, she would be resentful; if too affectionate, suspicious. He took the middle course and, his lateness glossed over, they all went in to dinner.

Christmas Eve and Christmas Day, packed with children, their own and those of all their brothers and sisters, along with assorted parents and grandparents, aunts, uncles, cousins, and the rest, had intervened; he had not been free for a moment. But now, as he stood facing the lovers on the stage, he saw that Pina in the hostess's chair was watching the boxes to her left, which she could do with less effort than to sit in the classic position faced round to her right. She was perfectly still and nobody else would have supposed she was not absorbed in the music. Her husband saw instead that she was steadily watching Harriet Piers.

Accidenti! he thought; now why? I haven't given her reason enough—or yet—to begin to be jealous. Is her imagination at work? If so, it had better stop right here. If she's going to jump to that even before I've so much as dabbled in the water! He was puzzled. He could remember incidents in the past which had gone as far as possible, to the extent of his own boredom and withdrawal, before Pina even guessed or found out or was told by some gabbling cow. This was different. He saw suddenly from her viewpoint too; why should this pretty American woman appear here all alone, if not to make mischief? How could her presence fail to stir everybody up? He bit his lips thoughtfully. Pina so far was simply keeping step with his own reactions.

Along to the left, Harriet Piers sighed with delight as the lovers turned, clinging together, to their nocturnal ecstasy, and the curtains fell on the darkened scene. The audience began to rise and stir. Lydia said, " Shall we walk or sit? " Some of the women in the boxes chose one and some the other. The younger ones liked to go to the Ridotto to parade and show their costumes, observe those of others, chatter and smoke; the rest, usually the grandes dames and dowagers, kept the old custom of sitting still and receiving callers.

" Whichever you like, darling," said Harriet. " You look so beautiful I'm sure Sandro wants to show you off." Lydia was wearing a gown of stiff, pale, water-green moiré embroidered with diamanté and pearls and corals, her bosom and shoulders rose white as foam from the sea-like fantasy and her fair hair capped it like a sunlit cloud. Diamonds and emeralds illuminated her neck and ears and arms; she was affirming her fame as the most beautiful blonde in Italy, and Harriet had a fleeting vision of what might have been— Lydia married to the moody young Princeton man who had been her first love. He had published one avant-garde novel and spent the next six years on a second one. Sandro, thought Harriet, may be a Milanese materialist but he's made a work of art out of Lydia and got an adoring wife and three delightful children for his pains.

They rose to go out. Harriet saw the Dalverio party doing the same. She was relieved, she did not want Pina Dalverio to stay behind while her husband circulated. She took her fur from old Dottore Tremezzi, the celebrated expert of the Brera, on whose board Alessandro Marchisi had sat for years.

The party was completed by Sandro's brother with his wife. They moved out to the corridor and up the stairs to the glittering white and crystal Ridotto, Harriet chatting with Dottore Tremezzi and marvelling at the spectacle of beauty enhanced by aggressively vigorous wealth. But presently she heard, " *Ah, buona sera!* " in Pina Dalverio's pleasant voice. " *Piacere . . .*" people said. " *Che bella serata! . . . buona sera . . . piacere . . .*"

Lydia had drifted ahead on her husband's arm, introductions were made, small-talk bobbed in the air. Carlo Dalverio bowed over her gloved hand with a conventional greeting and Harriet, turning to speak to someone, did not even catch his eye.

Two

THE TELEPHONE began to ring at half-past eight next morning. Harriet Piers struggled out of a sound sleep, rolled over, groaned, stretched, said, " Oh, God! " and picked up the telephone. " *Pronto!* " she sighed.

" *Ciao, tesoro!* " came gaily to her ear. It was Tia Ortolani, full of sparkle and ready to gossip. She was one of a few women who began their day at this ungodly hour, probably not so much because their husbands went to their offices at half-past eight as because they were of restless temperament. Harriet was used to the late mornings of a New York existence but she was eager to adapt herself here to anything that came her way in friendliness and sociability. She arranged her face in a convincing smile, she wanted this to carry over the wires. At home she always slept until half-past nine or ten and nobody would think of telephoning until much later. But she had had no children to get her up early and no job like many of her friends. The women she knew here did not have to deal like most Americans with their children's dressing and breakfasts, but a few were awake to see them before they started for school, and an occasional one, like Tia Ortolani, was merely supercharged with energy.

Everybody was " *tesora* " too. Harriet had been listening carefully for three months to the rapid-fire of Milanese chatter, and to this word so clearly the equivalent of the

24

British and American " darling " which also did not mean a thing. What did they say, she wondered, when they had need of a real term of endearment?

" So you will come to luncheon," said Tia Ortolani, " and I will tell you the rest because it was very entertaining." She had been describing the encounter of the Marchesa Paracelso last night with her husband's mistress, who was wearing a diamond clip which the Marchesa had relinquished only because her husband had said he could not afford the new bracelet his wife wanted unless he turned in the clip on the transaction. " And now he has to buy her another clip, bigger than Rosina's, and pay for the bracelet too—*dimmi te!* " and she rang off. Harriet wondered whether it would be any use to try to go back to sleep, but Angela appeared with her coffee and the *Corriere* and her letters. She had tried once or twice to explain to Angela that she did not always want to be roused so early but Angela somehow never believed her.

There was no use, either, in keeping to her usual breakfast of fruit and buttered toast and sometimes an egg; how on earth could she face a midday dinner a few hours later? It was easier to take what Angela was used to providing—one little cup of black coffee strong enough to rouse a corpse, and a dry little rusk which went to show that the Italians could produce something unfit to eat if they put their minds to it. There had been difficulty about the orange juice which Harriet decided she would not do without. To Angela it was a *bibita*, a soft drink; she served it with sugar, with water, with soda, with ice; she could not understand that the Signora meant to drink undiluted the juice of two or three oranges every morning. Her liver! And the cost! In vain Harriet Piers assured her, smiling, that all Americans did this, even the babies a few weeks old; Angela rolled her eyes piously.

Harriet opened a letter from her mother in New York. Mrs. Murdoch was taking a waspish view of this spending the winter in Italy, and Harriet sighed as she read. " You are missing everything," her mother wrote, " and getting out of touch . . . if you had any *reason* for staying over there, anything that would *prove* something . . ."

It was too easy to interpret, it was a patched net designed to trap her in exactly what she was enjoying her escape from. " Everything " was the usual series of benefit parties and subscription balls for fashionable charities, whose committees were composed of Mrs. Murdochs and their married, or divorced, daughters; a big way, thought Harriet irritably, of keeping oneself on the scene. A *reason*, in her mother's underlined scrawl, for being away; anything that would *prove* something . . . Mrs. Murdoch was vexed because there was nothing one could do to force a twenty-nine-year-old daughter with money of her own to decide quickly on another husband. Mrs. Murdoch herself was the widow of a third spouse (two previously divorced) who had left her dowered heavily enough to live in a luxurious residential hotel without a care in the world. Having made three different fresh starts in her life, each time discarding the furnishings tangible and intangible of a previous identity; sending to auction along with the chairs and the china some part of herself, brushing out old memories and associations like the trash she held them to be, she fitted perfectly the setting designed for her by the cleverest and most expensive interior decorator of the moment. Such rooms were not intended for the heights and the depths of anybody's interior life, they appealed in their glabrous elegance to those who flitted on the surface; and

Mother, thought Harriet Piers, is most certainly a flitter. I don't want to be. I don't know on the other hand just what I do want, but I am very lucky to have the time and money with which to find out.

Here was the telephone again; this time Carlo Dalverio.

" Are you awake? " he asked, with a hint of intimacy in his voice.

" Just keep talking," said Harriet, " and that will answer your question."

" You were beautiful last night. I took the greatest pleasure in looking at you."

" I'd no idea," she said.

" None, of course. That was plain. How soon am I to see you? "

" Where are you calling from, by the way? That double-talk from your office. . . ."

" From a pay-telephone in the Bar Tozzi, one door from the——"

" Yes, do explain. I might need the address some time."

" But when do I see you? To-day? "

" It's rather short notice."

" Why? "

" Why not? "

If I let him come, she thought, I'm not going to encourage him much. I don't want to be another of his toys. And there is the feeling I first had before the opera last night; it's like a little bell ringing. Pina was particularly cordial in the inter-missions, more than ever before, there was a kind of polish to it. Harriet said, " I hadn't planned to be in this afternoon, truly." There was a pause. He said, " Pina is going to ask you to luncheon to-morrow."

Harriet waited a moment. She said quietly, " Are you sure she wants me? "

" Do you mean, did I suggest it? "

" No, of course not. But did you? "

" No. Pina likes you and you've been with us before. Why shouldn't she? "

" I feel, I mean——"

She heard him laughing. " Cara," he said, " you make me say it. Do you think this is the first time Pina has ever dealt with "—he paused—" things? "

" My word, it's flattering," said Harriet with derision. " I'm so flattered I'm simply purring."

" Don't be preoccupied about it. Come to lunch and *buon divertimento*."

" The same to you. I will."

" And I may not come this evening? "

" Not *this* evening."

" Another, then. To-morrow."

" *Vediamo*."

" You are only playing with me! "

" And you? "

" *Brava*. I shall telephone to-morrow. The next day, every morning."

" The dear Bar Tozzi, your home from home——"

" What is your programme to-day? " he asked.

" Carlo, I can't give you an account of my time! "

" Women should."

" You'd die of boredom if they did."

" That depends on the woman. Where will you be at——? "

" Why? "

" One might meet, by chance."

" Not even by chance. That's enough now, there's always to-morrow."

" To-day is better."

" Good-bye," said Harriet, laughing.

By the time she had spoken to Lydia, and Pina Dalverio had telephoned her invitation to luncheon to-morrow, she had just time to dress before going to her daily lesson in Italian. " And as for your learning Italian," her mother had written, " I never heard such nonsense. What earthly use will it ever be to you? "

Harriet did not know and had not thought of it in that light. But what was the point of this sojourn if she were too indolent to pay her friends the compliment of learning their language, something well within her powers? How could one have the least sense of grace if one remained, like some Americans she had seen here, an unmalleable lump obstructing the flow and play of talk, forcing on their hosts the strictures of polite banality? Besides, Italian was beautiful and it was fun.

It pleased her that she could already chat and banter in it even when some people she knew, like Carlo, enjoyed speaking English. His was perfect; she wondered where he had learnt it; and she reflected how completely unacquainted with him she really was. This added piquancy to the soap-bubbles that they had begun to blow about, a harmless pastime if only she could keep it where she wished it. And while one part of her mind, dyed in the vat of her own murky experience, recognised an uneasy sympathy with Pina, another part rationalised that this was Pina's fate in marriage and that if Harriet herself were not the present object of Carlo's divertissement, somebody else would be.

There was a third member of her mind's equipage who

was busily posing her a question which she did not wish to answer even in such privacy; she had tried unsuccessfully to evade it. Just why, this irritating busybody kept demanding, was she hovering at all on the brink of a flirtation with a flamboyantly engaging stranger who was another woman's husband and whom, for every motive of taste and recent memory, she would really prefer to reject? Her answer to herself was halting and she was discomfited to find that she had an answer at all. But it existed, and to so honest a mind as hers it was impossible not to recognise.

She was curious; that was but natural. She was flattered, her desirability was being insistently confirmed by a recognised connoisseur, and she had never been flattered with this degree of suavity before. She would have enjoyed the assurance that she could continue to command the attention without having to pay its price, but she was realist enough to know that that would be impossible. And while she had been present here and there at the foreign scene with a good deal of grace for a number of years past, she had never really participated in it; she had been a spectator. The wish at this time to find herself on the other side of the footlights was surprisingly strong; it teased and intrigued her, and she could not imagine a more fascinating partner with whom to take the first steps—always remembering that it was a play, a permissible play in which most members of this society were or had been or would be at some time actors themselves. One must—how many times had she heard it! —abide by the rules, and there should be no awkward consequences. Was she to confess herself too gauche and too provincial to match all the others?

Going to her bath she stopped for a moment at the window and stood there in her nightdress surveying the element of sheer nastiness which overhung existence here like a minute quantity of arsenic in a stimulating tonic: the winter weather. One could die of it in one way or another and every year many people did. Right now it was scarcely any lighter outside than when Angela two hours ago had raised the heavy roll shutters. Though the flat was high enough in a pleasant building off the Piazza Sant' Erasmo to command a view of the Madonnina on an ordinary day, Harriet could not have seen her hand had she put it outside the window. For five months of the year this city and a vast area surrounding it lived in this nearly unrelieved dungeon of dark and fog, with which its people came to terms by shrugging it off. Aside from the rarity of an occasional clear day the only respite from the fog was streaming rain; when it rained there was no fog. A fine alternative; any way you found it everybody cheerfully agreed that the weather was hell. But the houses she went to were heated as warmly as even an American could wish, sometimes the fog lifted for a little while in the middle of the day, and millennia of this filthy climate had not spoilt the smiling dispositions and ready humour of the Milanesi.

In his office Carlo Dalverio studied a calendar. On Friday, the day after to-morrow, he and Pina were to take the children as usual to Cortina for the remaining ten days of their Christmas holiday. He himself, passionately fond of winter sport, would have preferred to go before Christmas but he would never have dared suggest that to Pina, voluntarily immobilised by the tribal traditions of the Verocchi which bound them in a ritual of gatherings at his own house, at her parents', at her sister's, her brothers', her Zio Massimo's. He never thought of one or another apart, it was like a polenta, too many-grained and too cohesive to separate. Then none of them would think of missing Santo Stefano at La Scala, and he himself usually required an intervening day or two to go over the year-end inventories and balance-sheets of his factories, the four wire mills and metal-processing plants strung between Bergamo and Lecco, which had grown so amazingly in the years since the war. They were no longer a one-family business, they were corporate; but his uncles and cousins, his widowed mother, his sister, his younger brothers, and he held most of the shares. Other industrial elements, woven in through marriages and heavy investments, some conservative and far-sighted, some sheerly daring, had broadened the complex and pyramided the Dalverio holdings, whose administration lay in the hands of Carlo in Milano. But the family were Bergamaschi by origin, of the mettle which had sent a grand-father to join Garibaldi in 1859 and to Sicily in 1860 among the youths who made that from Bergamo the single largest contingent of the hallowed Thousand. The Dalveri eschewed the sentimentality of talk about this cornerstone of family pride, but it pervaded their robust bourgeois spirit. Certain titled people had a tendency, now waning, to be snobbish about them, but such lines were fast becoming eroded by time and the restless force of money. Milano and all of Lombardy hummed with participation in the present; the past was a mellowing circumambience.

Carlo Dalverio's finger toyed with the cut-off switch on his private telephone. Of course it was a ridiculous fiction through which he assumed Harriet Piers had seen, that he could not speak from his office without being overheard. He had tossed off that phrase about Pina and himself the other evening as the surest way of overcoming any initial reluctance she might have shown about receiving him alone. A hoary trick, he sighed; but how am I to do the more difficult one of taking the family for the ski-ing I so much want myself, and also be in town to profit by their absence? It might, though, still be too soon for that . . . his expression was doubtful, there were novel factors to weigh. Expedients and alternatives began to chase one another through the narrower alleys of his brain, while he held its broad main avenue clear for concentration on the thick report in the folder before him.

Presently he looked up and stared across the room. For an instant he pulled at his lower lip, an unconscious habit which might or might not have had something to do with the slight heaviness of that lip, a sign of stubborn will and quick passion at once disciplined by the firm modelling of the upper lip; the whole mouth and chin were clear, sharply cut in unison with the straight nose, the lean cheeks, the fine eyes and brows, the moderate forehead above which the brown hair grew in the symmetry which informs the special beauty of many Italians, both men and women; their heads. Dalverio was weighing something; his eyebrows moved, almost as if in argument one with the other; then he shrugged, lighted a cigarette, and dialled the private number of his closest friend, partner and adviser in innumerable ventures, the banker Rinaldo Ortolani.

The Ortolani lived in the *piano nobile* of their ancestral palace, which was completely hidden from the commonplace street of their address. Trams clanged up and down, traffic roared, scooters and motor-cycles made their nerve-torturing noise. One came to an ugly nineteenth-century structure with a furrier's shop on one side of the entrance and a

c

picture-framer's on the other. It was dingy and brown and not even in very good repair. But it was only one room deep, a shell. Through the centre arch lay the courtyard, nobly proportioned, decked with wonderful wrought-iron and colonnaded with tenderly weathered marble. It was so planted that even now there were angles cushioned with the green of ilex and juniper, and at every season some blooming or leafy luxuriance belied the ugliness outside. The baroque palace of yellow plaster, its pedimented windows garlanded by faded stencilled frescoes, faced this tranquil court, and through the great centre doors of glass, covered only at night by the massive *portone*, one glimpsed the astonishing garden, a broad park with ancient trees, which lay on the farther side.

All this, Harriet noted, in the very heart of Milano where the land must be worth a fortune inch by inch; but while she was parking her little car she thought, Ah, yes! such a property would be a National Monument, nobody would be permitted to break up any part of it. Its owners could enjoy it and profit from any use they chose to make of it short of changing its structure; and no such family would part with it in any generation. She reflected upon the nature of this median between the confiscatory socialism of England which booted its old families from their homes and put the houses to the drab egalitarian uses of the day, and the merciless force of " progress " for profit in the United States, which tore down the fine houses and spawned millions of venture-capital rabbit-warrens in their place. The trouble was, she told herself, that both other worlds held probabilities of political stability not inherent in this one—but the Italians are unrivalled at sheer survival; and in any case, this is not the moment, nor am I the person, to ponder these things. She spoke to the smiling portress at her little window, who

said that the Signora was expected; and crossed the court
to the glass doors where a red-jacketed manservant waited
to admit her and usher her up the exquisite mosaic stairs.

" *Ah, ecco la bella!* " cried Tia Ortolani, as the man threw
open the door of the salon and Harriet walked into a bright
pool of laughter and chatter. It was not that there were so
many people but that they were all talking at once. Harriet
was given a glass of Campari while greetings were exchanged;
this was not a party, just friends whom she already knew,
members of the circle into which Lydia Marchisi had intro-
duced her. Lydia and Sandro were here, unusually for them,
as they preferred to lunch at home with their children; and
three or four others, a cousin from Rome, Tia's bosom friend
Detta Moroni and her husband, the Ortolanis' handsome
University son, on crutches from a ski accident at St. Moritz.
Tia's juicy bit about the widely disliked Paracelso woman
had been capped by a hilarious morsel of new scandal just
surfacing from the deep sea of erstwhile secrecy, and everybody revelled.

" And so you are liking it? " her host asked, after he had
seated Harriet on his right at luncheon.

" Loving it. I'm still so grateful, and surprised—if you
don't misunderstand—at everyone's hospitality. I hadn't
expected to be taken in amongst you like this."

" What else should you expect? We like beautiful women
and Americans and someone who appears to like us—quite
reasonable, no? "

" Just the same, can you imagine this happening—in
France, for instance? "

" No, but why should I try? "

From round the table they heard, " But she didn't go
there that afternoon, it was somebody else altogether and

the only reason for the fuss was that they both had the same suit from Gandini——"

" *Storie!* Nobody else walks like her! "

" Didn't you see them at St. Moritz, Gogo? They told me——"

" What can you expect, *tesoro*, he's an imbecile."

" Why does everybody copy him then? Look at the——"

" But for weeks, I tell you. Nobody's teeth take that much time——"

" Don't believe her, *cara*, she's never told the truth in her life, I ought to know."

" Fourteen thousand lire the pair! I'm told she gets them for four dollars in New York."

" I can tell you where——"

" You'll see, she'll be back next season, making the same *porcheria*——"

The talk whirled round and round, bouncing, frivolous, like a final pinch of salt or spice in the delectable food. Everything flowed so well together, Harriet thought, answering questions about New York from Gianni Moroni on her right who was soon going there. She was delightedly aware of the fine room with its superlative stucco-work mouldings and coves, the frescoed ceiling, the pale golden damask walls, the prismed girandoles soaring in the corners, their light cancelling the murk outside the beautifully curtained windows; the grave expert men-servants, attentive and precise, who made nonsense of the wail, even here, that servants were not to be had any more. It is absolutely unreal, she told herself, or it would be if it were moved intact to another country; but here it is right, here it is part and parcel of the life these people really live and—she sighed imperceptibly—I could all too easily take to it myself. At the same time some little chord of doubt, twanging faintly in her mind's ear, was echoing the question, what prices other than material ones were paid for all this; and by whom? Harriet was young and not specially wise, but for this she had good sense enough. For every grace and elegance, every facet of beauty and luxury and leisure, someone must yield or give or submit to some discipline; and since the natural temper of the men was to work hard, with the energy and enthusiasm of her own countrymen, who paid the balance of the reckoning after the men had furnished the money? She had seen a good deal of Lydia Marchisi's life in the past three months, and now Pina Dalverio came sharply to her mind, suggesting what was expected of these women, seemingly indulged and spoilt. She admired them keenly even while she knew them in many ways to be quite silly.

Ortolani was enjoying luncheon to-day, enjoying Harriet Piers's laughing talk, spiked with amusing little mistakes which made it charming to hear her speak Italian: she was bright, he saw, for she had picked up all sorts of little phrases and was giving Gianni Moroni a good time too. Ortolani was now not the least surprised about his telephone conversation with Carlo that morning. It had been such a crisp and skipping exchange of fragments as takes place between any two intimate friends, particularly Italians. No names had been mentioned and very little said. The banker at this moment was successfully concealing the rueful reflection that if Carlino hadn't undertaken this extremely interesting venture he would more than delightedly have done so himself. But he was a loyal friend and, in any case, it would be a stupidity to confuse the issue. *Pazienza!*—most things evolved in their own time.

Three

IT WAS almost six o'clock when Harriet let herself into her flat. The early winter dark had fallen two hours ago and with it a fog so vicious that its tendrils probed into the heart of town. Cautiously driving her car home the short distance from Lydia's house where they had gone together after lunch, Harriet thought with horror of the roads surrounding Milano, where the daily toll of fatal accidents filled half a page of the *Corriere;* and of the incredible insouciance of the Italians about this. They had nerves of iron and they prided themselves on rising above every challenge to their brilliant if often reckless driving. For her part, Harriet was relieved to be at home and without plans for the evening. She was looking forward for once to going early to bed, with perhaps a scrambled egg for her supper if she felt hungry enough late in the evening to get up and prepare it. It was not worth while to keep Angela waiting about; she had given her the evening off.

Angela before going out had closed the shutters, drawn the curtains, turned on some of the lights as Harriet, ignoring the maid's silent expostulation at the extravagance, had told her to do; had prepared Harriet's bedroom for the night, and had arranged in the sitting-room a mass of creamy-pink roses which had come during the day. There was no card with the flowers. Harriet bent over them to breathe their fragrance and put her cheek to their petals, dewed with pearls

38

of water and richening in the warm room. I wonder what
he wants me to think that unwritten card would have said,
she thought. I can imagine; but, as she went about hanging
up her coat, pulling off her gloves and eyeing some letters
which awaited her on the hall table, she found herself not
in the mood to imagine. She stood in the doorway of the
sitting-room, slowly looking round it, at the Italian Empire
furniture, the subtle and the dramatic colours, the well-
contrasted textures of smooth and rough silks, velvet, wood,
marble, glass; the enchanting group of old Capodimonte
figurines in their miniature Venetian cabinet. Good things,
beautiful, genuine things which Giulietta Scalero loves and is
not afraid to entrust to me. I like it very much, I am pleased,
it was a good idea to take this flat but—she stood perfectly
still while a feeling loomed, rolling and sweeping higher, even
suggesting the boom and roar, the rough salt savour, of a
great breaker hurtling to a beach—what am I doing here?

This was not the first time the feeling had overtaken her
and she was aware not only that it would not be the last, but
that each time it attacked her anew it would do so with
much greater urgency; she felt its insistence on an answer.
But how can I answer, how can I know? This is all part of
the same void in which I have been suspended for a long
time, and I am under no illusions as to how I wandered
into it. I did it myself. If she chose, she could review in
memory her childish, frangible marriage, sterile and studded
with strife; and also if she chose she could compound a train
of reasons for putting most of the blame on Norton Piers. One
did, said her mother, standing by while the rickety structure
teetered, buckled, cracked, and collapsed. Mrs. Murdoch
was adept at climbing out of this type of débris and springing
neatly to the top of a new and seemingly sound replacement,

strewing blame and epithets on the discarded husbands who were solely in the wrong.

But Harriet was not like her. At these times of troubled and questioning mood she tended increasingly to look the truth in the face and blame herself for five years of waste and futility. There had been seven altogether, but during the first two her husband was away at the Korean War, it had been a hasty marriage on the eve of his departure. Thank God, said Mrs. Murdoch, within a short time of his leaving, that you aren't going to have a baby. You never know about a war, it would be such a bore, darling, if anything happened and you were saddled with a baby. Mrs. Murdoch would have thought it the end, in her chirping vernacular, for some-one to want a child in the very event that her husband might be killed at war. But Harriet herself had no such depths of feeling about Norton Piers at that time, and when he returned home and set about compensating himself for the lost time, money, and pleasure that his country had exacted of him, he did it in a sizable way.

He was successful at business, avid for sport, amusement and motion; he was attractive to women, restless, thought-less and rich. Neither he nor Harriet looked upon their life as a reservoir into which to pour the components of a long and fruitful future. On the contrary, they treated it as a sort of Jack Horner's pie, out of which they pulled the noisy and glittering baubles of an existence as nearly like a continuous party as they could make it. When Harriet's share of the toys proved to be jewels, furs, sports cars, trips to Sun Valley or Nassau, it was all very gay; but when his proved to be pretty women Harriet exploded in tantrums of rage and jealousy, kicking the pie from the table and spoiling the whole scheme of the party.

It is not worth thinking about, she told herself now, as she went to get rid of the mussed-up feeling inevitable at the end of a long city day. She took off her smart grey wool suit, almost the daytime uniform of Milano, deceptively easy in cut, with its supple pullover of shaded soft greys beneath; treed her brown crocodile pumps; whisked off her underclothes, and left the lot in the *guardaroba* where Angela did her laundry, pressing, and sewing. She put on a dressing-gown and started the water for a hot bath, throwing in some borax to counteract the alkalinity of the water and a generous measure of scented drops which filled the room with cosseting fragrance. It is just as luxurious here, she reflected, as the way I have always lived, and in many things more so; but far fewer people here are so indulged, and I have seen enough of the miles of streets outside this select quarter, of the working-class outskirts like Sesto and Niguarda, the industrial towns clustering beyond them, to imagine what the people's homes are like. Dark and cold, she knew, because fuel and electricity were dreadfully expensive; cramped because families stuck together, partly for love and partly to pool their wages and make for all together a better life than their members could have had apart.

Stepping into the water, letting herself be lapped by steaming ripples, she saw the one clear thread which ran straight through this world from top to bottom, one key to every human pattern at every level from the grossly rich to the desperately poor; their family, their love for it which like all real love comprised most other emotions, even to jealousy and hate; their acceptance of its burdens which they regarded without protest or surprise. Perhaps, she mused, perhaps their religion is at the bottom of it, but many of them would deny that, and all are so steeped in their habitude that it would never occur to them to examine its origins.

As a result, she would be hard put to it to stretch her imagination to the concept of an Italian in her own situation: alone. Much of the time the fact did not trouble her, to many Americans it was more or less the norm, and with a mother like hers, certainly so. Her own childlessness was only to be expected in such a marriage as hers had been, but lately she had been looking back with open eyes and recognising deeper reasons for it than the life of selfish extremes, from pleasure to uproar, which she and her husband had lived. It had been easy to rationalise that it would be unfair to a child to bring it into such a situation. But she could put her finger now on other motives, and feel the force of their gravity even while conceding that it was as well no child had had to suffer the least consequence of the mess that she and Norton Piers had made.

This afternoon, lying on one side of Lydia Marchisi's vast double bed, where they had flopped down for their nap after coming in from luncheon, she had had fresh reason to look her own existence squarely in the eye. For a time they had both slept. But Harriet, on waking from that deep velvet sleep of mid-afternoon, which seems more profound than any other and carries deception in its soft sleeves, looked at her watch. Twenty minutes!—and she could have sworn, struggling up from blissful submergence, that it had been ten times as long.

Lydia, in a poem of a negligee, lay on her side, her hands folded beneath her cheek, drawing the deep, regular breaths of a child; and her beauty, free of the monitor which was her use and awareness of it, bloomed as spontaneously as a wildflower. Harriet lay very still on her back, careful not to rouse Lydia, though she smiled at the thought. Sharing this bed for ten years with her husband, Lydia would hardly be disturbed by such a light motion as anything that Harriet would do. But after a time Lydia opened her eyes. The room was nearly dark, these were the shortest days of the year, and half-past four on such an afternoon could look like night. Lydia yawned, stretched, and made a soft sound, too pretty to be called a little grunt. She pressed the bell for her maid who came to close the shutters and curtains and turn on the lights.

" Tea, darling? " she asked Harriet.

" Heavens, no! We've just lunched."

" Not just a cuppa? With nothing to eat? "

" No, really."

" Give me a glass of mineral water," said Lydia to the maid; " and the Signora too."

But when the girl had gone, silently closing the door, Lydia put the full glass on the table and lay back with her arms beneath her head. Harriet still lay without moving, tracing the delicate gilded mouldings of the ceiling with her eyes. It was so pleasant, so much part of a wonderfully agreeable fantasy; this waking just now had startled her briefly while shining little pieces fell into the pattern which told her where she was. But once awake and sharing Lydia's cocoon, it was tempting to slip away again into the stream of lovely unreality. She saw no reason for resisting.

Lydia said presently, in a thoughtful voice, " You know, I shouldn't be surprised if I weren't going to have another baby."

" Oh, darling! " To Harriet this sounded like the most beatific thing a woman could have to tell, but she had heard varying views from other people she knew, and her joyful exclamation became subdued to, " Would you be pleased? "

" I'm pleased with my family as it is," said Lydia slowly. " In all truth, we hadn't intended this, if it's so, but——"

" Would Sandro be happy? "

" Of course. And so would I."

" Because he was happy, or because you would really be yourself ? "

" Both. But there was a time when I mightn't have been. I used to——" She stopped speaking. Harriet did not prompt her. After they had been silent for some time Lydia said, " When I married Sandro I had no idea how much I'd have to change before I could be contented here. I had a lot of trouble in the beginning." She sighed. " So did Sandro. An Italian has no real idea what we are like. So long as he may be playing with one of us it doesn't matter much—but when he marries, that's different. They expect a great deal of their wives."

" Don't most Europeans? In the ways you mean, more than American men? "

" You and I don't know much about most Americans, Harriet. I never thought of that when I was still there. We were born and brought up in a certain way which would be called upper-class in any other country—but that's not said in ours. Women like your mother and my Aunt Kitten and the men they marry—people like you and Norton—that's not typical of American life. But marriage is marriage in Italy."

Harriet was silent, twisting an end of her hair round one finger. " They say themselves that it's changing here too," she said slowly. " You hear about all kinds of messes that people are in."

Lydia waved her hand. " Oh, I know. The Romans, some of the nobility, newspaper names—there are the same rotten spots on top of the pile in every country—on top where they show. But the real thing here is different."

" It's made a tremendous change in you."

" I know it. And I like it, that's what I meant. But it didn't happen all at once. I had to get used to lots of things more worrying than what would happen to my figure if I had a lot of children."

Harriet's eyes slid sideways to Lydia's face; perhaps some change of expression would tell her the answer to Carlo Dalverio's cynical speculations about his friend Sandro. " Lots of things? " she echoed. " Really lots? "

Lydia laughed a little. " It looked like lots to me. Whatever else, it was a lot to learn. What it boiled down to, I suppose, was deciding whether I'd grow up or not— according to Italian ideas. It wouldn't have been any use to cling to American ones. I had to fish or cut bait."

Harriet listened carefully, mentally applying the measure of Lydia's conclusions to her own situation and all that had led up to it. She was rather surprised but gave no sign of it when Lydia said, " Some of the same medicine wouldn't do you any harm either, darling."

For a moment the possibility of some flippant reply hung on Harriet's lips and died there. This whole conversation had turned unwontedly admonitory even as between the most intimate of friends; it was probing an area where Harriet knew herself to be indefensible and she did not propose the dishonesty of denying it. She said, " I know. I refused to fish or cut bait even at the level of marriage to Norton Piers. It's the most dreadful sensation of waste, Lydia, nothing but those burnt-out years. We're the same age, you and I."

" It wouldn't have done to have had a child in the circumstances."

" That's the way I explained it to myself. But——"

They were silent for a time, while Lydia gingerly tried the experiment of lighting a cigarette, thought better of it, and laughed. " I have news for *Papà*," she concluded. Harriet sat up and looked at the time again. " I must go," she said. She did not want to be there when Sandro came in.

" In time to be there if Carlino looks in on his way home? "

Harriet turned round, staring, and Lydia Marchisi saw ·the faint colour which swept up to her eyes.

" Oh, don't be shy about it, darling," Lydia laughed. " He's not supposed to have missed a new beauty in donkey's years, and his taste is perfect, so it's flattering."

" I don't want to have an affair with him," said Harriet abruptly. " He is absolutely charming, you couldn't be more right. But "—she bit her lip—" I can't help seeing it from his wife's point of view."

" Pina can take care of herself," said Lydia soberly. " She's had lots of practice. I don't envy her, but it's her life and she knows what to do about it. The main ˌthing is, could you play his game and do it well if that's what you want now? It wouldn't do you any harm so long as you didn't get confused and go sentimental or romantic——"

" I know."

" And if it isn't to be you, from Carlo's point of view it will be somebody else."

" I keep thinking about Pina, I tell you."

" So does he, darling. That's the whole point. Keep your eye fixed on that and you won't go wrong."

The last of the water had gurgled out of the tub, and

Harriet was combing and patting her hair into place while it was damp from the steam, still thinking of her talk with Lydia, and still swayed by the current of question and dejection upon which she had come home. The clearest strain in her reasoning knew well that this winter's interlude, whatever its yet undiscovered elements might be, was not part of her real future; and her reason, as well as her instincts, knew that of course she was to have a future, no bit of which she could as yet foresee. She was young, she was independent, she was perfectly aware of her good looks and her other natural gifts. The year since she had returned from that horrible ranch in the West had not been without its possibilities for a new resolution to her life, but she had learnt enough not to rush into anything which could have the least similarity to the botch which had been her own experience of marriage, and her mother's, and that of too many others she knew. Distance, suggested by Lydia Marchisi and friends in England, had seemed the best recourse, and she had been grateful for it. She had her distance, she reflected, getting into her dainty bed, comfortable with its reading-light and the pile of books, English and Italian, on the table beside her; but with it she had a measure of desolation. She lay back on her pillows, eyeing through the open door and across the little hallway the roses spreading their loveliness in the sitting-room. The telephone rang. She did not answer it. It rang three times, four, five. Having followed her intention to ignore the thing, Harriet now inconsequently picked it up.

" At last! " said Carlo Dalverio. " I have been ringing you all afternoon."

" I told you I would be out."

" ' Out ' can mean anything. Did it? "

" I found your roses here when I came in. They are so beautiful, thank you very much."

" Roses? "

Tit for tat, thought Harriet. " Then who has sent me a mass of heavenly roses——"

" No doubt the person with whom you were 'out.' "

" Lydia doesn't send me flowers." Harriet put a faint edge to her voice. " I send them to her."

He laughed. " *Va bene*. What would women do without their best friends? I tell you, the mere sight of Riri Minghetti——"

Harriet could imagine.

" May I come in for a moment? " he asked, quite meek.

" Now? "

" Well, not later! "

" Really, Carlo, I'm not free. I told you, not this evening."

" But only for a moment."

" No, not even for a moment."

" You are unkind."

" No I'm not. Come to-morrow if you like."

" Oh, I was going to do that anyway. Before we go away on Friday."

" I forgot, I am lunching with you to-morrow, that should be enough of me before Friday."

" Lunch, yes; and six o'clock too. Tell me, what did you do to-day? "

" But Carlo——"

" Where did you lunch? "

" At the Ortolani," she sighed. " Why do you ask so many questions? "

" Because I like to. I like to know everything. What are you wearing now? "

" An old tweed skirt, a baggy sweater——"

" For this engagement which keeps you from seeing me? "

" It keeps me from seeing anybody," she said. " I am in bed, with all the doors locked, and I am going to stay here."

" Then I am coming at once! "

" It won't do the least good. There's no way of getting in."

" You lack imagination, *cara*."

" No, seriously. I have a headache, I am tired, I feel like a bore. I need a rest. I'll see you to-morrow."

" You are expecting a lover," he said. " Every word you've said proves it."

" I am going to hang up this telephone now."

" No you're not. Who is he? "

" Do you think I'd tell you? "

" I can find out."

" Then why ask? They have a very inelegant phrase in the United States and I am going to use it. Good-bye, now."

" Not now, not yet, please."

It took her almost ten minutes to bring the conversation to an end. She put down the telephone, laughing. But then as she leaned back on her pillows, expecting the nonsense of the past moments to reverberate pleasantly and carry her along for a little while, she was surprised to find the whole mood gone. She lay thinking about what Lydia had said, and contemplating the thought of to-morrow with a good deal of concern and doubt. Well, she told herself finally, this looks like an imminent case of fish or cut bait and I wonder which I am going to do.

D

Four

PINA DALVERIO, whose name was Giuseppina, was beautiful, faintly unanimated, if not phlegmatic, for an Italian, but with a quality of calm which suggested the deep-rooted resilience of a tree. She was indeed, in her immovable attachments, like a plant, and even her looks, the lengthened ovoid head, the ivory skin, the glossy, bronze-tinged light-brown hair, the velvety eyes, brought to mind the thick-petalled flowers, the elliptical lacquered leaves of the magnolia which grows in every Italian garden. She moved with a rhythm almost imperceptibly slower than that of other women of her age, who were touched by the urge to be of the day and the moment and the world whose new ways and tastes flowed into Italy and out again, carrying abroad so many of its elements. She had a distinctive voice, throaty and suave, and she spoke in the manner of patrician Milanesi, faintly gargling her R's; but as in all else, her speech was more deliberate, and unlike many others she knew little English. She was untroubled by this. Many foreigners came to her house on the tide of Carlo's increasingly international business and she placidly assumed that those who spoke no Italian would speak French.

Harriet at the farther end of the table between Carlo Dalverio and Pina's brother Paolo Verocchi could not but compare Pina's matriarchal calm with the bubbling iridescence of Tia Ortolani and her friends yesterday. She had seen Pina among those other people and knew her capable of the chatter they delighted in, but she was different in her own house, and so was the talk. Here were present Carlo's mother, whom Harriet had not met before, his two children, Tonino and Lala, Paolo Verocchi's lovely and hugely pregnant wife, and the children's Swiss Mademoiselle. The winter holidays were foremost in their minds; the children, beautiful and beautifully mannered and dressed, were prodigies at restraining their excitement without being told and speaking only when they were spoken to.

The steaming, mouth-watering risotto with white truffles was going round the second time and Harriet refused it, but Carlo said, " Come now, you said you adored tartufi, and we can't have any nonsense about dieting here! "

" Risotto is very light, Signora," said Carlo's mother. " It does not make one fat."

Oh, no, of course not, thought Harriet, but she smiled at Pina and helped herself to a little more. " It's too delicious to resist," she said.

"I ordered the truffles for you," said Pina. "I remembered you like them."

"Are you enjoying Milano, Signora? " asked Carlo's mother, speaking across him to Harriet.

There followed the inevitable talk about Harriet's impressions of Milano, how she had happened to come, how long she was planning to stay, whom she had met, what she had been doing. She felt clumsy going through this with Carlo Dalverio's mother whilst he threw in an occasional word, but what else was there to do? And through the veil of convention she felt the warm, likeable personality of the handsome woman whom everybody called Signora Nora. They were such a large family, said the lady, smiling, that one had to have a label of one's own and Harriet too was to call her Signora Nora. She was the archetype of well-preserved, expensively dressed Milanese matron, robust of figure, with well-coiffed iron-grey hair and the fine features and dark eyes which her son had inherited. She must be well past sixty, thought Harriet, for Carlo is about forty, but she doesn't look it; she has the look of the perennial mother and grandmother who has been as she is for years and is never going to look any older.

"Tonino," said Carlo, to change the subject, " did you go to try your new boots this morning? "

"Oh, yes, *Papà*. They fit perfectly and they will be sent this afternoon. What time are we leaving in the morning? "

" You are all going in the big giardinetta with the luggage and the skis. Bruno will come for Coco and Maria at seven sharp," said Carlo to his sister-in-law. Her children were going with their cousins to Cortina because her new baby was due any day.

" Aren't we to go with you, *Papà*? " Lala's disappointment gave him a pang. " Not in your new Ferrari? "

" Not this time, my precious. I want Bruno to drive you because the fog will be very bad at first and he has more patience than your *Papà*."

" More prudence, you mean," said his brother-in-law.

" And for once I want Mamma to myself," said Carlo. " This is her vacation too. And besides, there's no room in the Ferrari for all you goldfish. But I shall probably pass you somewhere beyond Trento and if you've been very good I might stop and take you and Maria in the shelf in back. We'll see."

They had finished the meat course and were eating

tangerines and dried fruits and walnuts. The last few moments at table were always given over to the children, all the conversation was for them. Harriet asked Tonino if he was good at ski-ing and he replied with modesty, " Well, for my age, I think not so bad, Signora." He was eleven, his father murmured, laughing. " And you, Signora, do you like to ski? "

" I love it! "

This started a babble of enthusiastic questions. Everybody asked something: where did she ski, when had she learnt, was there good ski-ing in the United States, where had she skied over here, had she ever been to Cortina? No, she said regretfully, only to St. Moritz and St. Anton. And wasn't she going this year? Was she staying in the city all winter?

" Why don't you come to Cortina with us? " said Pina Dalverio in her calm, dark voice.

" Yes, why don't you? " echoed the children, with the enthusiasm for a loved place which made them want to include everybody in its pleasures.

Harriet smiled at Pina, keeping, she intended, exactly the same appearance of casual cordiality as that which had clothed Pina's remark. But she was on her guard, wary as to what this really meant; and conscious of the surprised discomfiture of Carlo on her left. He had not revealed it, he was saying, " What a good idea! " but his brain was responding to a series of telegraphic taps which spelt, she thinks this has gone farther than it has, she is bringing up her big defences already, she is prepared to see it through. My God! what women have to put up with, and what a woman Pina is! He looked at his wife with an expression of immense pride and admiration. In a strange way he had momentarily forgotten Harriet Piers and he heard, with a distant sense of relief, that she said, " It is so kind and hospitable of you, Pina, I wish I could come, but I am going to Rome to-night to join some American friends for the New Year."

" Ah, well," said Pina, rising, " another time, then."

" And *are* you going to Rome to-night? " he asked, as soon as Angela had shown him in.

Harriet raised her eyebrows. He could not have passed through the entrance hall without seeing her bags ready there. He probably thinks they're empty, she thought. He thinks I'm up to some kind of double-edgery and as a matter of fact, I am. She had declined to go to Rome when the Wainwrights had telephoned a day or two ago and begged her to come. " We're flying home on the first," Polly Wainwright said, " and there's nowhere else we can go in between, we haven't time. But Stan will die of boredom if we don't do anything but glare at each other over a bottle of pop on New Year's Eve. Do come down, it'll be an excuse for a party."

Exactly the sort of party she would loathe; the Wainwrights straining at their double leash, one or two characters from the expatriate fringes, somebody from the Embassy, somebody with a shop-worn title. . . .

But that afternoon she had rung them back and changed her mind, had begged off from Lydia's Capo d'Anno dinner to which she wanted to go, had booked her compartment in the sleeper. Why, she asked herself, choosing the clothes for Angela to pack, why have you let yourself in for this? Why go at all, and why go two days before the wretched party?

Only because at the moment it had seemed important that

Pina Dalverio never discover she had lied about going to Rome. Harriet had to assume that she knew exactly what Pina's invitation meant, and she had to act as though she had not understood. She began to ask herself why she should bother with this façade of innocence and manners. How much effort was she really willing to make, and what was she to get out of it? What would be the use of all this self-restraint and strict adherence to a code by which she had not lived before, and was not sure that she wanted to live by, now or in the future? She was moving on the edge of a situation in which all these feints and devices were taken for granted because they must serve in the crucial capacity of masks, and was she partaking of all this without even a good reason?

Her answer came with a rush; Carlo Dalverio had lifted her from her chair, wrapped his arms round her, and was kissing her mouth with intense, absorbed passion. Harriet was taken unawares. The prelude of verbal pyrotechnics, teasing, and playing for time had ended with a crash. For an instant she was too stupefied to respond and for another, too shaken not to. She thought dizzily, thank God he has my arms pinioned so I cannot put them round his neck, I have no intention of doing so.

" Cara," he said, " *come sei bella! Come mi piaci!* " and continued to kiss her. She could not get her breath. If I do not want this, I must make it plain right now; hurry, said something in her mind, hurry, or it will be too late. At last she drew her head away and freed her hands, to put them against his chest and hold him off, but his powerful sportsman's arms held her in an arc against his body, and he stood looking at her face, his dark eyes glowing. He was as eager, as delighted, as full of freshness and enthusiasm as if this were the most novel of pleasures for him. " Do you like me? " he asked her in Italian, pressing her closer and pleading with his smile, his eyes, his muffled, vibrating voice. " Do you like me? Tell me, tell me . . ."

" I—yes, I like you." She would have preferred silence but it was impossible not to respond. He knew his power with women, everything she had heard about it slid across her mind and vanished, swept away by his unfeigned ardour. He was like a boy, a preposterous boy, to be sure; but without a trace of the cynical detachment which the connoisseur is thought to bring to his pleasures.

" Tell me," he urged, his lips at her chin and her throat. " Tell me again."

She told him.

" In Italian," he said. " Only in Italian."

In Italian, then. It came more easily, it flowed. " *Oh! che meraviglia!* " he said, with surprise which in turn surprised her; his voice was altogether different from that of his poised, fluent English; it was deeper, rougher, a little husky, without resonance. This is not to be quick and easy, he thought, she is reluctant and needs persuading, though I do not know why because there is not the slightest doubt of the eventual outcome. But she will not like it if I hurry her now, and this is enough worth doing to do it well. Yet he had contrived to move, still embracing her, in such a way that she felt free; and he made an exclamation of delight as he bent his head to kiss her again and felt her arms go round him.

" *Cara!* " he murmured. " *Cara* Harriet! What a pretty name, how grateful, how different! Oh, how I like you! Tell me, tell me! "

" Oh, Carlo," she said, and put her forehead against his

chest. " That's such a lovely phrase. *Dimmi, dimmi,* you all say it as if it didn't necessarily mean anything."

" And you don't want it to mean anything? "

" I—I don't know. Yet. I don't know anything."

" Then you must find out. Think of the pleasure, think of all there is to find out. *Dio mio,* we are going to have the most beautiful time! "

He looked again at her face, the dark hair and heavy brows almost startling as the pale, clear eyes gazed at him beneath them.

" You are beautiful," he said again. He studied her face. " All that I see and "—his hands moved delicately down her shoulders, her ribs, settled at her waist, caressed her hips— " all that I don't. But I shall. Shall I? " He shook her a little as if to scold. " Shall I? "

" Do you think so? " He had to bend over her to hear.

" Silly! Silly Harriet! When? Tell me! "

Instead of answering she let him kiss her again. He found her warmer, he held her with bolder passion; he thought, perhaps I needn't be so cautious; he drew her slowly towards the divan. " Will you? " he whispered, with his lips in her hair. " Do you want to? *Vuoi, cara, vuoi?* "

She drew away suddenly and looked at him, startling him with the cool, musing expression of her eyes. My God, he thought, am I mistaken, is she cold, hasn't she felt anything, is it really as I have heard about such women? He was a little angry; she saw the thrust of his heavy lower lip, a movement of his brows which could have told her, had she known him well, that he had no patience with teasing women and would be furious at his own stupidity should he have blundered into this position with one of them. But she said, still with the

meditative look in her eyes, " I think—yes. But not to-day."
He was mollified, but puzzled. She saw it. She said, " Do
you mind very much, Carlo? I should like to give you
pleasure, I want to, and I know——"

" What do you know? " He held her tightly, gripping her
shoulders.

" That you, that I, that . . ." She smiled. " I simply have
a feeling of wanting time to decide something."

" But if you intend anyway to consent——"

" It isn't that. It's better not to talk it all to tatters. Will
you let it go until——"

" Until you return from Rome? Is that what you mean?
When will you be back? " He had not freed her from his
arms.

" Oh, early next week. But you'll be in Cortina. So
perhaps, later on——"

" But no more playing with me," he said, frowning. " Yes
or no——"

No more of my American misgivings, is what he means.
Unless I can carry this off like any woman here and keep
confusion out of it, he doesn't want a problem. He is right.
She remembered again Pina's smooth grace at luncheon, a
masterpiece of long discipline and practice. It will make me
feel a fool, she thought, looking at his face, to be treated like
the other women he has made love to. But I am not going to
be provincial and let it discomfit me.

" My God," he said, " is this the sort of moment when you
always do your serious thinking? "

She wound her arms round his neck. " Always," she said,
while he kissed her eyelids, the tips of her ears, the end of her
nose, the angle of her chin. He found her literally delicious
and he considered her hesitation and dilatoriness the sheerest

nonsense. It can just as well be now, he decided, and again tried to make the point conclusive. But she said, "No, please, Carlo—but I do like you very much."

He knew quite well that if she were not so appetising and a novelty he would not bother with her further. And of course, he told himself, she knows it too.

Five

HARRIET RETURNED from Rome on the *rapido* which arrived
in Milano on Tuesday evening. She was very pleased to
come back. She took almost a perverse pleasure in the keen-
ness of her preference for Milano over Rome. She could not
isolate every element of this preference, but much of it was
the knowledge that a certain ruggedness of mind, the faculty
to savour the pleasing and the beautiful amidst a mixture of
contrasts including the prosaic, the ugly, and the contem-
porary, were forms of originality, which she liked. Rome
presented its pleasures and splendours in such consistent
grandeur that, once past the status of reverent tourist, which
of course she had once been, one must be wholly a specialist
to support so much magnificence, history, panoply, society,
even so much blazing sun and turquoise sky. She was neither
scholar, historian, artist, nor participant in the convolving
spheres of the double *corps* and the grandest, most ana-
chronistic nobility on earth. To be a functioning member of
any of this would make one see it differently; but to observe
it from without, like some dallying or expatriate people she
knew, was meaningless. And the tourist's Rome she loathed.
Whereas her stay in Milano, unrelated though it was to
whatever she conceived as her real place in the world, and
this was a time of dubiety about that, was linked for the
moment to the real lives of real people. Only a transient
satisfaction, she reflected, and nothing to tie up to at all;

but it is better than racketing about like the people I have just seen in Rome.

A train was quite a novelty to her, for she was accustomed to flying long distances and herself driving shorter ones. Both were ruled out here at this time of year unless one were prepared to be grounded, delayed, or faced with mortal danger. She settled down in her comfortable seat in the new lightweight railway carriage, which in its open plan and abundance of aluminium fittings and plate glass seemed like the offspring of a venturesome motor bus and an absent-minded airplane. She had travelled to Rome in an old-fashioned *wagon-lit* and now she missed the cosy red-plush privacy of the classic compartment. She was disappointed when the guard told her that the train carried no dining-car; luncheon was served at one's seat, as in a plane. What a bore she would find that, expecting a slithering plastic tray dotted with dishes and cups of tepid, tired food. Her seat companion was a well-dressed, heavy-set man who carried a thick brief-case; when he had put his hat and overcoat in the rack, he bowed to her, sat down, and immediately immersed himself in the work he had brought with him. But Harriet was aware that he took occasion at intervals to glance her way. It occurred to her that this new sort of train might be regarded by a certain kind of man with considerable disaffection, it was so public; and she smothered a small laugh, opening the novel she had bought in the station in Rome. Not that this man looked like the sort of bore who scraped unwelcome acquaintance; he was dignified, clearly a person of importance, and in all probability he was a friend of Sandro Marchisi and of Carlo and of people they knew.

Harriet had spent the past days traversing the arc of a

resolution not to think about Carlo Dalverio, as the best way to approach the imminent moment for which she could not find a more accurate term than point of no return. She feared the workings of her hitherto romantic imagination should she allow herself to dwell upon him. She had never put this imagination to the test of reality as it was understood here; she had no doubts about the views of these people, but many doubts of herself and of the consequences of any mis-step that she might take. To go forward with this adventure would be to commit herself to a course of dissemblance, with all its pitfalls, which she had never before attempted; and to retreat would mean such discomfiture on meeting him inevitably in the circle of his friends that she would almost prefer to escape that by leaving Milano; a pity, and something she did not want to do. So for the relieving interval she took refuge in the childish device of shutting her mind to every aspect of the question except the ultimate one of asking herself whom she supposed she was fooling.

When the train had left Florence a white-jacketed waiter sped the length of the car, fixing a firm table to the arms of each passenger's seat. The man beside Harriet put his papers away and relaxed with a smile in anticipation of his lunch. The first waiter was followed by a second man with linen, silver, glass, and blue *Wagons-Lits* plates, with which he deftly set each person's place. *Aperitivi* appeared and Harriet took some Carpano; so did the man beside her. He smiled again and wished her good appetite. She returned the greeting. The wine man came along and she bought a quarter-litre of Chianti Antinori; her neighbour chose the same. The first waiter reappeared, with a great steaming bowl, swiftly ladling portions of *rigatoni* on to the passengers' plates. Harriet enjoyed watching the man work, his perfect balance in the swaying train, his lightning handling of the spoon and fork in his right hand, the bowl in his left. The food was plain, robust, and delicious; the *rigatoni* were boiling hot, mixed with an excellent salsa *bolognese* and plenty of cheese. When half the passengers were served the waiter rushed away to fetch a fresh hot bowl for the rest.

Harriet marvelled, and said so. Her companion nodded; yes, it was surprising what good, hot food could be served in this new way, but of course the public would stand for nothing less; one paid a premium fare for the *rapido* and there could be no nonsense.

" But the labour! " said Harriet.

The man shrugged. From his view, she saw, it was preposterous that such labour should not be taken for granted, both in available numbers and in willingness to work for the prevailing wage. Railway workers, like civil servants, bus drivers, and many others, were always going out on one-day strikes and it was a damnable nuisance; they should be grateful for their jobs.

Oh, oh, oh, said Harriet to herself. This was the under-side of the soft-surfaced carpet which was the part of Italian life that she knew; but while serious contemplation of social problems had never occupied her, she was not a fool. Reality in her orbit at home was high taxes and few, if any, servants; among her friends here, the opposite. Oh, they grumbled and worried; taxes were heavier and stricter now, the women complained about the servants and the men about the workmen in their factories, but one could not be oblivious to brutal truths pressing in their enormous preponderance. They were part of the same image as the one she had had last week when envisioning the people's homes; the Italy of the novel she was reading, the Italy about which most of its writers wrote, the Italy of hunger, misery, despair, and their spawn. When she read such a book it lowered her momentarily into a crypt of gloomy and uneasy thought, from which she was most likely to be lifted by some member of the working population, some cheerful, skilful soul like the waiter who was now serving her from a platter of fillet steaks with their garnish of fresh vegetables.

" But this is such a lot! " she told the man.

" Oh, no, Signora, I chose the nicest filetto for you, one must eat well on a cold day." He hurried on, doing his work as most of them did, with gusto. They liked to work, they had their faults, but their vigour and their quickness and their physical agility were a delight to see. She loved to watch them talk, nothing in the world could be so expressive as the least flick of an Italian's fingers. There was a certain circular motion, done with the relaxed hand on a loose wrist, accompanied by raised eyebrows and a judicious pursing of the mouth, which meant half a dozen different things and entertained her vastly.

The man beside her had been eyeing her book. Presently, as they were eating cheese and finishing their wine, he asked, " Signora, may I ask your impression of that book? "

" I have only read a little of it," she replied. " I had been told it was remarkable and I suppose it is, in its vividness. The dialogue is brilliant."

" And the subject? "

" Disagreeable," she said. " Have you read it? "

He shook his head. " Not even if I had the time. Any workman in one of my factories could write better about what Italian life is like to-day."

She realised who the man was, a textile magnate of enormous wealth, whose name was known everywhere. He had been pointed out to her. He said, " You must be the American lady who is the friend of the Marchisi? "

" Milano is really not so small as that! "

" Just small enough. And you speak Italian so well."

" Thank you, but of course I don't. I make mistakes and I don't let it bother me, I simply take pleasure in it."

" Many of us took pleasure in admiring you and your equally beautiful compatriot last Tuesday."

" Lydia is extraordinary, isn't she. Especially when so many of her friends here are really great beauties. I've never seen such a spectacle as the women at La Scala that evening. The clothes! The jewels! The furs! "

" But in America that would be outdone as a matter of course? "

" You've been there, surely. Have you ever seen an American gathering so elegant and—frankly—one that was such a display of wealth? "

He smiled as if to conceal some secret. " Perhaps not. But our women are much less intelligent than yours; they think about nothing else."

" Their families . . ."

A gesture said that this was not worth pointing out. " Their heads are perfectly empty," he said. " They are silly, they are vain, they are lazy, they cost a shocking amount of money." He paused, but seemed to have more to say.

" And? "

" We love it! " He spoke with the utmost gusto.

Harriet could not think of another reply, so she said, " You have given me quite a perspective from which to go on reading this book."

From time to time she looked at the window as they were covering the last stretch after Piacenza. The fog was a solid wall, but the train was still skimming the rails like a glider. The newspapers recently had carried accounts of several hideous disasters in the fog at level crossings. If one dwelt on this one would be beside oneself at this point in the journey, but nobody was. A few of the passengers were asleep or idly smoking or reading popular magazines, but most of them were like Harriet's neighbour, busy men who had brought masses of work along and who only began to put it away when they looked at their watches as they felt the train slow down for the approach to the Milano station.

The textile gentleman lifted down Harriet's fur coat from the rack and held it for her. It was a very good fur coat, as good as New York provided, and when she thanked him she slowly winked one eye. He laughed. She approved his not offering to help her as she handed her luggage checks to a porter on the platform; they bowed and he hurried away.

Carlo Dalverio was on the verge of changing his mind. This was not an unfamiliar thing, it had happened before. It was closely linked to his mood, to his whereabouts, and to the state of his relations with Pina. He was fond of her and proud of her always, but she came nearest to holding him completely when they were off with the children on holidays like this. He basked in the warmth of the children's happiness, of Pina's approval, and of the well-being wrought by this kind of life. They were lucky with the weather; the sky was blue, the snow packed and crisp, the slopes and slides and rinks in perfect condition. Every morning they rose early and set about the day's sport with fresh intensity. Each moment was filled; the children had lessons with champion skaters and ski-masters, later Carlo came down from the big slopes and took out Tonino and his cousin Coco for the last hour of the morning, while the little girls went to the children's practice slopes. Pina did not ski but she enjoyed this life, many of her friends were here with their families and those who were not sportswomen were pleasurably occupied with chic, with canasta and bridge and gabble.

At lunch-time, ravenous and tanned, they gathered round the big table in the sunny window overlooking the skating-rink, to eat an enormous meal in a chorus of ski-talk and plans for the afternoon, for to-morrow, for next day, even for next year, since the children were begging him to build a house up here like many people they knew, and he was seriously considering it. Pina remarked with a shade of doubt that perhaps they had enough houses already, what with Santa Margherita and Caldagna and Guello, and the farm near Trezzo and the old house at Bergamo, although they never went there, but Carlo brushed that aside. All houses were desirable investments; the only question was whether they would more enjoy a chalet-villa of their own or this life at the Cristallo. Then there was the afternoon nap, deliciously welcome, with Pina drowsing in his arms as he had drawn her from her bed close by his, replete with love-making and warm under the eiderdown. He lay in the dim room, drifting on the brink of sleep, with his wife's head pillowed on his shoulder, and vaguely he asked himself why this was not always as much as he could want. He had everything in her except high romance, variety, and excite-ment; wasn't he reaching an age where they should matter little anyway, and were they worth the trouble? He did not pursue the question to its conclusion because he knew the answer very well. He was not ready to change, and age had nothing to do with it. So long as he kept a sense that life held something which he had not yet experienced, so long would he be as he was; but at this particular time he could wish this were not so. He experimented with drawing a mental image of the American who had intrigued him, and he took some satisfaction in finding that for the moment the image had diminished in its appeal.

There would be passing constraint if he should delicately drop his pursuit of her, but he was skilled in these matters and he would manage it in such a way that there would be no slight to her beauty or her confidence. She was bound to have a lover soon, and shortly she would again be meeting the Dalveri, laughing and talking with him quite naturally and priding herself on her quick understanding that some unusual development between himself and Pina had made his withdrawal necessary. It was all quite simple.

It was also a lot of nonsense. All these thoughts were prompted by the fact that he was comfortable and content, enjoying himself, and at the moment without need for the diversions which spiced the routine of life at home. He knew himself; when he was back in Milano his present notion would appear in its true light, preposterous. He wanted very much to complete his conquest of Harriet Piers but the truth was that he did not want to have to leave Cortina to do so. It could wait. She had certainly not been impatient, if she was really interested at all. You imbecile, he reviled himself, silently striking his forehead with his clenched fist; you cretin, you giraffe! Why did you tell Rinaldo to get you out of here on Thursday? His usual impatience, he sighed; wasn't he old enough to have learnt not to spring at things on impulse? Well, he would send Ortolani a *lampo* as soon as he got downstairs; he would not interrupt his holiday, and next week would take care of itself. Tenderly he drew Pina to him and caressed her, which she received with a contented murmur; and in a few minutes he was sound asleep.

Oh, thought Harriet, as Carlo walked in on Monday afternoon; he is beautiful. There is no other word for it. It has nothing to do with anything else, he is simply beautiful, like a cheetah or a panther. His skin had the ruddy bronze tint laid on by winter sun and wind and cold, he strode in as if on a sweep of mountain air, he moved with the grace of the feline animal he brought to mind, wearing his brilliant, delighted smile. He was perfectly confident of his attractiveness and perfectly aware how his ski-ing holiday had enhanced it. He crossed the room in a couple of strides and took her in his arms. " At last! " he exclaimed, and his embrace was entrancing, his face still cold from the winter air, his mouth warm and urgent. His kiss lingered until she was out of breath. Finally they drew apart and he looked into her eyes and said, " I think you are glad to see me! "

" I think I am."

" Did you miss me? " He did not let her go, he was caressing her with his hands, softly, lightly, quickly. " Tell me. Did you miss me? "

She made a mocking face. " Not a bit more than you missed me. I had fun too! "

" You did! " His voice was sharp. He drew her to an arm-chair and sat down in it, holding her so that she dropped into his lap. " What did you do? With whom? When? In Rome? Whom did you see there? Whom have you seen here? Where? "

He stopped her peals of laughter with another long kiss, to which she responded so warmly that he sat up suddenly, took her hands in his, scowled and said, " Answer all those questions. Whom did you take for a lover? "

" No, Carlo. I am not going to answer any question I don't want to answer, and I must say you're taking a lot for granted by the way you ask them."

" *Come sei bella!* " he said, with a curious plangent undertone in his voice. " Look at me, *cara*, look straight at me because I want to enjoy your eyes. Open them wide. Very wide." He brushed the dark thick lashes with his lips. " Now smile, the funny smile which makes them close up. Now close them." He kissed the lids, pausing to look down at them and wait until they opened slowly and the wide, pale grey eyes were again looking into his. " What did you really do? " he whispered, his hands moving softly.

" You telephoned. You know. Don't tell me all that screaming was for nothing! Why are your telephone connections so frightful here? "

" The war," he said from force of habit; it had been said for nearly fifteen years. " But I haven't called since Friday."

" And I'm not accounting for Saturday and Sunday. Kiss me."

" With joy! "

They were silent, lost in the delights of discovery. Presently she said, " And thank you for all the lovely roses." She moved her hand from his embrace and waved at the fresh ones which had come to-day.

" *Cara*," he said, in a breathless voice, and asked a question to which she replied by burying her face in his chest. He stood up, holding her in his arms, walked over to the divan, and laid her down on it. He glanced over his shoulder at the closed door of the room, and she murmured, " She is out, I sent her on an errand."

He made an exclamation of delight and sank down beside her.

She had not dreamt, she had never had an intimation in her life before, that there could be pleasure so exquisite, perfected, sensitive, so veiled in tenderness, so bold in understanding, attuned like the finest vibration of a precision instrument to every shade of her sensibility. She was amazed, and after a long time, she said so.

" But *cara*." He stared at her. " How can one have pleasure if one does not aim first of all to give it? And you are wonderful, *wonderful* . . ." He broke off, as if choked by emotion; he did not want her to suspect that he in turn was surprised, why had he supposed that her fresh and girlish person, her light, firm body without a particle of needless flesh, would be less voluptuous than the ripeness that was more usual here? " Wonderful," he said again, " and how I like you! "

" I like you," she said, touching the fine, flat plane of his cheek. " I like to say these things as you do."

" Ah, it would be impossible in your language. Even you —*you* . . ." He gripped her shoulders and told her with his eyes that the past half-hour could be repeated now, this instant, but for the little clock ticking there across the room. " Even you could not make love in English."

" People have," she muttered.

" As we have? As we shall? "

She shook her head. She was aware that she had had the merest foretaste of sublimity.

Six

A DESIGN of ways and means had to be drawn, overriding her distaste, which she had to conceal like other evidences of her inexperience, for scheming, contriving, lies, duplicity, hiding. Though Carlo groaned how tiresome he found all this, Harriet saw that it was part and parcel of his habit, the spur of danger and excitement without which he could not ride the horse of everyday existence. He was a master at this feat of equestrianism. It was scarcely necessary for him to point out, with the realism which had always swept him over the shoals of recklessness, that if he and she were not lovers each would be involved with somebody else. " And each would have all the same problems," he said, " but none of the same rewards. Because this is not to be had just anywhere, Harriet. You are like . . ." He groped for a simile. " Like the finest possible musical instrument, the finest violin Stradivari ever made——" His graceful, graphic brown hand caressed her throat.

"—which is only wood and catgut until a virtuoso plays it," she said.

" *Cara!* " He was delighted. " But which virtuoso? " he added, sharply. There was that stubborn lower lip, pouting.

" The greatest, according to your preference."

" But which? "

" Do you really suspect me of having had a violinist for a

lover? You are incorrigible. I will never name any name to you, for any reason. Never."

He laughed. And she thought she was doing well not to let him discover how very few men there had been in her past. She was not sure why she felt this, but it was also the reason why her only break, prompted by rage and jealousy, from the bounds of her disordered marriage, had been brief and regretted; why in the past year she had shied away from commitment even to sheer adventure. A man like Carlo Dalverio either would not believe this or could not understand it; he would think her childish or priggish. She could not risk that, remembering a time not vastly long ago when it had been true. She could not help knowing what Italians usually thought about American women in her situation and, again, she wanted to take care not to be so jejune as to argue it with or without words. She was fastidious; and in Carlo Dalverio she had a man who so exceeded the extremest qualifications for pleasing her that any experienced woman would tell her it was essential he not find this out. She checked her words, her glances, her acts, even her posture, at moments when her forthright character urged her to be herself, and her clever, adaptable mind counselled otherwise. This was the preceptor which told her to keep her touch light, her wits sharp, her perceptions lightning-quick.

It was less difficult than she had feared to carry off ordinary meetings with Carlo among friends, even in the presence of Pina, because he spoke only English with her at such times, just as he had from the first. Sometimes when she was speaking Italian with other people he would turn and compliment her gravely on her progress, which put her under a special challenge to keep the least glint from her eye, the flicker of a tell-tale expression from her lips. She hoped; but of course she could not be sure. Carlo told her frankly that he assumed Pina knew, because Pina almost always knew; but if we do no stupidities, he said, and she is never allowed to feel that she is not in command of the situation, there will be peace.

" And," asked Harriet uneasily and with diffidence, " has there ever—ever not been peace? "

" I am afraid so, *cara.* Pina is jealous——"

" I knew that within a week of meeting her."

" And me."

" And you."

" But Pina knows this which I always tell you. It is life, there is nothing we can do about it, I am as I am. Some day I shall be too old or too feeble or even too indifferent to want pleasure any more."

" I can't imagine it."

" *Eh, be'.* But it must happen, like everything else. That will be when Pina has me all to herself and that is what Pina lives for. That, and the children."

" I'd never have the patience. Or the discipline."

" You also have not kept your husband, *cara.* This is not to blame you," he added quickly, with an apologetic smile. " It is only to explain women like Pina. I suppose they exist in all countries but I do not know other countries well and I do know my own. I know how much Pina will stand and how much she will not. I know when I hurt her and I am sad that I hurt her, but as I said before, that is what life is. So long as Pina knows the ground is solid beneath her feet she will be, she will act, as she does now."

" I couldn't do it! " Harriet felt a wave of intense admiration for Pina. " I think she's magnificent." Prodded by the humiliating memory of her own behaviour in the same circumstances, she spoke with spontaneous sincerity; then she saw that quite without design, she had pleased him very much by saying what she had.

" Well, she is," he agreed. " And even though you are more beautiful and interesting and novel than——" he hesitated.

" Than others that there have been? " she prompted softly.

He nodded, with a helpless little laugh. " Clever also. Ah, you please me so much! " He swooped down and pinned her with a long kiss.

" Come, come," she said sidling away. " Finish what you were saying."

" I don't remember," he lied.

" Something about me "—she drew the kind of imperceptible extra breath which enables one to carry off a phrase one is not too sure about—" and my predecessors, shall we say? "

" I am not enjoying this conversation any more," he said, reaching to draw her towards him.

" But finish it."

He shrugged. " However greater your charms may be, and Pina can see what they are, you are foreign, you belong elsewhere, you will eventually go home, and for this reason Pina can be more patient about you than she might be, and than she has been, about others. *Now* have I talked enough?" And he seized her with the mock roughness which set her blood and bones tingling, and coolly drew the zipper down the long back of her dress. " There," he said, pushing the dress from her shoulders and tracing their delicate curves of bone and muscle and fragrant skin with his lips, " that is better than silly talk. And that. And that." He pursued his voyage of discovery, telling her, in quick, excited words, new, secret, playful words, about the treasures he was uncovering, and asking her to rejoice with him because they were so marvellous.

So among other people, Carlo speaking English, quickly became a person different from Carlo in whose arms she lay, looking up at a face illuminated with sensual delight, and communicative as no face she could ever have imagined. To respond to this, to be led into realms unknown before, to hear what he said in this lovely language of words spoken and rapture unspoken, to be taught to answer in every sound and every sense was more than she had ever had or hoped for.

And still she did not know him very well. Every morning he telephoned, to talk so long that she wondered at the methods of Italian business, imagining him to be fending off a troop of associates, secretaries, and busy men arriving for appointments, all cooling their heels in ante-rooms. She should have realised that his habits and his routine had been established years ago to make breathing-spaces for the arrangements of his private life between the great major fixtures of his family and his work. He had energy and to spare for all of them, and enthusiasm too; he neglected nothing; but time and the opportunity!—that had always been the problem. He had solved it in his own way and Harriet, studying the lesson of feminine resemblance to the ostrich, warily learned to disregard the part played in his life by what she herself had called her predecessors. It was best to keep her head in the sand, a tactic proved by his way of teasing, accusing, probing the crannies of her past and even of the present, for each day he demanded to know whom she had seen since he had last seen her, and whom she was to see before they met again. She parried this and played his game of darts with increasing skill, and kept him inquisitive and amused; but she sensed that the least back-thrust from her, the slightest venture towards a question as to his whereabouts and his doings present or past would be rebuffed with coldness if not with sullenness.

Sometimes she felt quite exhausted by her constant, watchful effort and sometimes she wondered why she was making it. Italian women and other foreign women did all this with ease and bravura, for its own sake; many Americans did, but she had never been one of them. Now she was committed to play on a scene where failure or defeat would be too ignominious to endure, and she found herself in the arena encumbered by a sackful of instincts and habits, the American amalgam of romanticism, materialism, and prudery which demanded that a love-affair prove something, be something more than a special type of friendship and a glorious physical experience. Or, if it made no claims to anything higher, it was defined by a series of slang phrases, flippant or smutty, which outraged her. These she had always angrily rejected, in mind as well as in fact. Her inner self was not so cool, so poised, or so worldly as her outer one, upon which she thought she could rely anywhere. She still had to fight down the impulse to demand that men and life be as she wanted them. But she also perceived that if she wanted Carlo Dalverio at all, she would have to do as other women had done who had won him for varying lengths of time on his terms and his alone.

The great factor on which her fate would hang was the injunction not to fall in love with Carlo Dalverio, not to be in love with him any more than he was with her. She had never attempted this; she had practised what she had heard derided as the American infantilism of refusing to make love without being in love or believing oneself to be. Now it was all to be different, and if she did not learn to measure the difference and act accordingly, she would not only drive him away but she would make a fool of herself. She had noticed in a very short time that all the verbal wealth he lavished on their love-making and taught her to use with delight, was devoid of reference to the emotion of love. This was a strange discovery in a country where the word *amore* was probably pronounced oftener than its equivalent anywhere else. Italy throbbed with song, from its temples of music to its back alleys and juke-boxes, and *amore* was the burden of these hundreds of thousands of arias and songs. Sometimes, putting her hands to her head in sheer bewilderment, she wanted to ask what it all meant, but she was astute enough to suspect she would be better off not to find out.

One morning in the middle of January, Harriet and Lydia Marchisi went to try on some hats that they had ordered. Lydia's milliner, who had a salon in the Montenapoleone, was a handsome, smiling, hard-working woman with the efficiency and sure hand of lifetime saturation in her métier. She went frequently to Paris to bring back the choicest models from the great designers, and her copies were better in materials and workmanship than the originals. But her real speciality was her own originations in a type of wildly flattering small hat, usually made of feathers, designed to be worn in the boxes at La Scala on the evenings when one dressed only a little, in contrast to occasions of grand gala. A superb, slightly mad, short black dress was then in order, worn with one of these wicked hats and long antelope gloves of a shade to match it. The whole scheme enchanted Harriet, it was so altogether a Milanese speciality. In New York if one should dress like this it would be to dine in a restaurant which would exactly resemble any good restaurant in any metropolis in the world. Most such cities also had their opera houses, but only Milano had La Scala, generative of a whole way of life with its unlikely combination of casual intimacy and grandeur, its argot and its conventions, its moulding of taste in matters ranging from great art to fripperies like these hats which the two women greeted with exclamations of pleasure. The modiste and the vendeuses hurried about; the feather hats were pronounced perfect; and of course there were more models newly arrived to be brought out for trial and discussion. Hats were Harriet's foible because she wore them well and it amused her to cultivate them when many women of her age went bare-headed. But she said, " This has got to stop somewhere, Signora Ricci, it really does, I've never been here that I didn't buy something I never intended to."

" But with the Signora's beauty and chic——"

" Don't stoop to that," said Harriet, laughing. " The trouble is your hats. You don't have to flatter anybody to sell them. Let me see that cloche over there," she said to a girl, " the poison-green one——"

" Oh, no," said Lydia, " that colour——"

" We can make it in any colour, Signora, I've just done it for—*ah, buon giorno, Signora!* " and Pina Dalverio walked in.

She greeted everybody with a calm smile and said to Harriet and Lydia, " Tell me, what have you been choosing? "

" I was just about to show the ladies your new cloche I've finished." A girl came from the workroom with it. Pina sat down and they fitted it to her shining nut-coloured hair. In a coppery shade of brown the hat was perfect on her, she was one of the extremely few women who could wear brown well and give it high style. Harriet watched her studying the hat from every angle, watched her smooth, imperturbable features, the deliberate movements of her beautiful hands. How sure of herself she is, she thought, how perfectly she carries this off; my God! if only I didn't crumple inside at the sight of her. I hate it, I feel like a worm. Lydia and Pina were chatting, absorbed in the hats, and Lydia's expression in its way was also a study, a wide, photographic smile turned on nobody in particular. It felt to Harriet like a bright curtain drawn across the panes of her own disquiet, to protect her and give her time to rally a degree of poise and grace equal to Pina's. She had seen Pina several times in the past ten days, in the same pattern as before; for some reason she had felt surer of herself with time to prepare for those meetings. This was their first chance encounter and she was distressed to find it much more awkward. She would have thought it easier to see Pina without Carlo present, but she found to her astonishment that she was wrong. And to Lydia, for all their intimacy, she had not said a word confirming the *fait accompli* between herself and Carlo. Lydia must have sensed that matters were as they were, which in one way was a reassurance to Harriet, but in another might mean that if Pina and Lydia already knew this, many others might or presently would, in exactly the same way.

Harriet was putting her hair in order and Pina Dalverio, finished with her fitting, came over and said, " I'm glad I've found you here, I telephoned this morning but you were out."

" At my Italian lesson," said Harriet. She wondered if Pina had also telephoned during the long time when the line had been tied up by Carlo.

" I wanted to ask you to join us on Wednesday evening. It's *Tosca* and a friend of Carlo's will be here, an Englishman."

" Why, I should love it. Thank you so much." Harriet smiled gaily.

" That will be a help," said Pina, with a self-deprecating shrug. " You know how little English I speak and I never want this man to be bored. Carlo is very fond of him, he knew him in the war."

The war, thought Harriet, how extraordinary. I can't imagine Carlo in a war, or any of these people. Yet there could not be one of them who had not been through everything; Sandro and Carlo and all their friends were about the same age, and nobody ever mentioned the war. Harriet was also wondering why Pina should not speak her beautiful French with the Englishman, which she must often have done if he was such a good friend of Carlo's. Then it occurred to her that if the man had been through the war here he must speak Italian, probably better than Harriet herself; why had Pina put this on the footing of Harriet's doing her a favour? This invitation and other recent ones now appeared to Harriet to be devices manipulated by Pina as parts of a panel of instruments for measuring the exact state of the situation and keeping the controls in her own hands.

Or, she reflected, as they all rose to go, drawing on their gloves and moving to the door in a chorus of smiling good days from the milliner and her staff, is Pina pursuing the tactic of inviting me often, hoping that she is ramming me down Carlo's throat and betting he will soon be tired of me? A quick flash of pride rose within her, she hoped not to her face where it might betray her with tell-tale colour; she wished she had pleaded another engagement, but she was

F

trapped now. The easy sociability of a few weeks ago seemed a long way off, and she looked back upon it wistfully.

In Lydia's car they sat silent for a time. Harriet watched the people streaming into the streets from every shop and office, amidst a cacophony of descending iron shutters. It was just twelve-thirty and they were all hurrying home to their midday dinners. They crammed the greenish-blue trams and buses so tightly that one gasped to see them leaping to footholds where one would have said there was not space for a fly. Lydia's chauffeur was stuck in the traffic behind a filobus, where a group of young men packed in the rear were looking out at the glittering Flaminia with the two beautiful women in it; from their smiles and their gestures of heads and hands it was too easy to imagine their remarks about the car and its occupants. Harriet could not help laughing. " How they do enjoy everything! " she exclaimed. " Can you imagine taking an interest in anything if you had that trip to face four times a day? "

Lydia shrugged. " They're so tough and energetic and gregarious it doesn't occur to them it's a hardship. They all want a Vespa or a Seicento, but not to be by themselves; for sport. And they're getting them, too, more every year. You've seen the road along the lake, and heard it, every Sunday. That's why I like it best in winter."

" Will you be going this week-end, darling? "

" I think so. The children love it and Sandro's such an angel he indulges my whims. Actually, he likes it himself now he's got the habit. Everybody we know thinks I'm mad to keep that house open all year round. They can't understand our week-ends, they say the lake is '*triste*' in winter, when that's apt to be the best time of all. They say it's the only American taste I've kept. Well——" She turned and looked into Harriet's eyes. " I've been wanting to tell you, darling . . . any time it might help you to say you're there with us, say it."

" Oh, Lydia——! "

" And also—you won't think I'm prying? "

" Darling! "

" If you should want to go there—you know, by yourself—it's always possible."

" You are too wonderful," said Harriet softly.

" No. But *you* have to be."

" You were, just now, with Pina."

" I am really fond of Pina, we've been very good friends for ten years."

" And yet you've just said—— "

" What am I to do? " Lydia's blue eyes were troubled. " Some aspects of this could be painful. I can't help Carlino's being as he is and it's none of my business what he does or with whom—until that involves you. Pina doesn't care that you and I are like sisters, but what that means in this case is that I'll have to do what I can to protect everybody."

Harriet grasped her hand with a quick surge of love. " Thank God you're here," she breathed.

"—just so everybody behaves," murmured Lydia. She looked hard at Harriet. " You're not going to get in deep, darling? Promise me you won't get hurt."

" No. My eyes are wide open—to here." She stretched them as far as she could. " I haven't asked you how you're feeling."

" Oh, fine. I'm past the icky stage already and ravenous all the time. I'm dying this minute," she said as the car arrived at her house, " and we're going to have tortellini in pasticcio for lunch! "

In the afternoon Harriet left Lydia's house on foot, planning to do several errands on her way home. She had learnt a lot of short-cuts through arcades and little slices of streets threaded between and behind the main arteries, and she enjoyed walking all over the fan-shaped north-eastern quarter of Milano, whose base was the Duomo and whose two outer corners the Brera and the Conservatorio. In this area nearly everybody lived whom she knew, and every shop and place of business was situated to which she was likely to go. Everything was stirred together in an agreeable jumble of houses great and small, palazzi old and new, where no zoning laws existed and no distinction was made between residential and commercial tenants and property. It had been startling at first to find that some people she met lived at the same address as the man's place of business, which usually meant that he or his company owned a palazzo with offices on the lower floors and a magnificent penthouse apartment on the upper ones. New York had no exclusive claim to penthouse life and its accoutrements; one needed only to be high enough to look out and see how prettily the Milanesi did themselves, how many charming awninged roof terraces there were, green with trees and planting, and furnished with the kind of imaginative nonsense at which they excelled. Even the vile winter weather was no discouragement because of the lovely long autumn and spring unknown in the United States. It was a good life, Harriet reflected; a very good life—for the rich, whether they lived in mellow beauty and state like the Ortolani, in old-fashioned luxury like the Dalveri, or in the smart style and spirit of the remarkable skyscrapers which had sprung up since the last war.

She reached home at the end of the day, tired enough not

to feel very sanguine in mood. On the way up in the lift she recalled a similar evening not so long ago when she had also had no plans and had been glad of it. To-day she was at some pains to hide from herself what she was really feeling; that an evening like this was good only in proportion to one's own resources of mind and taste, but even more, to the natural relationships which gave reason to most people's lives and which she had to admit she was without. Even when she was married to Norton Piers the idea of an evening quietly at home had been almost absurd; he proposed a restaurant, a play, a film, a hockey game, anything rather than repose and tranquil companionship, of which he was incapable. But Harriet believed that she was capable of it now and would like it and make something treasurable of it. The corollary, then, was the uneasy question which some other woman might not ask herself: where was Carlo Dalverio leading her, where other than to a dead end? This was a passage of her life when she should be assembling the materials for a permanent dwelling-place; not such a jerry-built pleasure-dome as her mother expected of her, but a real house to live in, with thick walls and a leak-proof roof, and a cellar and an attic to hold the leisurely accumulation of memory and sentiment and shared experiences good and bad which gave full dimensions to other people's lives when her own, especially at this moment, felt like a rough sketch on flimsy paper.

She opened the door of her flat, saying, " Angela? " and pausing for the maid to come and take her coat. But Angela for some reason had not heard. Harriet dropped the coat on a chair with her purse and gloves and picked up the letters that had come, looking through them as she went to the sitting-room. The curtains were drawn, the lamps lighted, the little glass cart with ice and bottles ready in its corner. And near it, comfortably settled on the divan with a cigarette and a drink, reading an American picture magazine, was Carlo. Harriet stood open-mouthed, deciding how to respond to this. The thing not to show was the spark of delight which touched her when she saw him. He pretended to ignore her for a time, then he put down the magazine and sat shaking with laughter, holding out his arms.

" But how did you get here? " she asked. " You didn't say——"

" No, I rang up after lunch and Angela said you'd be out until about now. So I told her I'd be along and she was expecting me."

" *She——!* "

" Our servants have hospitable ways. When a person has been received before they assume he is welcome."

" Oh. And I suppose she gave you coffee? "

" Naturally she did. Then when I learned you would be here alone for the evening, I told her to run along."

" Carlo! You *what?* "

He had pulled her down beside him and was busy revisiting his favourite nooks and corners about her head and throat and breast; he lifted his face from hers and said, " I told her to go to the cinema, she was happy as a lark."

" And gave her money, of course——"

" The poor girl! But her gentleman friend, what is this subtle term for it they have in your country? Her friend is the *cameriere* of the Longoni downstairs and as they are away at Sestriere, you can see how welcome my suggestion was."

" But Carlo——"

" But *cara.* You are going to fuss because of what you

think she will think, and though centuries roll and you pretend people are not as they are, she will think what all reasonable adults think and if you continue to be kind and generous with her, may I ask what you have to fear? "

" But servants talk."

" Of course they talk. Don't you? Don't I? If they were deaf, dumb and blind they would still be perfectly aware of everything their employers do, and if it were otherwise— come, this is ridiculous. Come to bed."

" Well," said Harriet slowly, " now that the opportunity presents itself——"

" ' Itself——! ' I created it, I alone with a stroke of genius. Come, we have several hours and I have seized them by the throat."

" Hours! " Harriet felt a surge of pleasure.

" Pina is dining at her sister's and I had to beg off to take a man from Stuttgart to dinner who is here on business. I must say he is the most appetising, fragrant, irresistible, the loveliest—— Ah! you are wonderful, you have the body of a girl and the eyes of a sphinx."

" I wish they were," she murmured, as they moved towards her bedroom, their arms about each other. " I wish I had such wisdom."

" Be wise later, be wise some other time," he said. " Hurry. Let me help you." His fine, muscular brown hands were as agile, as skilled—she felt with fleeting revulsion—as a good maid's; he is too experienced; but she was lost at once in the splendours roused by his own physical beauty, his marvellous wholehearted eagerness which swept thought and second thought into lucent space, where flames soared and a vast orchestra thundered. But the flames did not burn and the sounds did not deafen; they revived, redeemed, and in ebbing left beatitude. She was too moved to remember to pretend insouciance. He lay with his head on her breast, murmuring, " My God, my God, you are miraculous, it is too beautiful to be true! " Once again she blessed his exquisite language which had a phrase and a nuance for every part and every echo of this experience; it released her from the constraint whose shackles she now knew she had always worn before. Suddenly he gripped her shoulders hard, raising himself on one elbow and looking into her face. " Tell me," he said, " tell me. Why are you so extraordinary, what is your secret? "

She turned her head to escape his eyes and murmured, " It might be my teacher."

He gave a great cry and in a little while swept her away again.

They slept and when they stirred, smiling, to think about the time and let it bring them back to reality they saw that it was almost nine o'clock.

" Well now," said Carlo, " you will be very hungry and here we are, faced with things as they have to be. It would be so pleasant to go and have something to eat."

" We can go right into my kitchen and have something, since you have taken care of Angela's evening. I can cook eggs."

" Suppose you go and look into the question," he said.

She put on a negligee, arranged her hair and face, and left him to dress. As she turned on the lights in the kitchen she stood and stared. A large tray had been set out on the table, ready to be carried wherever it was wanted, with everything laid for supper for two. On platters and dishes were an assortment of raw and cooked ham, various sausages, pieces of devilled chicken, lobster in aspic, a *paglierina* cheese, and a small bloc of *foie gras*. There was a basket of bread and *grissini* and the flute glasses on the tray prompted Harriet to open the refrigerator and find what she already guessed, a bottle of Dom Perignon. Carlo appeared in the doorway, very spruce and beaming with pride. " See what a good provider I am? " he said.

" How did you do this? Did you sent Angela out for it? "

" I am hungry," he said, " and you are my hostess. Let us not discuss domestic arrangements. Where shall I carry this tray? "

She told him and gave him the champagne to open. They sat close together at the round table in her small dining-room, and ate ravenously and laughed and teased each other.

" If I hated everything in your country, including you," said Harriet, " I would still be seduced by the food. Where did these divine things come from? "

" From Peck's naturally. There is a *salumeria* in every fourth doorway in Milano, but only Peck is the be-all and the end-all."

" I'm glad it began and I hope it never ends. Carlo, tell me about your English friend whom I'm to meet to-morrow. Were you at school there with him? Is that where you learned to speak such good English? "

" It was a type of school, I suppose," he said, " but not in England."

" I know, the war, Pina said so. Of course I am trying to get you to talk about it."

" And of course I have no idea of doing such a thing." He leaned over and kissed her nose and the deep hollows of her eyes, which gave him an uncommon pleasure of a sort he had never felt before. " I must go now." She pictured him, arriving at his sister-in-law's to pick up Pina at just the hour when he would have finished a leisurely dinner with the man to whom he had to talk business.

" It was lovely," she said, at the door, while he was putting on his overcoat.

" It was. It has made me want something I hadn't planned on."

" Do you plan so exactly? " she asked, instead of showing the curiosity he expected.

" Oh, I am very efficient, I have a big business to run and lots of other concerns to fit in——"

" Be careful. Don't say too much! "

" *Cattiva!* What I should like," he said, putting his hands on her ribs under the light peignoir, " is to take you to Bergamo with me next week when I go."

" You are going to Bergamo? "

" I go regularly—at least once every fortnight. And in winter I cannot get back the same night on account of the fog. So I stay there. Would you like to come? "

" Oh, Carlo! " She was afraid she sounded too happy; she caught her voice on the edge of a tremor.

He held her for a moment, looking into her face. His glowing brown eyes, his fine skin, his subtly sculptured mouth, his whole head which might, she often thought, have belonged to a model of Donatello's were for the moment hers and absorbed in her.

" *Ti piacio io?* " he asked softly, as if for the first time.

" *Tu lo sai,*" she said, as he turned to go; and when she had shut the door behind him she stood leaning against it, staring at the wall. What a language, she thought. To translate it was to make nothing of an infinity of meanings. Did he please her, indeed!

Seven

CARLO DALVERIO stood as usual in the back of the box, regarding with satisfaction his beautiful wife and his beautiful mistress, his mother between them, and his friend Douglas Nevile seated behind them. His uncle, Andrea Dalverio, completed the party. Pina had chosen each guest for a good reason, Carlo's relatives because the whole Dalverio family held Douglas Nevile in unique affection, and Harriet Piers because Pina had charted a fixed course through potentially troubled waters and intended to hold to it. Carlo looked at the two exquisitely dressed heads, each wearing a delicious folly from the milliner whom he knew as he knew everything which made women decorative and desirable; and he thought, *per bacco!* if people are peering at us and beginning to sharpen their tongues on us, they will at least admit I have superlative taste!

He was always proud of Pina and confident of her wisdom and patience. Her intuition had always been swift and shrewd, but in this instance he believed now that she had sensed his attraction to Harriet Piers before he himself had realised it. Pina was hot-tempered and jealous; he marvelled with regret and a useless feeling of guilt, how she was facing this exaction greater than any he had put upon her before. Her actions had been almost too perfect, too finely judged and controlled; yet what else was she to do? And he vowed not for the first time that he would come through this without hurting her in any way that he would not be able to repair. He was deeply attached to her and he would take more pains than ever before to make her sure of it.

As for Harriet—he smiled, with tenderness and a little ruefully. She was so young, and she did not know it; artless, and she did not know that; her efforts to play her part with skill and bravado were sometimes audacious and sometimes touching, but always intelligent; she would be nonplussed and distressed if she should suspect that he saw all this. And occasionally he came up short with a flash of real fear lest she fall in love with him. If that should happen she would really be hurt and there would be little he could do to solace her. He had to escape into the sophistry that this was an experience inevitable at this turn in her life, and that chance had made him the man with whom she was to have it. It was damnably unfortunate that she was so conspicuously alone. Much better had she been married or even a widow, those were natural situations in the sight of everybody here; but a childless American divorcée—that was almost asking for the harshest pronouncement that would be made. And here was Pina doing everything in her power to maintain the façade of particular friendship, an extension of her real friendship with Lydia Marchisi. There were aspects of it that could make him feel a fool if he allowed himself to glimpse them, but he knew better than to lapse towards that.

He thought his party seemed more spellbound than the performance deserved. The cast was uneven, the Scarpia like most of them, could not project a convincing fusion of grand seigneur and savage malefactor, but the soprano was delivering an enthralling *Vissi d'Arte*, and Dalverio listened critically, reflecting upon the mystery of that impalpable quality beyond the concrete such as a voice, a type of looks, a perfection of technique, a physical personality, which could make art and supernal experience out of material essentially banal, reducible to the abhorrent through overfamiliarity. He thought specifically of bungling students and bad singers who elected this aria for every test they had to meet; and of a literal infinity of women with whom a sexual encounter was equally drab; whereas a singer like the one on the stage or a woman like Harriet Piers could infuse experience with such freshness that she wrought an illusion of marvellous novelty. He was, of course, ruminating upon the mystery of genius, and upon the further mystery that even the most incontestable genius could not affect alike all who were present when it passed their way.

The soprano placed the two candelabra at the dead Scapia's head and feet and the crucifix on his breast, moving with schooled, fluid grace despite some portliness; she held the dark illusion she had created whilst the drums rolled and she left the scene with the curtains falling and the applause beginning. The house lights came up and everybody stirred, changing position, talking, discussing, and exclaiming.

" Come, let's go and smoke," said Carlo. " Mamma, I know you want your coffee."

" Why don't you four go along? I don't want coffee now. Zio Andrea will keep me company and I see Maria Lavigna already on her way up to visit us."

" I do envy you," said Douglas Nevile to Harriet as they went with Carlo and Pina to the Ridotto. " Spending a whole winter here."

" Yes, I am lucky. And it was so unplanned, it just happened. But you come often, I understand."

" I do some work for clients here. Patent-licensing, largely, there's a lot of that now between one country and another."

Harriet assumed that Carlo was one of the clients and she smiled at Pina's intimation that Mr. Nevile spoke little Italian. He did speak it, with an atrocious accent but considerable fluency, and Harriet could not put her finger on Pina's reason for saying what she had.

Nevile was a tall, sandy-haired, thin-featured man with fine blue eyes and a relaxed grace of manner, reserved but amiable; he was, like Carlo, charming in his way and Harriet was entertained at the vast difference between their ways, Carlo all glow and sparkle and kinetic magnetism, with easy confidence in his own attractiveness, Nevile equally confident in a broader, less egotistical sense, quiet, interesting and understated. It was plain that the two men were very good friends, linked by shared experiences which had their roots in the grace under pressure which has become one of the inspired definitions of men in our time. Harriet perceived that Douglas Nevile knew a Carlo who was sealed in a certain time-capsule difficult if not impossible for anyone now meeting him to penetrate, and she found herself wishing somehow to share in Nevile's knowledge. She had also become aware in the short half-hour at Biffi Scala where they had all met before the opera, that Nevile had immediately grasped the state of matters between herself and Carlo, a subtlety of perceptiveness clear in his grave friendliness towards Pina and the quiet twinkle of his eye whenever it caught Harriet's. Or was that only a special communicativeness between two Anglo - Saxons engendered by their enclosure in an alien, no matter how sympathetic, enclave?

They turned from the bar, chatting with various friends who drifted up to it and away, greeting Nevile along with Harriet and the Dalveri, with pleasure at his reappearance and inquiries as to how long he was staying. Clearly he knew most of Carlo's and Pina's friends.

" Do let's stroll through the Museum," he said to the three. " I've not seen it this year and there's always something not to be missed there."

They went in and wandered through the lovely rooms, whose integration into the theatre brought immediacy to the calligraphy, the manuscripts, and the personal mementos of the immortals who lingered on there. " It's one of the best things in Europe, don't you think? " said Nevile to Harriet. " But in such a warm, natural way. It doesn't seem a museum."

" No," said Harriet, " and there are times when it seems particularly like this one's house or that. I always feel as if Rossini had just gone out and left his things behind."

" What a nice thought," said Carlo, and Pina agreed, smiling.

" Somebody should write a good book about Rossini," said Nevile.

The bells rang for the last act and Harriet exclaimed, " Oh, we must hurry, we mustn't miss the lights going down." They laughed and she said, " I know, but I love that moment so."

As they came out to the lobby after the opera Carlo bought the last gardenias in the basket of one of the old pensioners from the Casa Verdi, pausing to chat with her for a moment. Harriet saw unintentionally the large denomination of the note that he held folded inside his palm and slipped into the old lady's hand, and the tender private glance that Pina gave him as they moved along. For an instant Harriet's eyes smarted; she turned her head sharply as if to look for someone in the crowd, and swallowed hard. A moment later she noticed in the eyes of Carlo's mother, Signora Nora, a thoughtful, penetrating expression which seemed to comprise a number of feelings; it was affectionate, concerned, inquiring, and when the brown eyes for an instant looked into Harriet's they conveyed kindliness but also, unless Harriet's imagination or conscience were hypersensitive, a faint censure. Harriet knew it for a warning, a warning which admitted that this woman's son like other men must have his pleasures, but that no component of those pleasures would survive any disturbance to the immutability and well being of her family. If she had known Signora Nora better Harriet might have yielded to a sudden impulse to grasp her hand for an instant and in pressing it, pledge deference to the inviolable; as it was, she could only look clearly into the woman's eyes and pray that her message was understood.

They strolled across the Piazza and through the Galleria to Savini's for supper, hungry and smiling and all talking together. Carlo and his party were greeted with affection which proclaimed that this fine old restaurant with its warmth and brightness and its air of burnished nineteenth-century luxury was and always had been a fixture in their lives. The older members of the staff came to greet Signora Nora and Carlo's uncle, everybody was made comfortable, the proprietor himself, attended by two captains, prepared to take the orders. Carlo said, " Let's see what our guests will have." Harriet smiled and shook her head at the caviar, the smoked salmon and sturgeon, and the beautiful antipasti wheeled up on their carts. Nevile did not look at the menu.

" Lots and lots of *prosciutto* first, please," he said, " and then *risotto al salto*."

" Ditto," said Harriet.

" Bravo! " said Zio Andrea. " The right choice." He stroked his full, old-fashioned moustache; Harriet thought him a darling, with his smiling pink face and white hair.

" The same for everybody," said Carlo, without further inquiry. It was the perfect, classic supper and so simple that only a great restaurant could produce it to perfection. Nobody could say just why. With all the millions of Parma hams in Italy, said Zio Andrea, why is it that Savini's ham is unique, with its chiffon texture and its faint flavour of peaches? And why, when a million Milanesi eat risotto most days of their lives, can one kitchen come forth with these crusted, sizzling discs of deliciousness whose origin was the frugal obligation to use up the remains of the midday meal, and whose final destiny this masterpiece which nobody else could achieve?

" It must be the old question of reducing matters to their elements," said Douglas Nevile. " One perceives perfection best at the level of fundamentals. It may exist in elaboration but then it can begin to be its own enemy."

" How long will you be here this time? " Signora Nora asked him. " When are you coming to me? "

In the course of talk about the rest of the week Harriet heard that to-morrow was the wedding anniversary of Pina's parents, which meant a full gathering of the Verocchi clan that would preempt Carlo and Pina for the evening. So she was not surprised later when Douglas Nevile as he escorted her to her door while Carlo and Pina waited in the car, asked her to dine with him, and she told him she would be delighted.

G

When Carlo telephoned next morning he asked, " How did you like my English friend? "

" Very much indeed. And I think," she added, " that his powers of observation are acute."

" So are yours. Cara, you were beautiful and you are discreet."

She might have blurted that such an evening as last night was becoming increasingly difficult, hedged round with little spikes and warning markers and signals to which one must pay the minutest attention while keeping one's footing and picking one's way without ever seeming to look. But, she thought, this must be even truer for Pina than it is for me; and she stifled the impulse to tell him so, though she knew she would please him. The trouble was that her admiration for Pina's behaviour was purely of the mind; her heart could not concur without stumbling. And this above all she had to hide.

" You have not been listening," said Carlo in his tone of reproach. He had been talking to her in ardent, breathless little words descriptive of her physical beauties and the particularity of his delight in them, and he wanted her to answer in kind. Instead she had only breathed, " yes . . . yes . . ." So he was a little cool when he asked whether she was dining with Douglas Nevile this evening.

" Not only that, but I will jump ahead of you and say you are not to be tiresome and jealous about it. He's *your* friend."

" He really is my friend," said Carlo soberly. " But if I were in his place I suppose I would react in my normal manner to a tête-à-tête with anything as beautiful as you. Ah, I am terrible, bad, wicked, evil, treacherous——"

" You are," she said, " and if you don't stop talking like

this you will make me begin to suspect you of crimes I hadn't ever thought of." As she said that, she was shaken by a sudden click of her wits which brutally asked her to consider whether there were other women beside herself in his life right now. My God! she thought, with a shudder, it's perfectly possible and I've been infantile not to think of it. For an instant she felt heartsick and mortified.

" Where are you dining, the Barca d'Oro? " Carlo was asking.

" Mr. Nevile didn't say. But Carlo . . ." Her voice was very serious and he realised it. He was unused to that. He said, " Well? "

" I want to ask you something—please. Promise me you won't try to leave Pina's family party and come to join us late somewhere."

She would have seen, had she been able to, a darkness come over his face but move away as he recognised the pure good sense and kindliness of what she had said. He was touched; eh! he thought, I am fortunate.

" I promise," he said. " And are you coming to Bergamo with me on Monday? " His voice became eager and warm again.

" Yes, I am coming."

" All of you? Each and every one of my treasures? "

" All of them. Everything." Oh, my God, she thought.

" You want to come, very much? "

" Very much."

" *Cara*."

" Darling."

" Don't be too charming to Douglas," he said fretfully.

" Don't be silly," she replied. " I——" And she clapped her hand over her mouth. In the glass across the room she saw a look of horror on her face. What had she almost said!

"You want what?" He never missed anything. "What were you saying?"

"I want him to talk about you," she said. "Why else do you think I'm dining with him?"

"I will tell him to talk about himself," said Carlo. "Of course I shall be seeing him during the day and by this evening he will have had his orders."

"Hah!" said Harriet, and with another ripple of amorous talk they finished with the telephone.

It had been an interesting evening and it would have been one even had they not had Carlo to talk about. At eleven o'clock they were still sitting over their cognac, Douglas Nevile enjoying his cigar and the company of this uncommonly pretty woman who was gracefully subordinating the present, which could only be the tacit admission of her relation with Carlo, to the past when she had been a child and Nevile a young man whose experiences he was rather flattered to be begged to relate. In one's middle forties, and by a person from another world and definition of age, it was surprising how one could let oneself be drawn out, well as he understood that it was Carlo's part in the experiences that she wanted to know.

It was, after all, an unusual story. Carlo at the end of 1940 was a sub-lieutenant in the Italian forces in the Egyptian desert, and Douglas Nevile a captain assigned to secret intelligence with the Seventh Armoured Division of General Wavell's armies which crushed the Italians at Sidi Barrani. In the course of certain interrogations of Italian officers in the vast prisoner-of-war camps at Mersa Matruh, Nevile had been struck, he said, by some element of personality in young Dalverio which set the chap apart from the mass. " It sounds absurd, put in a few words now, but it wasn't then and it was my job to look for certain possibilities. I found that Dalverio had no use for Musso or any of his rot, that he belonged to a family of strong anti-Fascists, who at the same time kept out of politics, put one foot before the other, and minded their own business—very profitable business, of course. They weren't the type to risk all for love, war, or any other high flights such as we or you are prone to. In short, they were Italians, with the usual realistic views and the usual ability to put up, shut up, and survive. Their son was in the army because everybody's son was in the army. He had no use for what he was doing. He didn't believe in it and he scorned the whole jackal performance."

" Was his father still alive then? " asked Harriet.

" Oh, yes, very much so."

" I've got the impression," she said, " that his father died in some way connected with the war but I don't know quite why I think that—I've had a feeling that Carlo would be reluctant to talk about it if I asked."

" I expect he would. His father was splendid in his own way." Harriet understood that Nevile would come to that in due course.

Nevile went on to relate that his first impressions of Carlo had been put to stringent and protracted reappraisals, and that Carlo had passed every test of his potential reliability. " In the course of all this," said Nevile, " we stumbled on the sort of coincidence it would never occur to one to invent. Going back as we had to into Carlo's family history we found that the Dalverio grandfather had fought with Garibaldi. It happens that a distant cousin of my own was one of those

Tuscan Englishmen like Hugh Forbes who also joined Garibaldi at Rome and in Sicily. In the circumstances it was a bond between Carlo and me. I dare say it meant more than it would in ordinary times. At any rate, when we were preparing for the invasion of Sicily early in 1943, I asked for Dalverio's release because I needed such a man in particular jobs that I was going to have to do, and he was the man I wanted."

" And did they release him? "

" Not without the greatest trouble. It took a long time and I never quite believed we could pull it off. Finally they gave in and paroled him in my custody—most irregular, of course. He was assigned me on my personal responsibility."

" So that your life was in his hands."

" And his in mine. I never made a better bargain. He was invaluable. He was with us, with me, actually, from Sicily in July until the end. He was in the greatest imaginable danger. He belonged to nothing, in the event that he was captured. Nobody would have been able to acknowledge him. He had no uniform, no papers, no identity. He simply melted into the population wherever we were, dressed in rags and living I can't think how."

" A spy for you." Harriet was sitting spellbound, her chin on her clasped hands.

" He was whatever we needed—reconnaissance, messages, information, anything that could be done by an Italian, a peasant or a workman or whatever, and not by one of us. He was not only on his own among the people and in case he fell into the hands of the Germans or the Fascists—he wasn't even known to any of us except to a strictly closed list."

" Didn't he ever emerge—even towards the end? "

"Towards the end, yes. After they had organised Mamma Mia and——"

" What in the world was that? "

He laughed. " Of course, it does sound odd. The Military Mission to the Italian Army. That was after they had come in with us, though they didn't really get into action until January."

" Which January? " She spoke without thinking how queer this would sound to a man whose whole life was marked by the calendar of those years, when she had been a school-girl and could now remember little of her remote impressions of the war.

" 1945," said Nevile. " Carlo expected to go back to an Italian unit in action on the Po, but the previous autumn he heard that the Germans had arrested his father."

" Where? " asked Harriet, with a slight gasp.

" Right here in Milan. Carlo's father had been doing what a good many Italians did, hiding Jews and political fugitives, helping them escape to Switzerland, looking after their families. And helping the partisans with money and supplies. All behind the façade of business as usual. They were quite matter-of-fact about it."

" What happened to him? "

" They sent him in a transport to Mauthausen."

" A concentration camp."

" Yes, in Austria. A bad one."

" Did they—did he——? "

" No. He didn't die there. Many did, very many. He was still alive there when the war ended and Carlo went and brought him home."

By the ensuing silence Harriet realised that Carlo had brought home a dying man, and presently Nevile said, " He didn't live long. He was never able to eat, not at all. I saw him before he died that summer, only a bit after the war ended."

" So Carlo did stay with you until the end."

" He was fanatical after they'd got his father, and even I don't know everything he did. He was a brave, resourceful man." Nevile smiled rather sadly. " It's not often one knows an Italian in just the combination of circumstances which brings out those qualities. They're very different from us."

" Cynical."

" Yes, and rational. All the silliness about them, the gestures and the panache, the hot tempers—it doesn't mean a thing. Underneath it's cold reason. They'll fight when they care what they are fighting for, but they very seldom care. Once they do care they can fight, and their endurance is quite unbelievable."

" They care about their families," said Harriet quietly.

" And not much else, which isn't surprising in view of their history."

" I like them very much."

" So do I. But for quite other reasons than the usual, the superficial ones. Sometimes I find them irritating. Their bureaucracy and procrastination drive one mad. Then balance that against their energy and their efficiency—and their charm——"

They laughed. Suddenly Harriet said, " Do you know Pina well? "

" I don't think so, really. I doubt that anyone does except her family. Of course I came to their wedding."

" When was that? "

" In the autumn of '46. You can't think how extraordinary it all looked to me. I'd left here a little over a year before, when Milan was like every place else, rubble and ruins and all that. Even then, though, they had shops open and trams and taxis running when nobody else had. And when I came for Carlo's wedding I could scarcely believe my eyes. Lots of ruins still, but everything going full tilt, Carlo and all his friends making money, everybody beautifully dressed and well fed, the war might never have been. They'd even rebuilt the Scala and opened it—less than a year after the end of the war. Incredible."

" There was American money and help behind that."

" Of course. But the labour was theirs, that driving energy —I believe they'd have got it done anyway, without the American money. And there we were dragging along at the very bottom of things, grim and rationed and nothing done. Those ghastly queues and coupons."

" I know. Even I know about that. I was in England in 1947. And even I had sense enough to ask who won the war."

" It's curious, you know, I never expected then that I'd have a friend here such as Carlo has been. One gets through a war, surprised to be alive, and goes home——" he shrugged."

" He's devoted to you."

" As I said, one doesn't expect it. Or perhaps I mean, not of an Italian."

She smiled, gathering up her gloves and purse. " I know," she said.

Eight

CARLO SANG most of the way to Bergamo. His repertoire was an idiotic mixture of love songs old and new, arias, American and Italian jazz, and a string of dirty little ditties whose words Harriet suspected he improvised. He knew he was acting like a boy and he was loving it. He taught Harriet some of his songs and prompted her to fill in when the songs were funnier as duos. He drove his Ferrari with diabolical speed and swagger, causing Harriet to marvel, between suppressed gasps and starts of terror, that this frightening form of juvenilism should persist in the Italian man. Like most Americans she was a natural excellent driver and Norton Piers had been one of the early leaders of the sports car craze, so that she had driven the fastest kinds of cars all over the United States and in Europe. But she knew, with a secret Chauvinistic scorn, that Italian women except for a few among the gilded youth, were not expected to drive cars well, if at all; that the men considered women drivers—good ones especially—an affront to their masculinity, and that to please Carlo she must seem to be inert and unversed in this subject unless she should have something to compliment him about. Her feet tingled with the effort not to push them through the floor when he roared past a file of trailer trucks on the brow of a curving hill, singing at the top of his lungs and glowing with happiness. He does, thank God, keep both hands on the wheel, she said to herself; but so far the keynote of this trip is Don't Look Now.

" *Ri-cor-da-te Mar-cell-i-no*," sang Carlo, with the bouncing verve of Carosone himself, and Harriet, infected with his gaiety, also felt that in herself it was only thinnest and brightest veneer. What lay beneath she was not quite sure; certainly an uneasiness she had not expected to feel, and on every side the echo of the injunction not to look now. Yet she was afraid to be so reckless as not to look. Her absence from Milano had begun at the week-end at Bellagio with Lydia and her family. Carlo early this morning had driven from Milano to Lecco, where the largest of his factories was. Harriet had come there in her little car the short distance from Bellagio and met him at a certain garage on the outskirts of the town, just after the noon whistles blew. She had left her car there, and to-morrow morning they would reverse the plan, when Harriet would go back to town in her own car alone. There was not much leeway for a catastrophic slip, but she could not feel easy in mind, and she was troubled that Lydia was in any degree related to the situation. She had said to Lydia when they were strolling on the terrace, gazing at the dark sparkling water and the glorious sight of the mountains in their winter dress, " Sometimes I wish I'd never got into this."

" Sometimes I wish it too," Lydia replied. " But you have, and we needn't go over the same old ground again—it will be all right if you keep your head."

" I'm perfectly sure that Pina knows. Each time I've seen her she's been calmer and smoother and more remote. I realised on Wednesday evening that she and I have never looked each other straight in the eye. Do you know how grotesque that is? "

" For you, it is. For Pina, I tell you, she's been through this many times before and she'll have to go through it many times again. Stop writhing about it, darling, or you'll lose your footing and then there will be some kind of mess. Do it, or don't."

Well, she was doing it. But she had not reckoned with the perfectly silly factor of terror at Carlo's driving which was actually brilliant no matter how it looked; he had the car wholly under control and she knew that as well as he did. And the sun was shining as they sped along the road skirting the river Adda, with the shimmering plain, green with new winter wheat, on their right, and the peaks of Sopracornola sparkling in snow, on their left. The road, said Carlo, had long been a *porcheria*, too narrow and twisting for the heavy industrial traffic that filled it, with an ancient interurban tram-track on one side and a sharp-edged ditch on the other; *Dio*! the accidents! But lately it had been rebuilt, it was well surfaced and spaced with the gay red and white markers of the province of Bergamo, and he knew every centimetre of it like the palm of his hand.

" And there's no fog now," said Harriet happily.

" Not at midday! "

" I don't see how you people stand it. The strain and the tension, and having to time everything by it."

" Sometimes that has its uses," he said, with a snicker. " It's true that most of the time the fog is impossible after four in the afternoon and Pina cannot endure the torment if I drive in it. She prefers me to stay in Bergamo."

Even, thought Harriet uncomfortably, at the cost of this sort of thing. She only said, " But think—I've had two days of glorious sun at Bellagio."

" Exactly. When it is glorious there the fog is worst of all in the Pianura."

" And the moon at night too! "

" The moon also to-night, I think," he said. " The wind seems right."

" Where are we going to stay? " she asked, with a note of shyness which caused him to glance at her and smile as at a child.

" You will see. In a very old house in Bergamo Alta which has been there for many centuries."

" Not a hotel? " She felt uneasy.

He laughed. " A hotel? Me—in Bergamo? My dear child."

" Oh, I thought——"

" Just thought you could disappear into a large beautifully appointed suite like any tourist and have a caller. Not in Bergamo. There are several quite comfortable hotels used largely by business men, most of whom I know. I own one of the hotels and all the people in the others know me. Not that a mother's son of them would care what I did or with whom, *cara*, but—*ecco*." The gate was closed at the level crossing at Sala, and he stopped the car. The gatekeeper was not in sight, nor was anybody else. It was the hour when people were eating, leaving the road and the surroundings deserted. Carlo took Harriet in his arms and kissed her, with tenderness and a depth of feeling startling in contrast to his boisterous mood roused by fast driving and the exciting presence of Harriet in a new setting. She was shaken, this was one of the most unexpected things he had done. She was familiar with his kisses and caresses in every phase of pleasure and passion, but at this gentleness, almost poetic in its harmony with the calm countryside and the smiling sunshine, she was wonder-struck.

He saw in her eyes what she felt. Then she closed them, with a slight motion as if to turn her head for escape into the eternal necessity to dissemble. But he said, " Open your eyes, *cara*. Do not be afraid."

" Of what? " she whispered, looking again into his eyes, very dark now and deep with feeling. She saw their expression change a little, a faint contraction cross his face as if of muscles bidden to brace themselves.

" My God, I am not quite sure," he muttered, and kissed her again.

The train came shrieking down the track, and the gate-keeper from her house, to turn the crank which raised the bars. They started again and the remaining half-hour of the way Harriet listened, fascinated, to Carlo's descriptions which she prompted with questions that surprised him by their acumen, of the work of his factories and their relation to the whole industrial complex of this region. She had not known what it was that the Lecco factory made. She was astonished when he explained that it produced most of the steel wire used in Italy for making the spokes of bicycle and motor-cycle wheels. It also made most of the metal stripping used for umbrella-ribs and the metal framework for many light articles. When she asked about the relative quantities of these products she was open-mouthed at his replies; they might not seem large in the United States, she said, but they were enormous here. Yes, he nodded, an umbrella was a joke in a sense, but Italian umbrellas in recent years had become a large export like thousands of other small manufactured articles; and the cycle industry was no trifle by any measure. Much of his wheel-spoke production went up the lake to Mandello to the big motor-cycle works which employed so much of the labour of the region.

Suddenly he glanced at her and said, " How should you be interested in such things? Why do you know enough to ask questions about industry? "

" Oh, I don't know much," she said, " but I've been taught—what one needs to understand."

" For what? A woman . . ."

She laughed. " Money, darling. How can one understand investments if one doesn't know anything about business? "

" But a woman," he said again, shaking his head. " What have you to do with investments? "

" I manage my own."

He was incredulous. " How can you! " he said, almost jeering.

" Well, I was made to, by my grandmother. Haven't you ever heard that more than half the invested money in the United States belongs to women? "

" Heard it," he said, jerking his head, " but who could believe it? "

" Well, it's true. And my grandmother was the only child of a rugged old roughneck who made his money in mining— oh, it's all such ancient history, Carlo."

" No, go on. I'm fascinated. What kind of mining? " He was no longer driving like a racer.

" Copper, lead, silver, various gambles in Nevada and Colorado. He left it all to his daughter, and she really had a head for business."

" Which grandmother was this? "

" My father's mother."

" Then why have you the money? What about your father? "

Harriet sighed. This was the sort of thing she knew no Italian would understand and would disapprove with his whole soul if he could understand.

"My father," she said. "Well—my grandmother didn't think much of him. I suppose it was her own fault, she brought him up—but the way he turned out, she simply left him an allowance to live on and left her money to me with directions that I was to be taught to take care of it."

Carlo's face was a study. Harriet was not sure whether he was more astonished or more affronted.

"I'm sorry," she said, with a little laugh. "I know it sounds horrifying here. But it's not the least peculiar in the United States."

"And where is your father now?"

"He lives in Mexico."

"I thought your parents were in New York."

"My mother is," she said, resigned. "Don't make me spell it all out, Carlo. Everybody's been divorced and remarried, on and off the merry-go-round, and "—she looked at him with an expression which moved him sharply—"I loathe it."

"*Poveretta*," he murmured.

"Compared with your lives here, it's a shambles."

"But if you were Pina," he said, with sudden pungency, "if you had Pina's life to live, you'd have divorced me long ago."

"That's what I did," she said quietly, "and here I am. There Pina is. Oh, look, Carlo, is that Bergamo?"

"Yes, but don't look down there to your right. That's Bergamo Bassa, modern Bergamo. Look up there." He pointed to the left, where the soft pinkish mass of an ancient town clung, gently moulded to the shoulder of a mountain.

" Bergamo Alta. It's nice, you see, the old town is unspoilt and the modern one has room to grow."

" And your factories here——"

" *Basta* factories! I'm hungry! "

" Tell me what you've got here," she insisted, " you made me talk."

One of his factories made cylindrical steel products, he said: drums and tubing and such for the chemical industry; another made metallic parts for small machinery, anything which moved or turned or rolled; electrical appliances, for instance, but an infinity of things. How many coffee-grinders do you suppose are manufactured in Italy, and we make the ratchet gears for most of them. Gears for any kind of small machine. " And now," he said swinging the car to the left and starting up a long, climbing street, " keep quiet, because I am worn out with talking and I want my lunch."

The street rose towards the upper town, branching at its end right and left. He followed the right-hand turn, sweeping up in a series of curves and pausing at the gateway in the old city wall to let another car come through. Harriet looked at the lion of San Marco on the arch and asked whether Bergamo too had been part of the Venetian Republic.

" For three hundred years it was; the westermost part. It was fortified then, all this was walled."

It is fortified still, she reflected, in its own beauty. She had seen many of the celebrated hill cities of Italy and learnt their histories with more than the usual tourist's interest; but this, of which she had heard nobody speak in the same terms as Assisi, Arezzo, Gubbio, Todi, Orvieto, had its own quality of wholly unexpected enchantment. Perhaps that was Lombard; she wondered why, looking at the shuttered houses squeezing the narrow streets, their faded tints soft as cushions

H

that one might reach out and touch. The shops were closed, the streets deserted, the people had eaten and were shut in their houses resting. Carlo drove past the Piazza where the domed cathedral and Santa Maria Maggiore presided over a square whose gracefulness and intimacy made Harriet think, this looks like a cosy place; but she said nothing. He swept round back of the Piazza and stopped before a very old house, faded to a creamy, sandy tone that was neither xanthous nor grey, wonderfully garnished with wrought iron and spread across the crest of the rise between similarly beautiful neighbours.

He leapt from the car and came round to help her out. The central doorway of the house was a great pane of glass, and through it she saw a small balustraded courtyard, with doors right and left to the interior, and beyond the balustrade the sight which made her stop, her eyes enormous, and gasp, " Oh! How divinely beautiful! "

Carlo led her through the courtyard as an old manservant dressed in a red and black striped jacket with brass buttons came forward from the entrance at the right, beaming at Carlo and bowing to Harriet with easy grace.

" We're starving, Domenico," said Carlo. " Tell Anna we will eat as soon as she is ready. Come," he said to Harriet, " this way."

" Oh, just a moment," she begged. "Please let me look!" She was standing at the graceful balustrade, looking down over the terraced fall of gardens clinging to the bottoms of the houses, green even in the midst of winter; and at the descending planes of the ancient roofs moulded to the hillside up which they had come; and beyond them to the sweeping Lombard plain, with the modern city of Bergamo filling the foreground and the richest farmlands of Italy spreading away as far as the eye could see. She found the sight one of those beauties too moving to make possible any words; she reached for Carlo's hand and stood there squeezing it, gazing before her.

" Yes, yes, I know it is beautiful, I am glad you like it," he said, " but please won't you come upstairs before I drop dead of starvation? "

She let herself be led away, still looking over her shoulder at the view; but when he took her inside and started up a wide, shallow stair curving through niched and vaulted walls, and opened a high, richly decorated door, she stood in the great room and said, " I had no idea. I never imagined."

The room was dim, soaring and vaulted at the top, with a frescoed ceiling of the Venetian school, tumbling with colour and glinting with gold. The dark rosy silk walls were hung with portraits and old-fashioned landscapes; the floor of exquisite hardwood mosaic was laid with small, precious rugs; the furniture was old, grown into its setting over a span of continuous age so long that one epoch blended imperceptibly into another; even the ugly and clumsy things of the last century were effortlessly absorbed.

" How lovely," she whispered, looking slowly all round the room. " How perfectly lovely. Carlo, is this your family's old home? "

He nodded, leading her to a small dining-room opening from the salon. They sat down, Harriet waiting eagerly for whatever he had to tell. " My grandfather and his brothers were the last to live here. The next generation, my father's, began moving to Milano."

Domenico began to serve their luncheon.

" Your Garibaldi grandfather? "

He smiled, pointing to a portrait. " That one."

"But he hasn't got a red shirt! That's a different uniform."

"No. The red shirts were earlier and also later. This uniform is the *Cacciatori delle Alpi*—see the hat with the feather? The Alpini wear them still. Of course the portrait is a pasticcio, it was painted years later. My grandfather joined the Cacciatori when he was fifteen years old—in 1859. It was not the thing to do, you know, among good families."

"I didn't know. I thought——"

"Oh, people were proud of it later. We have all been taught to be. But many Italians will tell you that the Cacciatori and the Thousand were just a rabble."

"So were the Minute Men."

"Well—so are most libertarians. The Bergamaschi always have been, they have always resisted tyranny."

Harriet remembered her evening with Douglas Nevile. But she only said, "Who lives in this house now? It's a big house...."

"I keep this part of it—just a small flat; and the rest is rented to various people. There are a few old relatives tucked away in it, of course."

She was looking preoccupied, her expression was full of uneasy concern. He knew what she was thinking; he might have been impatient with another sort of woman for such thoughts, but no lady, he knew, could help feeling as this one does. She looked at him then and said what she had all morning refrained from saying. "You mean that this flat here is just yours?—that Pina and your children never come here?"

"Never, *cara*. If it must have a definition, you would have to say it is a *garçonnière*. And yet, to me it is not quite such a flippancy as that." He looked for a moment round the room. " If you wanted to believe that I use it more because of my business and because of my sentiment about the place, which Pina does not share, than for my much-advertised sins, you would be right."

That last might or might not be true; but there was no doubt of his attachment to the house and to the ancient groundwork of his family. One thing appeared clear, and she said it with relief. " It does make me feel I know you better," she said. " Like——"

" Like what? "

" Your friend Douglas Nevile told me some interesting things last week. More interesting, even, in the light of all this."

" People will talk."

" I'm afraid you're so right." They looked at each other with comical resignation. " Tell me, how old is this house, Carlo? "

" It must be—*ma!* Some of it sixteenth century, some much earlier. Bergamo is old."

" That always seems so wonderful to us."

" Will you have some cognac? " he asked, when Domenico had served their coffee.

" I don't think so, thank you."

He touched her cheek. " I want none either. I do want——" His brown eyes glowed. " Do you? "

She did not feel like talking about it. They went back through the salon towards another pair of tall decorated doors at the far end of the room. Walking along with him, spellbound by aged beauty, his arm across her shoulders, she wanted to be lost wholly in this moment and in the enchanted past; she wanted no intrusive thoughts flung off from the corrosive wheels of actuality; nothing of the mundane. He might have spoken the truth a moment ago, but she could not evade the crudity, shoving, grimacing at her in spite of his reassurance; the idea of other women who had come here with him, and the probability that Pina never came because if he were to have such a retreat at all, she much preferred it be away from Milano. Desecration, thought Harriet, heartlessness; those women!—how I hate to be one of them. I want to be different, I want to be a rarity and cherished, I want to be myself. Suddenly the voice of pure reason, like one crystal drop, tinged in her mind's ear. If Pina can put up with her lot, it said, you can put up with yours.

" Now you will sleep," said Carlo, bending over to kiss her again. He went to knot his necktie at the looking-glass; she lay and watched him finish dressing. He ran the comb through his thick hair, which, Harriet said, had the purely Italian genius for growing exactly as it should; put on his jacket, feeling in his pockets for the things he carried; and fastened his gold watch on his wrist. Harriet loved his wrists, strong, flexible, delicately shadowed with dark hair.

" It is three o'clock," he said, " and I must go to work. Can you occupy yourself for the afternoon? I shall be here by seven-thirty. Shall I send the car back in case you want to use it? "

She smiled. " No, thank you," she said. " I've got my plans all made."

" I suppose you are going out to buy a factory." He wagged his head.

" Wicked. I am going out to walk all over this lovely old town and I am going to the Duomo and the Cappella Colleoni and——"

" Well, that is very commendable. And you will be good
and tired later so I will find you meek and complaisant and
can do whatever I like with you."

She shut her eyes, smiling, to hide if she could the unspoken
retort that he could do whatever he liked anyway. When he
had gone she lay still in the vast double bed with the linen
heavy as leather, and the hard woollen pillows which she had
come to like, her arms folded beneath her head; and she
stared at another fine painted ceiling and took stock of herself
and her situation and found that she had no answer for
anything.

Late that night Carlo drew his arm from beneath her head
and quietly got out of bed. He stood looking at her for a
moment in the light from the shaded lamp on the table; then
he put out the light and she heard him crossing the pitch-
dark room to the windows. She heard the heavy curtains as
he drew them, the thick scuff of the casements, the clank of
the iron latch and the creak of the shutters as he pushed them
quietly open. He stood looking out, silhouetted against the
white light of the moon. Harriet felt the air, delicious and
not very cold. She saw him, a beautiful creature of hard
flesh and muscles, reminding her more than ever as he stood
naked in the pale light, of a marble of Donatello or Michel-
angelo. He would not feel cold, she thought, for he had not
grown soft since the years when the cruellest cold was part of
his lot along with hunger and hardship and danger.

He turned from the window and came over to her, catching
up a blanket from the foot of the bed. " Come," he said, " I
want to show you something." She threw off the bedclothes
but before she could rise he picked her up in his arms,
dropping kisses wherever they fell upon her body; and
setting her on her feet, he wrapped her in the blanket and

led her to the window. They stood silent. Carlo holding her
in his arms.

Spread before them they saw the tender mass of ancient
masonry, mute behind its blinds and shutters, one block of
pink or ochre nestling against the next, as if for company and
comfort, the groups and clusters melting together beneath
their dark, low, serrated roofs; only the campanili of the
churches rose above the gentle levels to draw the eye up and
out towards space. The milky, faintly misty white light lay
across it all, spraying it with lustre, spreading down from the
mountains in a wide, shallow sweep to the distant plain
below. It glowed with light and silence. Any sound, any
motion, would have been desecration, but Harriet felt tears
of sheer ecstasy sliding down her cheeks and Carlo's arms
trembled faintly as he held her, standing there and gazing
at the shimmering white globe and its radiance streaming
across the beauty it had illuminated for a thousand years.

Perhaps they stood for twenty minutes, perhaps less; but
when they stirred at last, to turn towards the room, they saw
that the bed lay full in the white light. Carlo took the
blanket from her shoulders and laid her down, staring at her
face. " You will not be too cold? " he whispered, and she
shook her head. His eyes kept their rapt, solemn expression,
something she had never seen before; every flash and play
of his mind and his appetites had shone in his eyes and she
had learnt to know them well, but this was new. He lay
raised on one elbow staring at her, from the tips of her feet
to the wide arcs of her dark brows, tracing with finger-tips
like feathers the lines and curves, the light and the dark, the
moulding of fine flesh and delicate bones. He was silent,
while she looked at him, knowing now that she could no
more keep her heart from showing in her eyes than her body

from his gaze. He knew he should have spoken, he should for reason's sake have broken the spell of this beauty shining in celestial light and brought it back to earthly pleasure; he should play, he should shout, he should get on with it in all its joy and heat and gusto. He was dumb. He looked into the wide, pale eyes, wide with helpless admission of the truth. His mouth trembled, he let his eyelids fall; he heard his voice choked and struggling, say " Harriet! My love! " and he felt he had crossed into a country where the old charts and guideposts might be useless.

Nine

But life went on as before; and since in all his experience he had never yielded to the power of romance to shake judgment, disrupt order, and make misery, he was not going to do so now. He was not going to allow Harriet to surrender to any such assaults either. Though this bade fair to absorb him more than any love-affair he had ever had, it too would be kept within the bounds of the good sense and realism by which he had always lived, fortified by generations of equally sensible forefathers. In Bergamo even at a moment of revelation he had not needed to remind himself of this, and he had sensed from the first the particular dangers waiting to confound a man who committed himself even by a word to a romantic adolescent, which sane people supposed all Americans to be in matters of love. Look at their books and magazines, look at their films, listen to their songs—*Dio!* look at their lives! Look at Harriet herself and that pasticcio of a family of hers. In fact, she had no family, she had only a mess of broken trunks and boughs, and trees uprooted like the tragic sight of the ruined park at Cernobbio a year or two ago after the tornado; nothing to give her strength or shelter. *Poveretta!* he thought, as he had done before. It was too soon to judge how she would consistently behave, but she had learnt so much, so well, so quickly, that he hoped for the best. Still, he was alert to the dangers.

The time since Bergamo had held no surprises, thank God;

their separate returning to Milano had gone without a slip, and how much more Pina knew than she had before he did not know and did not want to speculate about. Driving back to Lecco where Harriet was to take her own car, they had talked quietly, agreeing that the time had come to be seen a little less often together in the frame of social engagements; on the other hand, there must be no sense of a break; it was a thing to be judged carefully whilst they made their way through the mined terrain where any misstep could detonate a scandal. It is not Pina, he said, who would precipitate a disaster so long as we act with discretion and I keep her reassured.

" I know," she said. " It is other women." She looked at him for a moment, her lips pressed together, very reluctant to say something. He touched her gently and said, " What is it, *cara*? "

" Sometimes when I have seen women," she was thinking out her words carefully; " sometimes—oh, you know where they gather——"

" At Sant Ambroeus," he nodded, " over those sweets, and at the hairdresser's; and they meet at Pirovano, and Ferragamo—yes, I know what you mean. And they look at you in a certain way——"

She nodded. " And they're jealous. Much more plainly than anything Pina ever shows."

" They are curious, rather, perhaps," he said.

" No, jealous. Two or three whom I recognise by sight but haven't met. I can imagine exactly what they are saying."

" And why? "

She nodded again. " It would be too much to expect me not to sense that."

It would, he thought. Obviously certain former mistresses of his would be brutally curious about her, and some jealous, and all indifferent whether they embarrassed her. On the other hand, those who had settled down to real friendship like Tia Ortolani, were the greatest help; people wove these webs of mutual understanding out of the filaments of long ago, long after any current had ceased to charge them.

" Well," he said, " what you say may be so. But so long as Pina remains as she is, that is your protection as well as mine, from real trouble or scandal."

Harriet said she hoped so. She was feeling shaken.

He had not gone to see her every day, partly because he wished not to make it too much of a habit, and partly because when he did not go to her he went straight home as soon as he could finish at his office. If Pina was secretly unhappy at the reason for his extra attention she was also consoled by it. And such was the confutative nature of man that while his hours with Harriet were growing into the most ecstatic experience that he had ever known, his love for his home and his children, and his tenderness and gratitude to Pina were deeper than they had ever been before.

When he came into Harriet's flat one afternoon late in January she was finishing a conversation on the telephone.

" Fine," she said. " I'll be there on Thursday afternoon. No, but I wanted new ones anyway, and I can get Heads up there. Anything I can bring you? "

She held up her lips to Carlo, with the telephone still at her ear.

" All right, Sadie, from Pucci, but it'll probably cost as much right here. 'Bye, darling."

When they had embraced until they could forget the need

of it for the moment, he asked, " Where will you be on Thursday and who is Sadie? "

" St. Moritz." His eyebrows went up in peaks. " Those are some friends of mine from San Francisco, Sadie and Robert Keyes. They've just landed in Paris on the polar route on their way to St. Moritz."

" But what is this, so suddenly? " He scowled, but she moved into his arms and with all the little things he liked, with words and certain sorts of kisses, she tried to please him. She held his face between her hands and with her lips caressed his eyes, his brows, the corners of his mouth, the silky tops of his cheeks, whispering in English, " Darling, oh, darling."

" Not that! " he said, in Italian. Mostly they spoke Italian when alone except for this one word of hers. He held her hands tightly and said, " *Not* darling. Sadie is darling and Lydia is darling and everybody is darling——"

" Everybody is *tesoro* here," she said. " And I got so used to thinking I would never be able to tell you what I felt or call you anything I meant——"

" So you call me darling in English because it doesn't mean anything. I see."

" Don't tease me," she whispered. " Don't scold."

" *Va bene*. What am I to you? What do you want to call me? "

" My love," she said, her lips touching his. " *Amore mio*. But I was afraid. You don't mind? " Her voice was timid.

" No, I don't mind," he muttered, " God help me. Now what is this about St. Moritz? "

" These are ski-ing friends of mine, and we made a plan long ago to meet for a week at St. Moritz."

" When, long ago? "

She could not understand why he catechised her so closely and why he made such a play—if it was a play—of jealousy. Can't he see, she thought, that I could not look at another man?

" When was this? " he repeated.

" Months ago, when I wrote I was going to stay here for the winter. Usually we meet at Sun Valley. And I'd forgotten all about it because—oh! " she cried, " you know why! Oh, *darling*——! " And she clung to him. " Oh, I'm sorry, I forgot all about the silly word, I only want—— "

" Yes? " he said, with the note of excitement, and she saw it in his eyes. " What do you want? "

She whispered in his ear and he stood up and carried her to her room, all in a swift sequence like a wind in the dark.

" So now tell me this thing about St. Moritz," he said later, lying with his arm under her head.

" Well, as I told you, I've had something else on my mind, and I'd forgotten just when I had said I'd meet them. And as it turns out, they've had to come early because of a law case he has to be back for. So they've got the rooms booked for Thursday, I can't imagine how, and to tell you the truth——" She turned her head and looked at him quietly.

" What? "

" Don't you think," she said slowly, " it might be wise if I were to be away somewhere for a week and you here—you see? "

He did see, and she was right. " But what shall I do? " he said, in the queer fretful tone which if one did not know him well one would think petulant. It had a feminine quality preposterously out of key with everything about him. " A week, you say, and St. Moritz—*per l'amore di Dio*! I shan't have an instant's peace. How can I tell what will happen there? "

" Nothing will happen," she said. " Nothing. Don't you understand? Nothing can possibly happen."

" Why? The whole *porco mondo* is there! "

" But what difference can that make to me? Don't you understand? " she said again.

" Understand what? "

She bit her lips. " If I say it you'll be cross," she murmured. " My God, I go mad trying not to say it! "

" Not to say what? " He was eager again, and excited, leaning over her intently.

" What I mustn't say," she said, almost wailing. " What doesn't exist in Italian, and if it did, I still shouldn't say it."

" Say it, then, say it in English."

" Oh, no." She shook her head sadly. " No."

" Say it! "

" Very well," she said in English. " Listen to it, since you insisted. I love you. *I love you.* Don't you know it? Oh, Carlo, don't you know it? " She was almost in tears.

" Yes, I know it, my poor child." He had heard her with emotion, he was very moved but he was prudent too. He held her, caressing her face with one hand and tingling with pleasure when she kissed his fingers as they touched her lips. " I know."

" And it was not supposed to happen."

" No, it was not."

" But it has."

He saw in her face what she was trying to hide, the longing to hear him reply with the words which his language was too wise and too spare and too subtle to indulge in.

"Be good," he whispered in her ear. "Be good, be patient. *Anch'io, ti voglio bene, tanto bene. Oh! come sei bella!* " he cried, as if for the first time. " *Come mi piaci!* "

And Harriet thought, with that shred of her mind not engulfed in the vortex, we are right back where we started.

He telephoned her at St. Moritz every day, sometimes twice or three times. He kept such close track of her days and nights that he might almost have been there himself, as he had of course, many times. He knew exactly when one went out to ski, when one came in, when one gathered for cocktails before luncheon and dinner among the darlings and the pet-names who formed the bejewelled lid of the world's most extravagant human snuff-box. He liked an occasional dip into that world but he did not want Harriet in it without him. He should have been there, they both said, it would have been heaven; but since he was not he had to content himself with her answers to the minutest questions he could think to ask. He knew every slope and every mountain and if he was surprised at the ski-ing he heard she did, he kept it to himself. She must be very good indeed, far better than he had imagined, and he was tormented by the desire to be there with her. Then those damned parties; who was there? "Who is paying court to you?" he asked, every time they spoke. "Who is flirting with you?"

"Nobody, Carlo, nobody, believe me."

"Nobody?"

"Truly. Nobody."

"But they can't all be blind, they can't all be pederasts!"

"Oh, my God, why is *this* a good connection from Milano?"

"The line to Switzerland is always good. Tell me, what

are you wearing now? " She was dressing for dinner. She told him.

" And under that? " She told him.

" And under that? " She hesitated and he began to tell her.

" Carlo, Carlino! This is a hotel . . ."

" The better for them. If they listen they will hear me kiss you . . . here. And here. And here."

" This is terrible," she breathed.

" What is terrible? "

" You know."

" *Cara.* Is it, really? " His voice throbbed.

When she went back to her dressing-table her eyes looked as though they were full of belladonna, and her hands shook. She sat still, staring into the glass, until she was calm enough to pick up the little brush and go back to smoothing her eyebrows.

Then the day before she was to leave Carlo said, " *Cara,* listen. Don't come back to Milano to-morrow."

She had a horrible vision of some disaster there, even of Pina having overheard him on the telephone. Surely he could not be so bungling. She felt sick and he heard her gasp.

" No, no, be tranquil. Nothing is wrong. On the contrary." She waited. " I can get away for two or three days——" Her heart gave a lurch.

" But not here," she said. " You know who is——"

" Of course, of course. Not there. The Arlberg."

" Oh, Carlo. Not St. Anton. That's dangerous."

" No, Lech. Do you know anyone who goes there? "

She did not.

" Then when you leave St. Moritz to-morrow go on to

I

Zernez. Be at the Esso Garage there at one o'clock. On the farther side of the town, just before the bridge."

Oh, my God, she thought, I hope it's all right. He must be thinking the same thing. There were no amorous palpitations in this conversation. He understood, it was wonderful how quick he was.

" Don't worry, *cara*," he said. Like any man he hated explanations but he wanted to put her at ease. " Pina's aunt in Brussels is very ill, she's the widow of a rich baron and Pina is her favourite niece. She's got to go there to-day."

Harriet breathed a sigh of relief. It flashed through her mind that whenever Carlo was away from Pina he telephoned her every day, and she did not see how he could do that from Austria. But he must have met that contingency somehow; Harriet dared not let herself think of everything.

When he saw her next day standing beside her little car at the garage which was closed for the lunch interval, looking exactly as though she were waiting for a mechanic, he could have shouted for joy. In those pants and boots and a fur-hooded parka she was a sight to see. Her figure was that tantalising thing, legs and hips slender as a boy's, feminine in their grace and in the contradiction which made no sight, when it was perfect, more exciting. Her face glowed inside the frame of spiky fur, her eyes were rapturous, and when he drove the Ferrari to the edge of the road he was out of it almost before he stopped it.

" Oh, come here, come here! " he cried, pulling her to him and running to a corner back of the service shed, where they were out of sight of the road. " Oh, *Dio*! " and they embraced as if they would never have the opportunity again. " You are more beautiful than ever, more beautiful than— oh! my God, I am mad, I am wild with joy! "

" You are beautiful yourself," she said, smiling at him, surprised that she could keep tears of delight from her eyes. He was bareheaded, dressed also in ski-pants and a black wind-breaker jacket, its open neckline filled with a dark red scarf.

" Harriet, *cara*! *Amore mio*! "

" I can't believe it. Oh, I'm so happy."

" Tell me, tell me everything."

" Everything."

Presently they went back to the cars. Carlo moved Harriet's things into the Ferrari and fastened her metal skis on the detachable rack alongside his. They locked her car and left it parked while they went to a Gasthof and ate thick tasteless soup and veal and potatoes and spinach and dark bread and huge pieces of cheese, sitting close together in a dark corner, talking, talking, in words and without words, and drinking a bottle of Dôle. When they got back to the garage the man was there and Harriet waited in the Ferrari while Carlo took her keys and went to arrange something. He had his own tank filled, and they started for Landeck.

" What did you do about my bug? " she asked him.

" Arranged with the man there to drive it down to Lecco on Monday."

" Oh, lovely." So they could be together almost all the way back.

The road was clear, there was not in fact much snow on the level ground, but Harriet said that the ski-ing had been excellent, although the weather was looking doubtful now. It was grey and might probably snow; it might even be bad all the time they were up here.

" And suppose it is? " said Carlo.

" We couldn't ski," she said, like a child reciting a lesson.
" And what would we do? "

" I don't know—teacher. You must tell me."

" Shall I tell you? "

" Not unless you want me to have a fit. Seriously, do you think we'll be all right at Lech? "

He nodded. " It's still January. Nobody else will be quite as smart as we are except perhaps some royalty who want to be incognito. Only the best skiers go there anyway and then later than this."

" Have you been there before? "

" Once. It is magnificent, the best I ever saw."

" I know, I've heard about it at St. Anton. But I'm worried about the weather."

" We can risk that. I don't think we have to risk people. They don't get to Lech until later, the real season there is March."

" I know. But going through St. Anton I'm going to lie down in that hole in the back. Somebody may be there."

" It may be getting dark by then. But I am not going to worry about anything. I want to enjoy you in peace."

If there is such a thing, she thought. They were approaching the frontier. " Why do you suppose this last stretch of road is so terrible? " she said. " You'd never know you were in Switzerland." She watched him weaving the car along the unpaved single lane, stopping at the turn-outs if he had to, and bumping over the frozen ruts. The road was cut in a narrow shelf between the mountains on their left and the steep ravine on their right with the frozen River Inn lead-coloured at the bottom. " At least the road is frozen now— but have you ever done it when it was pure mud? "

" Wouldn't you if you were the Swiss? It's always been

like this but I expect they were particularly satisfied with it in Mr. H's day."

But on the Austrian side the road was wide, fine and new, and he could make time. They marvelled at the tunnels of the Flexenpass, as well done as the Gardesana, Carlo said; and the Austriaci do a good job of keeping this road cleared. It was not quite dark when they came over the top of the pass and down into the valley where the village of Lech with its broad, low houses and cheerful lights, all but buried in snow, greeted them with the charm of a Christmas card.

"Heaven!" said Harriet, her eyes sparkling. "Utter heaven."

And Carlo had not told her about the enchanting Post-gasthof where he had taken the Bemelmans rooms, dear to the writer-artist whose family home this was, the bathroom walls of the suite painted by him with a whimsical itinerary of his travels. There was a fire in the little sitting-room, the bedroom was spacious and cosy, and Harriet was like a child in her delight. "I can't believe it," she said over and over again. "It can't be true, it's too perfect." It bore no relation to anything that was part of his world or of hers; it was a separate one for them to share wholly and alone.

In the morning when they opened their eyes, buried in goosedown and bliss, they looked at the closed shutters and then at each other.

"Shall we look?"

"Let's get the suspense over."

He went to a window and opened the shutters. From the bed Harriet saw only that the sky was cloudy but Carlo said, "Too good to be true. It has snowed in the night, a light powdering. Perhaps four or five centimetri—Dio! how lucky we are."

" Oh, how heavenly. They'll know downstairs what it's going to do, too."

" Speaking of downstairs I shall go down ahead of you and look around and sniff."

They had their breakfast, sitting up in the two low beds pushed close together. Carlo whenever he moved in the night had been giving the three-piece mattress the rough edge of the foulest oaths he knew, cursing tedeschi of every stripe from the Rhine to the Danube, and fighting the short, square featherbed which warmed either his feet or his shoulders, but not both.

" But I am here," she said, " and we have better ways of keeping warm."

" That's just the point," he growled. " It's the principle of the thing. *Imbecili! Cretini!* The only part of me this damned thing warms is the part that doesn't need it! " and he threw it on the floor. Laughing, Harriet retrieved it later, for the room was cold. She pinned the two featherbeds end to end with safety pins and this covered them in one bed completely.

" And how can you eat all that stuff? " he exclaimed, watching her calmly put away three semmels with butter and jam and three cups of coffee with hot milk. He had eaten a bit of a roll and gulped some coffee, saying, " Augh! " She giggled, she had never seen him so violently Italian.

" Austrian coffee is good of its sort, and you know it," she said. " And I need this when I'm ski-ing. Besides, I——" And she put her face down to her cup, knowing she was blushing. What a thing to do, what a time to feel like a bashful child.

He roared. " Of course it makes one hungry! "

She looked at his share of the huge tray. " Oh," he said. " Me—my appetite is special." He leered.

" Go away," she said, pushing him gently. " Go and get dressed. We want to get out."

He came back to report that he believed they had nothing to worry about. It was a small place, not yet full, and there was nobody here whose name he had ever seen before, also no English or American one.

" I shouldn't mind for myself," she said, lacing her boots. " People practically expect this sort of thing in my situation."

" You are perfectly sure," he asked as he had last night, " that you really want to start off with the Rüfikopf? "

" Absolutely." She beamed at him.

It was the toughest peak there was, in principle only ski-masters did it; but she knew about it and she said, " I'm in practice. There's no better time than now, suppose it snows all to-morrow? "

It rose straight up like a crag-topped wall behind the village; the Seilbahn, the lift, was only a few steps from the hotel. He watched her face as they were going up in it. She was interesting to him in a new way; she sat looking up at the peak, then following the drop with her eye in a practised, appraising manner of which she was unconscious. She smiled at him when they said a word now and then but she was not really thinking about him. They heard someone saying that the peak was nine hundred metres above the village; over twenty-seven hundred feet, she thought, as they stepped out. The drop before them was almost perfectly sheer for half its length; then the slope turned more gradual as it broadened out and swept down between clumps of firs to the level of the valley.

" Who first? " said Carlo.

" You say."

" No, you."

" Okay, I'll go."

She fastened her skis quickly, took her long poles, and without a trace of hesitation stood poised to start. He watched her closely. There was relaxed precision about everything she did which bespoke the expert in a degree inapplicable to most women. She must be very good. She sniffed with excitement and with a motion almost casual in its ease, she moved off on her left ski. God almighty! he breathed; but the right one came together with it like the blades of scissors and they stayed together as he watched her go straight down the sheer drop. Could she? She slammed straight down until, just before he could bear it no longer, his heart bumping in his chest, she began to *wedeln*, checking her speed; he stood open-mouthed, watching her little behind moving like a pendulum in short rays, with perfect synchronisation of hips and knees. Her track was like feather-stitching in new snow, dotted by the pricks of her poles; he had never seen a more perfect one. Past the steep drop she swept round in a perfect parallel and a dust of snow and stood looking up waiting for him to join her.

He had never had such a thrill. He had seen the Olympic women and she was fully in their class, the best, in fact, that he had ever seen.

Ten

ONE DAY was sunny and the sky was blue, which gave their pleasure the last scintilla of perfection. They had not been so greedy as to hope for that. The rest of the time the sky was grey but they were lost in a quality of bliss so extreme that they told each other many times, " This is impossible. It can't be real. It can't be true."

" Indeed," said Carlo, " life is not like this and so we must consider that we have gone to another world or another incarnation, where time is suspended and nothing has any reality except this "—he touched her face—" how beautiful you are, how extraordinary everything you do."

" You are the same for me."

" And we have shut out everything in the universe except each other and a minor concern whether the big snowfall will hold off. It is fantastic."

" You mean," she said, " you have never had such an experience before? "

Her eyes were incredulous.

He thought for a moment before answering. They were sitting in their own corner of the Stüberl downstairs, on the padded bench surrounding the big green tile stove, having their leisurely drinks at the end of the day. The place had the untheatrical theatricality of the Austrian *Landhaus*, its walls studded with antlers, its beams and wainscot, tables and benches of dark polished wood, its little leaded casements with embroidered curtains, its floor pocked by the spikes of mountain shoes. It smelt of beer and frying onions and beeswax and the dry sprucewood burning in the stove. Carlo spoke finally.

" No. I have never had such an experience before. For one thing, I have not known a woman like you. There is no other."

" *Amore mio*," she murmured, " it only seems so." She felt tearful and drove the feeling away, smiling.

" If there are others, then they are probably Americans too," he said, " and I should never have thought I would like that. A woman as a rule should not—" he paused and motioned to the barmaid to fill their glasses. " She should not do things too well."

" Can't there even be one thing she does well, just one little speciality of her own? "

" Well, one." He rolled his eyes. " But you . . ." He threw up his hands. " And I like it. It pleases me. It interests me. I would never have believed it."

" It is nothing," she murmured, " except we please each other."

" Besides, you are intelligent. This too is new to me. You know perfectly well, I don't have to tell you, I've had a horror of intelligent women. They are bores."

" I don't know anything," she said mournfully. " I didn't even go to college and most American women—girls—do."

" And does it give them anything you have not got? I tell you, they are pretentious bores. While you—you have learnt something. You know something."

" In recent weeks, perhaps yes. The real test whether I've learnt anything is—you know." She stared at him. Presently she whispered, " Carlo, sometimes I'm afraid to go back. Back to Milano—or to anywhere."

He leaned back, stretching his legs and looking at the toes of his gaudy red and white slipper-socks. He smoked his cigarette to the end and crushed it out in the pottery ash-tray. He turned his head to look at her.

" You had no child when you were married," he said slowly. " Why? "

" I—it's hard to explain in a way. It wouldn't have made sense."

" And did it make sense as it was? "

She shook her head.

" You were not living life," he said. " You were married but you were not accepting the fact that marriage is what it is. It is not this which you and I have," he said, touching her cheek tenderly. " This is also part of life, and it is not marriage. Marriage is nothing without children. And without trouble. If you did not know that and know what marriage should have been, you were afraid then too."

" I suppose I was," she said softly. " I hadn't thought of it that way."

" And you must not be afraid now. You have no physical fear, you are phenomenal in that way. Why should you have any other? You must not be afraid of anything, afraid of the world or of going back to it, because that too would mean you were afraid to live and that cannot be true of you now. You have grown too much for any more of that."

She was spellbound. This was a Carlo whom she had not known at all. In the light of his tastes and his habits and his capers it was almost unbelievable. She put her chin on her folded hands and gazed at him with the clear eyes he adored.

" I could not imagine being married to you," she said, " even though we are in heaven together."

He nodded slowly. " That is right," he said. " Any such idea would be completely unrealistic. If you could imagine it, or were trying to, it would mean that you were still a child, and children fear many things which we do not. I too, I love to be with you, I want to be with you all the time, I cannot get enough of you. But I am not going to spoil that by confusing it with anything else, or by being afraid to live it for what it is; and I am not going to let you be afraid if I can help it."

" Oh, you are wonderful," she said. Her eyes were full of tears. " I didn't know . . . I didn't realise . . ."

He shook his head slowly. " I am not wonderful, *amore mio*. I am a man, a very sinful man, guilty of unkindness and selfishness and many things that I am ashamed of."

" But a man. Not a boy."

" Eh, I said you are intelligent. Come," he said, with a flashing change of mood. " It is past time for another of those epicurean *Abendplatten mit Kompott oder gemischtem Salat* —my God, my God, no wonder the tedeschi are what they are."

" People eat mostly frozen food in my country," she said.

" And that is what makes you such an icicle in bed. *Andiamo*."

The next day, their last of ski-ing, he had a silly collision on a level stretch with a youth who turned unexpectedly, and in falling Carlo sprained his right wrist.

" It is nothing," he said in their room, while Harriet bathed it with hot and cold water: but they saw that it was beginning to swell. More because he wanted to avoid explanations at home than because of the pain, he consented when she insisted he let the doctor come to look at it. The doctor strapped it up and said it would be all right in a few days, but he told Carlo to use it as little as possible. When the doctor had gone Carlo scratched his head and made a face. " I suppose the driving to-morrow would not be good for it," he said.

Harriet was silent, looking at him with an apologetic little smile. He shrugged.

" Would you hate it if I drove? " she asked.

" Of course not. You shall," he said, but she saw him wondering how she would handle his car, which was a very expensive custom body mounted on the Ferrari chassis, only slightly modified from the racing car. She thought better of begging him not to worry, that did seem pretentious.

Their last night was yet another revelation in a broadening sphere of wonders, profound with contrasts and the interweaving of mood and feeling, action and reaction, tumult and stillness. Their relation had changed and deepened in quality and expression and in the acts and the words which could sweep from outrageous play to hushed solemnity. They were wholly at ease, more than intimate, more than passionate, infinitely relaxed. She had given up the futility of abjuring the words she wanted to say, and he the pretence that he did not feel for her what he did. Both knew what this portended in the short weeks to come but Carlo had shown how they must meet it and that was what they would do.

The fat chambermaid came pounding in with their breakfast at six o'clock as they had ordered, and Carlo went as usual to look at the weather. It was still dark and from the look of his back, standing there with arms akimbo (why do only Italian men do that, she thought) she knew what was happening.

" Snowing," she said.

" *Corpo d'un dio. Maledizione. Che porcheria.*"

" Why? Shut the window, love, it's cold. So it's snowing —think how lucky it hasn't broken until to-day."

" With three hundred kilometri to drive? God knows what we'll find in the Maloja."

" Oh, the Maloja," she shrugged. " That's nothing."

For himself that was true, he thought, but for her? Well, the hell with his wrist if he thought he ought to drive. He would see.

He saw at once. She did not ask a question. She had observed everything while riding with him, the gear-shift, the controls, the unfamiliar instruments. She adjusted the driver's seat, warmed up the motor gently, turned on the lights and the windscreen wipers. The snow was falling thickly enough to keep a curtain steadily across the road but he saw that she was perfectly relaxed; she backed out into it without a swerve or a spin of the wheels. " It isn't slippery, just thick," she said, and little else for a long time. She was wearing soft suède boots with rubber soles and her feet were as light and accurate as a cat's. She sensed in a moment the right balance between a safe speed and the compression-ratio of the engine which normally made a very high speed the best performance of the car. Very quickly he relaxed and sat smoking, looking at her every few minutes and admitting with his eyebrows and shoulders that there was nothing to do about this woman but concede that she could do superbly what women had no business doing, and make him take delight in her doing it. For some reason it intensified her femininity.

" And it doesn't come easily," he muttered once, but she

had either not heard him or pretended not to. At Martina the Swiss frontier guard told them that chains were necessary in the Maloja and they both nodded and said yes; but when they started again she laughed and said, " I bet you haven't got chains."

" Chains," he snorted. She would have carried them for the places he drove in winter, but they did flourish their bravado so!

She was perfectly cool the twenty kilometres of vile one-track road, turning off or backing unconcernedly into a turn-out when they met the trucks which always had work to do up here. When they reached the Maloja the snow was falling less heavily but the clouds were down so low that there was no visibility at all. The surface was slippery with grainy snow frozen as it fell. She slowed down and said, " Does my driving make you nervous, Carlo? Do you want to go down this yourself? "

" No," he said. There was an odd note in his voice. " I want to see you do it."

He doesn't like it, she thought, and if I'm going to do anything to discredit myself this is where it will be. She went down as she would have done had she been alone, with extreme care, probably with much more caution than he would use, she supposed. Not until she was at each one could she discern the markers on the right by which to gauge her place, and not at all the red mid-line of the road. She knew the pass well and she had so much natural road sense that she felt the serpentines in the rhythm that skilled drivers know. She kept the car at the same slow even speed by judicious choice of the lower gears. They got below the cloud-line more than half-way down but the grainy snow was still falling and she was still wary of it. When the road

flattened out before Castasegna the snow turned to streaming
rain and when they stopped at the Chiavenna frontier Carlo
sat surveying the sodden chill of his native land and burst
into a roar of laughter, saying " *Bell' Italia piena di sole!* "

" Anyway," said Harriet, " we can have coffee in that bar
over there. *Coffee*, Carlo! *Bell' Italia!* "

" And a *grappa* to toast an amazing driver."

" Oh, come, don't be silly. Anybody can do that."

" Any American? "

" I suppose so."

" Do you know that you've driven the entire way without
touching the brakes? "

" Well, my goodness," she said in English, " what kind of
damn' fool would? "

Angela was glad to see her, the flat looked cosy and charming, there was an accumulation of letters and messages which
she saw as the most immediate of several devices for keeping
busy; she had been telling herself on the way in alone from
Lecco how essential that would be. Be occupied, keep busy,
see more people, keep the time filled if it only means running
about spending money in the shops. But keep busy and don't
yearn, don't dream, don't maunder, don't think if you can
manage not to. Oh, it is not difficult at all to tell oneself
what to do. The question is, how well can one hope to do
it?

While Angela hurried about, disposing of luggage and
running her bath, Harriet went to the sitting-room with her
hands full of letters, to get accustomed to being here again.
She stopped with a little gasp in the doorway. The room was
filled with flowers, the pale roses that he always sent, sprays
of lovely white lilac from Holland, a faience tub in the corner

with a tall plant of mimosa in full bloom. Its fragrance was divine, moist and caressing; she stood breathing it, her eyes filmed with tears. He had known how she would feel to find herself alone again, he knew everything, he understood the all-gone sensation which she was determined to keep at bay. And how could he have managed this, he could only have arrived in Milano a little while before she had, driving in from Lecco in sheets of rain. It was past nine o'clock now.

The darling, she thought, smiling weakly at his ridiculous objection to her calling him that, when it meant as much to her as if she had invented a whole new language to express what she felt for him, which at the same time shut out every other being on earth. This was not going to be easy; but his tenderness, added to all he had said that evening at Lech, was fortification much greater than she had expected in the beginning. She had needed no admonition that to be in this situation with a man like Carlo meant pain in many degrees less than the inevitable great pain of final parting when it came. She knew well that she had to face an intervening series of little deaths but she was surprised to find that he understood and was trying to soften their impact. It never occurred to her to wonder whether he was feeling the same pangs, he was so supremely practised and wise about all this. He telephoned then for an instant, to make sure she had got home and to reassure her with a word of love; but he could not speak, he whispered, when she tried to thank him for the flowers; he would ring her as usual in the morning. She wondered with anxiety if Pina were already at home and had seen him arrive in ski-clothes; most probably not, he was merely surrounded by his household. His children would long since have been in bed. He had mitigated some of the

K

odious conspiratorial feeling for Harriet by not discussing Pina's plans, but it was obvious that Carlo had arranged to arrive home ahead of Pina, and that in turn meant he had somehow contrived to communicate with her without betraying his whereabouts. Oh, it is all so complicated and I do wish I hadn't . . . no, you don't! she answered herself. You don't wish anything of the sort. You are mad about him and you are prepared to see this through. She put her face into the cool yellow cloud of powdery blossom, drinking in their scent, then she went to her room and got ready for bed.

And it proved a little easier than she had hoped to keep the days crowded. She blessed her pleasant new friends for their spontaneous hospitality and the readiness with which they suggested this thing to do or that. She decided to give another " cocktail " early in March, like the one she had given in December, as the only practicable way to reciprocate so much kindness. She became aware that Tia Ortolani was inviting her oftener and seeing more of her than anyone but Lydia; and when the reason dawned on her, beyond that of Carlo's friendship with Rinaldo, she saw no cause to refrain from asking him. He came now every day in the late afternoon, and stayed until almost eight. They never felt ready to be parted when the moment came for him to leave, but Harriet sped him away with the gayest smile, the lightest touch, she could muster. Often they met later in public, at some evening party or at La Scala; they took the most elaborate care never to be apart together, never to say a word that was not intended to be overheard. It was a trying feat, but only a real fool could fail to carry it off. Harriet knew quite as well as Carlo that they were deceiving nobody. The luxury of relaxing into verbal and human intimacy, beyond all the rest, was a life-saving respite; and at such a time she could ask a question like the one about Tia Ortolani. If anything, he was pleased.

" You see? " he said. " I told you, you are intelligent. Yes, what you think was true—for a few weeks long ago. Tia is older than I am, nearly ten years older. She was very unhappy about something that Rinaldo did, and this was also before I knew him very well. It was long before I was married. For this reason, if Pina knows it at all, and I suppose she does, she does not hate Tia as she does——" He shrugged.

" Certain other women. And, of course, me."

" *Cara*, Pina will not indulge in any overt hatred of you now. She keeps more controlled than that. Pina only allows herself to hate when——" He stopped speaking and lighted a cigarette.

When he has lost interest in a woman, Harriet told herself with a suppressed shudder. For an instant she saw him from Pina's view. In that light he was heartless, he was cruel, he was selfish. She drew her hand across her eyes as if to shut out the equally horrible idea of how he appeared to women whom he had dropped. But she relaxed quickly; he had become good friends with some of them, his gratitude to Tia Ortolani was as gentle and real as his tenderness to Pina herself, to his children, to his mother, to Harriet. It was when she thought of his mother and his children that Harriet knew him capable of real love; just what he felt for his wife, for Harriet; what he had ever felt for any woman with whom he was amorously involved, she did not think herself wise enough to say. She had a certain sense of stability with him for the moment, but the moment was bounded by the first of April when her lease would terminate and she would go away—for the best, she knew, even while it wrung her heart.

She was surprised by an invitation to luncheon from Carlo's mother, and even more surprised after she had accepted, when Carlo told her that he and Pina were not to be there. Zio Andrea was there, the dear old gentleman with the beautiful white hair and moustache; and Carlo's elder sister Maddalena Corti with her husband and their eighteen-year-old son who was so like Carlo that Harriet almost gasped to see the same beauty in its pristine form, a man indeed and not a boy, but a clear slate with everything yet to be written upon it. The party was completed by an elderly Marchese Boninsegna and his marchesa, patrician people with fine aquiline heads and courtly manners, whose conversation was the most interesting that Harriet had heard in Italy. He was one of the great bibliophiles of Europe, known everywhere for his library and his scholarship. Harriet found herself wondering about the origin of this friendship which was somewhat uncharacteristic of the alignment of groups and classes as she had seen them; it was not equality of birth or community of intellectual or social interests which explained the warm and obviously long-standing affection between the Boninsegna and Signora Nora. Gradually through fragments of talk less erudite than that about books and art and history Harriet came to grasp what the bond was. It was philanthropy. She had heard little up to now of this, intrinsic to a tradition and an ancient civic pride which marked certain Milanesi. All that she had seen of good works were a few big parties and entertainments for the benefit of one charity or another, where the women appeared in gowns and furs whose prices would have maintained the beneficiary of the occasion for months on end; exactly the same thing as the theatre parties and balls which filled the winter in New York, run by committees of fashionable women—or those who strove to be—among whom Harriet's mother considered her presence important.

Everything about these people and this setting was different. There was a dark, dowdy heaviness about Signora Nora's house which at the same time was infinitely pleasant. The luncheon table was in the old-fashioned family style, covered by a polished damask cloth laid over a thick pad; the Ginori china, like the silver and the glass, was discreetly ornate and of the very best quality; a chandelier hung low over the oval table around which two solemn elderly men-servants in dark livery and white gloves moved in silent procession, serving perfect, classic Milanese food.

Harriet was fascinated, not alone by this glimpse of Carlo's old home but by its contrast to the house in Bergamo; and had she not known it already, she would have understood that Signora Nora was the real Milanese in the Dalverio amalgam, the daughter of long-established bourgeois wealth derived from and reinvested in banking, industry, and—Harriet had heard recently—hydro-electric power. There was a late nineteenth-century flavour about her house, her looks, her voice, her guests, for they spoke with a certain elegance of phrase and an idiom different from the crisp babble which Harriet heard elsewhere, just as the big luxurious flat of Carlo and Pina, with its beautiful, expensive décor, its shimmer of pale colours, crystal, and dramatic lighting was the quintessence of the best present-day taste.

In the drawing-room as they rose, about to take their leave, the Marchese paused before a large photograph which stood alone on a table, Carlo's father, for here were the eloquent eyes, the masterful mouth, the fine lean cheeks, tempered and sensitised by years and wisdom. The Marchese put his hand on Signora Nora's forearm and said in an undertone, " I think of him always, my brave, dear friend." Harriet looked away, reluctant to intrude, apprised by a few words of the identity and nature of the men who had quietly risked their lives for conscience and decency.

She found herself alone for a moment with her hostess, as the Boninsegna departed. Holding the hand of Signora Nora for an instant longer than the clasp of leave-taking, Harriet said, " Thank you so much, Signora Nora." She looked into the wise dark eyes as she had once imagined doing, and she said, " I shall be leaving Milano in a few weeks." She paused and saw with relief that the implication of her words was fully perceived. There was no change in Signora Nora's expression, it was bent upon Harriet with severe gravity. " May I come and see you before I go? "

" Any time, Signora," said Carlo's mother; and for a moment she smiled.

Harriet sat still for some time before starting her car, staring at nothing. If she had wondered on arriving why she had been invited, she knew all too well now.

Eleven

" Can it be only seven weeks? " said Carlo. He put out his hand and laid it on Harriet's cheek, holding it still while she turned her head slowly until her lips brushed his fingers. " Only seven weeks of this we have had? It seems a lifetime."

" Like a jail sentence? " she said with a shaky laugh.

" Oh, *stupidina*, you know what I mean."

They were leaning on the balustrade of the terrace overlooking the lake at the Marchisis' house at Bellagio. This was another contrivance, one of so many that the details of some were becoming confused in retrospect with those of others. Yesterday they had been at Bergamo again and to-day Carlo was supposed to have gone from there to Cremona on business. If the matter at Cremona really required his presence, he said, he would make a quick dash there and back from town one day soon. But this was the third week of February, the fog was tapering off, and there would be no reason—no opportunity, he said wryly—to stay overnight when next he went to Bergamo.

" I know," said Harriet. " It feels as though things were closing in on us."

" If we could only go ski-ing once more! "

But they could not, for it was the height of the season everywhere, and unless they could go very far away, farther than the Dolomites, the Engadine, the Arlberg, the Valle d'Aosta, the Apennines, they were sure to encounter people they knew. Carlo could find no way of stealing the time that a greater distance would entail and still, no matter how far they might go, there was risk. In sheer frustration he had thought of something so preposterous as proposing to Pina a long week-end at Cortina and manœuvring for Harriet the deferred invitation that she had declined before, but second and saner thought showed him how grotesque this was. Pina in any case would not have concurred, he knew now; he was becoming uneasy about Pina for the first time in his life. She was still polite, still very correct; she had not invited Harriet for some time past, but such meetings in any group of people move in random sequence; weeks can elapse without gatherings at a certain house after there have been many in succession. They still met elsewhere, and Pina's extraordinary imperturbability was unchanged—at least, he believed, so far as Harriet or most others could discern. But he knew how to interpret what he saw in certain people's eyes; the scorn and reproach of the Verocchi, the mean threat in the rat's beads of that hateful Minghetti woman, the worry and sorrow in the wise eyes of his mother. He knew too that the crux of their censure was not so much his infidelity as his choosing a northern woman, an American particularly, who would never understand the rules, written and unwritten, of the code. These signals where he saw them were like tiny flicks of fire in the brush-clad slopes of a mountain in dry weather; if there were any way other than renouncing Harriet, he knew he could stamp them out before they spread beyond control. But he was not going to renounce Harriet and so he had to risk the spreading of a brush-fire, fed by the dry plants of fear and jealousy and malice and spite. And Harriet, even before she was to leave Milano, might get burnt; he knew who the few friends were who would fight the fire and do their best to shield her, but those would be nothing against the legion who would ally themselves with the Verocchi and make her position untenable. He must not let her stay until any such crisis threatened her. And he must not let her know that he was worried. He must not let her know anything, indeed, more than she could sense by instinct; above all he must not let her know what she meant to him. For he could hardly believe it himself.

They wandered off the terrace on to the steep hillside which overhung the little harbour of Loppia, with its sleepy boat basin and the collection of fauns and swans, urns, cherubs, and carefully damaged copies of statuary which were lying out to weather in the stone-cutter's yard. It was high noon of a heavenly day; a north wind in the night had burnished the mountains, sharpening their outlines, deepening the shadows of their purple velvet robes, brightening to blinding brilliance their capes and crowns of snow. The water was dark dazzling sapphire, glittering and live with whitecaps, the shores the freshest green of spring. Each cypress stood out like a thick dark pencil sharpened to an artist's point. They walked slowly along the soft green slope, where lemon-coloured primulas bloomed in clumps amidst their furry leaves, and Harriet cried " Oh, Carlo! Look! " as they came upon some violets in a sheltered spot. She stooped to pick them, and then some primulas, making as they moved along a little bouquet which she carried back to the terrace and handed to Luigi, Lydia's butler, when he asked if they thought it warm enough to have their aperitivi out here. He would put the Signora's flowers in water at once but, he asked apologetically, had she looked to see if there were ants? "

" Oh, no," she laughed. " Surely not ants at this time of year? "

" At any time, there are ants, Signora," he said, bringing out two basket chairs and placing a low table between them. " It is a beautiful day," he said, with the delight which all these people took in every detail of their weather, their landscape, their world. He had never lived anywhere else, nor had his wife Giovanna the cook, nor the gardener and his family nor, said Carlo, laughing, any of the few thousands of people who had populated this promontory since the time of the highly disputable Pliny who had evidently managed to inhabit more places—" and for all I know, more beds, than your own George Washington in his day."

" But George Washington was not Italian," said Harriet, making a mouth.

" And so he did not use beds as the rest of us do, one sees."

Luigi poured glasses of Carpano for them and hovered for a moment, sniffing the air.

" It is not prudent to sit outside so early in the year, Signora," he said. " One takes cold."

" Only for a little while, Luigi. The sun is so glorious. We shan't sit out again after luncheon."

" *Per bacco*, we shan't," said Carlo when the man had gone.

" No wonder Lydia loves this place so much. She says she'd like to live here the year round."

" Well, Sandro would not; and Lydia if she is wise will live as Sandro prefers because he is no more special than the rest of us. But they are lucky to have these servants here all the time. That's unusual for these days."

Domenico in Bergamo was different, he was an old retainer, but Lydia's household here had been established since the war. Harriet did not say so, but she knew that Lydia had insured this comfort from the first by buying Luigi away from one of the hotels where, as head waiter, he had earned enough during the season to hibernate peacefully the other half of the year, doing a little smuggling on the side.

" Don't you ever open your house up at Guello? " she asked. She turned her head to look up and back towards the top reaches of the mountains which divide the lake into its two long arms.

Carlo shrugged. " Pina does not like it. It is old-fashioned, it was my father's house. Mamma uses it sometimes. And we used to come occasionally in the spring or the autumn when the children were small, but there's not much for them to do there. They adore Santa Margherita in the summer."

" Do you? "

He looked at her, weighing his reply. Then his face set in an unfamiliar way and he said, " I did. I used to like many things that I shall hate when "—his eyes narrowed as if to shut out a bitter prospect—" I no longer have you."

" Oh, God," she breathed.

He turned sharply in his chair and said, " Harriet! *Amore mio*! Must you go so far away? "

" After the first of April? "

" After the first of April." (And pray God, not before, he thought.)

" Oh, my love, haven't we managed not to talk about it? "

" Managed, yes. But think ? In this sense," he said roughly, " I have never thought. But now, now I do." His eyes had the dull look of despair which told her that he would suffer as much as she when they had to part. She had never really believed it before. She clung to his hand, holding her head turned sharply away until she had fought down her tears.

All afternoon they lay in the shaded room which she had come to feel was almost her own, so fond had she become of it since last September when she had settled there for her long visit with Lydia. She told this to Carlo, and added, " Now that we are together here it will mean so much more. Everything, in fact."

" *Cara*, don't think already in terms of memories."

" I try not to. But also I have to think that way, in order to keep my footing. I tell you. I *will* be realistic."

" And that means you will go straight back to New York when——"

She wound her arms round him and lay so close that he had to strain to hear her words, whispered against his shoulder. " Shan't I have to? " she said. " You know that the first of April is none too soon for me to leave Milano. And go where people think I belong."

He was silent for a long time. When he spoke his voice was dull, he spoke in a tone that she had never heard before; even as she listened, she thought remotely, this is without authority, this is beyond his control. He said, " My love, my dearest. Could you not go somewhere else, some place where I could see you? Paris—London——"

And how, she managed not to say, could you always be flying to Paris or London or anywhere at all? She only clung to him without answering. " Need you go to America? " he said. " All that way—after the first of April? "

She raised her head and braced herself on one elbow, looking at his face. She tried to speak, choked, rallied, and forced out the words. " By that time, beloved," she said, " I think I may have to get out of your life or something terrible could happen."

So she does know, he saw; and what is the use of hiding anything?

But the only wise measure against worry and dread was to keep them at bay with any means at their command. It seemed to Harriet that never in her life had she really laughed before, for such irresistible reason as Carlo's non-sense and pranks, and even without any reason when they looked at each other, making owls' eyes over some hopeless aspect of their situation, and bursting into boisterous laughter because they knew that if they did not laugh they might be tempted to weep. Harriet had been right when she said it seemed as though things were closing in on them. Carlo did not mention Pina but he did not need to. It was enough to watch his face when he made some suggestion that they devise a way to go to one place or another for twenty-four hours within the scope of a business trip of his; and then to see the curtain of frustration which dulled the depth and sparkle of his eyes when he dismissed his own ideas as im-possible. Harriet understood that it was now really dangerous for her to be out of town at a time when Carlo was, that no feint could insure protection if Pina should yield at last to the furious impulse to inform herself as to Harriet's whereabouts.

It was with burning retrospective shame that Harriet faced this. There came to her mind from the limbo partly of real oblivion and partly of wilful forgetfulness the memory of her-self not so many years ago, savagely tracking down some woman with whom Norton Piers was involved, using any means that came to mind, informants knowing and unknow-ing, the telephone in all its deviations from false wrong numbers to false names and messages; yielding to the drive of desperate jealousy and icily sure she was within her rights.

Nothing in Pina's conduct had yet suggested that she would resort to the same devices but Pina was a jealous woman, jealous by nature and surely by this time, jealous of Harriet Piers to the verge of frenzy. Where Harriet had once marvelled at Pina's phenomenal poise, her amazing discipline and bitterly acquired wisdom, she now marvelled that there was anything left of them. Harriet felt herself standing on the brink of catastrophe and Carlo, if he grasped this, no longer attempted to reassure her. Pina, he had always said, will do nothing so long as she feels the ground is firm beneath her feet; what then had happened to make Harriet sense that that ground was beginning to crumble?

She began to feel torn between the prospective agony of parting from Carlo, and the wish, as desperate, she thought, as the death-wish that one could not escape hearing about in these harassed times, to get the whole thing over with, to get away and be done with this Milano and all that had happened to her here. But whether she lay in transports in Carlo's arms, or whether she exchanged an imperceptible glance with him across a room full of people, she lived with the truth which he himself had stated in the moment of surrender that he had fought off not only in the case of Harriet but in his whole life before. The measure of its power and its awful despair, she knew, was his turning from his own language to hers, and saying quietly, " This is love, real love, because it is recognition, not infatuation."

"—that we have always known each other," she said

"—that it is true in spite of the fact that we are strangers."

" Strangers——? "

" In every way that touches reality. In every way that concerns life outside our private selves."

" And we shall remain such strangers," she said, while she

felt pain as though her heart were shrieking in protest, " as long as we live."

" Perforce," he said, and closed his eyes because he could not bear to look at hers.

So it was by instinct that Harriet knew that the Verocchi had begun to rise up and rally round Pina, re-enclosing Carlo inside the stockade. He had seldom said on leaving her where he was to spend the evening unless they were to meet at some party or occasion, but now when he stood in her little hall-way, putting on his overcoat or delaying that finality for a last embrace, he might mutter, " Another of those deadly family dinners! " and with irrepressible mischief, toss off a gesture or a grimace mimicking the long nose of one uncle, the big belly of another, the pious rectitude of Pina's widowed sister, the bustling authoritativeness of his mother-in-law. And they would look for a moment deep into each other's eyes and see there the mutual exhortation to courage; and they would break into peals of laughter.

The Ortolani were giving a ball for their daughter Maria Luisa on Shrove Tuesday, which fell at the end of February. It was sure to be a beautiful party and very gay, a party for which to have a new ball gown made, and to get the big jewels out of the bank, which in some cases meant running up to Lugano, since certain families preferred to keep their treasure there. In the preceding fortnight Harriet had followed along with the preparations and arrangements so far as they concerned her; she too had ordered a new gown and accepted Lydia's invitation to dine before the ball, in a party of sixteeen which Lydia thought out very carefully. But while Lydia was thus occupied, for reasons so cogent that she shrank from mentioning them, Harriet had been traversing a long

road into an ominous country; and, arrived there, she paused
to get her figurative breath and look back from the lonely
plateau to see as though in the distance the imminent festivity
which she had half forgotten.

She was brought back with a thump as Lydia said to her,
when they were alone a few days before the party, " Darling,
I think you ought to know."

"What?" asked Harriet, with a nerve ticking in her temple
and a wilfully blank look in her eyes which could not fool, but
might rebuff Lydia.

Lydia sighed and was plainly at a loss for how to answer.
But she summoned her courage and said, " Well—Pina."

" What has she done? " Harriet's tone was too defiant to
be good sense.

" She tried to back out of our dinner next Tuesday. She
said she preferred to give a small dinner of her own, and
perhaps in the end not go to Tia's ball. Neither she nor
Carlo, of course."

" Was this because she doesn't want to see me or because
she is angry with you? "

" Well—both. She was pretty bad with me. She accused
me of being treacherous and helping you to be with Carlo—
of course I told her it wasn't so. I felt horrible, but we've
been over all that."

" It won't be bothering you much longer," said Harriet
with bitterness, " or Pina either."

" Oh, darling, I was so afraid it would be like this."

" It is. And it's bad. I feel an utter damned fool for letting
it happen but I don't know how to un-happen it—except I
shall be leaving so soon now. Why the devil didn't I leave
weeks ago! "

" Oh, God," said Lydia miserably. " Hindsight."

" I'd much rather not go to the ball myself," said Harriet.
" You can imagine how festive I feel."

" But you must. I told Pina they must, too. I had a hard
time persuading her. I don't know whether she believed me
when I swore I hadn't covered for you—but she's beginning
to lose her grip. And for Pina that wouldn't mean just a
plunge into hysterics. She'd do something."

Harriet jumped up from her chair and stood at the window
looking out at the street along which people were stepping
at the brisk pace which was native to New York, but
surprising here. The place hummed with the same kind of
energy. No wonder she had felt natural here from the first.
She turned from the window and stood leaning against the
sill, her hands clasped behind her.

" Look here," she said. " All I've heard and all I've seen
of Pina since I met her, have been how cool and tough she is
about other women. It's not so easy for me to face it, but I
know stories of some of Carlo's escapades and how Pina
behaved about them. I've felt like a dog because of her
having to put up such a front on account of me. It's hell, it's
not the kind of thing we're good at. I couldn't have gone
on with it if I hadn't always known exactly the day when it
would end. And she knows too. So why is she suddenly
different now? "

Lydia looked at Harriet as though to beg her to use her wits
and stop being wilfully obtuse. But Harriet had put herself
behind that barricade for some reason and she was not to be
forced out. At last Lydia sighed and said, " Oh, Harriet. If
I haven't needed to have the truth about you and Carlo
spelt out, if I know it by sheer instinct, can't you imagine
what Pina knows? She knows as well as you do that this is
different from anything that ever happened to Carlo before."

L

Harriet said nothing. Lydia said, " If Pina can't sense the difference between Carlo in one of his usual affairs and Carlo desperately in love, who could? Of course she's beginning to panic—she's phenomenal but she's not superhuman. And that's why I'm terrified she'll do something."

" What? "

" I don't know, but if she does it will be a scandal. That's why you've all three got to appear at Tia's ball and do a good job of it."

Harriet swore in a style of Americanese that Lydia had not heard in years. Then she said, " There's that damned party of mine next Thursday too."

" Of course you've asked them."

" Of course. Like everybody else I'm indebted to."

" Well, it's the same thing. I hate to tell you, darling, but both times everybody will be watching you, watching like buzzards. I've seen other . . ." And Lydia stopped speaking, shutting her mouth with a sharp breath and looking at Harriet with pain in her lovely eyes.

" Go on," said Harriet, turning her head. " Say it. You were about to say something about other affairs of Carlo's . . ." And she shivered.

" I just told you," said Lydia almost in a whisper. " I know this isn't merely an affair, that's the trouble. Not just what it was meant to be."

" Never mind that," said Harriet harshly. " It's too late, the milk is spilt—what were you about to say? "

" That when—when things have got critical in lots of cases, any case, leave Carlo out for the moment—people gather for the kill. They watch and they wait—oh, I don't have to tell you. And this time they're not going to have anything to gloat about if I can help it."

Harriet put her cheek on Lydia's and held her close for a moment. "Darling, I'm desperately sorry—and in a way, ashamed—that I've put you in such a spot. But you are wonderful."

Lydia sighed. "Anyway, we'll get through Tuesday——"

"And Thursday. And then I'll concentrate on getting ready to leave. By the way—have you any special cues for me for Tuesday?"

Lydia shook her head. "Just good sense and watch Pina without showing it. And pray."

"I wish I could. Like a lot of other things you've taken to since you came here."

At the dinner party Harriet sat on the left of Sandro Marchisi, with a young Count Boninsegna on her other side, a nephew of the old Marchese whom she had met at Signora Nora's. The Count had recently returned from a stay in the United States where he had been on business. Most of it was in the far West and since he was an ardent sportsman he had been ski-ing at Sun Valley and Squaw Valley.

"And I've heard about you there, Signora!" He was delighted to have something of this sort to compliment her about. He had heard so much about her wonderful form and the competitions she had won that she began to quake, sick with the thought that he might go to Lech and hear enough more to put all the pieces together. But what would it matter, she thought, it's so badly torn anyway.

Pina was seated at the farther end of the table on the same side as Harriet, to spare them the possibility of seeing each other, and Carlo also far from Harriet on the opposite side. She blessed the Italians, or anyway Lydia, for keeping the English and American custom of the host and hostess at the far ends of the table, instead of facing each other across the centre as in France. Suppose that were done to-night!—I should be cross-eyed by the end of dinner, she thought.

Lydia had put Pina beside the Belgian Ambassador on her own right, who had come from Rome for the ball; and Carlo sat beside Teresa Restelli from Torino, who was young, frighteningly beautiful, very fast, and married to one of the richest men in Europe. She flirted boldly with Carlo, who led her on just enough to make Lydia hope in despair that all these people were laying their bets that the Restelli would be Carlo's next flare after the American had gone—and perhaps before. How great a fool could Lydia be? She need only glance at Harriet, fine-drawn as a Romney, in a wonderful white and black gown and a diamond necklace all lace and frost, the delicate taste of forty years ago, which made modern blobs and chunks and eye-smackers vulgar by comparison. Her grandmother's, Lydia knew, and Harriet had always refused to have it re-set, like the other pieces in the same style which suited her better than the massive jewellery that she sometimes wore like everybody else. Harriet was pale, but pallor was a cachet; and her eyes, wide and clear, were set about with so much of the artifice that was to-day's mode that one could not tell in a great room like this, under such brilliant lighting, what part of the deep, blended shadows were skill and what the hints of suffering.

A lordly staircase is a breath-taking sight, and Harriet as they all moved up the sweep of marble and mosaic at the Ortolani palace, between a double row of flunkies holding lighted tapers in long golden wands, was lifted for a moment from her tense, cautious thrall and transported by sheer enchantment. How lovely was the world, she reflected, for which such houses and such dramatic perfection of setting were designed; how drab and crude to-day's life when seen from behind this masque which for an evening had been raised to hide it. Was it possible that men and women two centuries ago had lived their inner lives with the studied sureness and splendour which had framed their outer ones? No, she knew; women have moved up these stairs ever since this house was built, shaken by the same fears, tortured by the same pangs that I feel now; and they have moved through the intricacies of evenings like this one, calm, beautiful, mannered, gay. The world changes and it does not change, this one perhaps more positively in each respect than any other I can know; I am the problematical element, the alien one, and I am not going to betray that when there is so much exquisite precept by which to be guided. She raised her head and came up with a radiant smile to greet the Ortolani at the head of the stairs.

The party was sufficiently large to fill the sweep of salons just short of crowding them; the band was superlative, the champagne also, and the gaiety that capricious intangible which cannot be forced, arranged, or insured. Harriet was kept whirling by a succession of partners—and what beautiful dancers they were!—but by prearrangement Carlo danced with her hardly at all. Nothing would have induced her to tell him what had passed between herself and Lydia but she knew that he had guessed it. He had to play a difficult role fraught with pitfalls, as Pina must and Harriet herself, delicately feeling their way amidst the dangers masked by all these sparkling eyes and smiling faces. Nothing that they did, well or badly, would deceive anyone. It was part of the very excitement which kept such a party tingling that people knew the tensions which ran like cables buried in the dark conduits of men's and women's private selves, carrying the

electric charges which could touch off disaster as readily as
illumination and delight.

Carlo had done his part to dress the ordeal with grace,
balancing his notice of Harriet between perilous extremes, the
preposterous feint that he had abruptly ceased his attentions
to her, or the crudity of pursuing them as in the beginning,
defiant of eyes and opinions and tongues. Each of the few
times that he danced with her they had taken only a few
steps when one of his intimate friends, Sandro or Gianni
Moroni or the host or someone else, came up and wafted her
away. Carlo then returned to dancing with his dinner
partner or with other spectacularly flirtatious beauties;
occasionally with Pina; and Harriet when she glimpsed him
with the former caught herself thinking that if he could
divert Pina's alarm from herself by making love to one of
them, she would thank God on her knees for it. And I, she
remembered, I used to be jealous!

Lydia did not dance much, but sat like a minor queen
holding court from a golden divan in a corner, her blonde
beauty refulgent and unique even amidst such a redundance
of beauty. It required only a glance between them now and
then to inform Harriet that all was well, that people's
attention had long since spread over the kinescope of the
whole party and that for to-night at least nobody would
listen for the mute triangle in the human orchestra unless
someone should be so blundering as to strike the instrument
maliciously. The supper passed off well, a buffet of edible
works of art of which Harriet did not eat a morsel, and after-
wards Lydia availed herself of her faintly visible madonna-
like state to move towards departure. It was past three
o'clock.

They had agreed that they would leave together and when

Harriet, dancing with Roberto Boninsegna, saw Lydia rise she asked him to take her over to join the Marchisi.

" Oh, please! " he said, " not yet. Don't go now. I shall be enchanted to take you home."

But Harriet did nòt mean to stay without Lydia. " Well," she said, " we must anyway say good night to them," and she noted thankfully that she had not seen the Dalveri since an instant at supper when Pina's eyes, the one-time eyes of amber velvet, had lain upon her with the flat glass-like stare of a lioness. Harriet, laughing and chatting with a group of people, turned her head to reply to some bit of banter, grasping the excuse to evade that baleful glance; but now as she moved with the Marchisi and young Boninsegna through the crowd towards the head of the stairs, she saw that Carlo and Pina, coming from the opposite direction, would reach the stairs at the same moment.

This she had not counted upon. She had feared in any case to make herself conspicuous by leaving early, when the ball would go on until broad daylight. But she and Lydia had planned to drift away together, and any revision of their idea could only be communicated by telepathy. The two groups converged where it was impossible to avoid meeting and Lydia said, laughing, " I've overstayed my leave. I was given until two o'clock, and look at Cinderella now."

" But Signora Piers is not under orders," said Boninsegna eagerly.

" Nor are we," said Carlo. " Except I've got to go to Modena at eight o'clock this morning. And I'm too old to go without sleep altogether."

The remark was so out of character that Harriet, anxious and wary behind her laughing masque, did not bother to think whether he was lying. She had heard nothing of

Modena before. People stood all around them, talking, laughing—and watching. With the imperceptible skill by which one can sometimes take advantage of a step forward or backwards, she got close enough to Lydia to exchange a private glance. Lydia's meant " Stay! "

Boninsegna was still at Harriet's elbow, hopeful and gallant; she had not committed herself to leaving, and she took his arm gaily, complimenting Lydia on her dinner, and bowing to the Dalveri.

" I don't want to miss the rest of the party," she said. " It is so beautiful, and I can't think when I shall ever be here to enjoy another." She included Pina in her wide, smiling look at them all. The flat stare came back into the topaz eyes, a look of pure hatred. Pina nodded stiffly and started down the stairs.

Twelve

CARLO TELEPHONED in the morning, much later than usual. Modena had been a lie.

" Have you slept? " he asked.

" Oh, darling. I'm so uneasy. No, to tell you the truth. Have you? "

He made a mocking noise. " What time did you go to bed? " he asked.

" Six o'clock."

" *Cara*, it was brave of you to stay. But there was nothing else to do."

" It was such a beautiful party and I've never been through such hell in my life."

" And you were so beautiful! Oh, *Dio*! You were so beautiful."

" If I had any spunk left in me I'd be saying something about the other how-beautifuls. The Restelli is a block-buster."

" *Lascia stare* la Restelli. It was only very intelligent of Lydia to have her. Tell me, *amore mio*, how do you feel—really? "

" Can't you hear? " Harriet fought off a quaver in her voice.

" Listen, my love, I am coming for you in an hour."

" But Carlo——" She felt sick with the memory of those tawny eyes going flat.

" I don't want to explain. I have nothing to explain."
His voice roughened. " I am coming for you and we will go
somewhere outside town and find a trattoria and eat
pastasciutta and a *costoletta*——"

" It's Ash Wednesday."

" Well, fish then. But I've been to church. And then we
will come back and spend the rest of the day in bed."

" Is there anything you haven't thought out? " said
Harriet, surrendering to the quaver.

" If I answer that we will both go to pieces. Tell yourself
something for me, my Harriet."

" What? " She was very tired and very near to tears.

" What you say, in English. Tell yourself as many times
as you can. It is true and I mean it. Be ready in an hour."

It was the last day of February and perfectly beautiful.
Carlo was waiting at the door in a taxi when she came out
of the house; they drove to his garage and got into a car
there. It was not the Ferrari, it was a Millecento, utilitarian,
completely unnoticeable.

" Whose is this? " asked Harriet, as he started out through
a labyrinth of side streets and alleys in which she was utterly
lost, well as she had learnt to know Milano. She spoke
English and so did he.

" Oh, mine. It is used for errands and people in my office
drive it." He came out finally into the Viale Zara, far beyond
the centre of the city.

Harriet had been silent. She had managed for a week,
since the worst tension had begun, not to say anything of this
sort, but suddenly she felt as though she would burst into
tears and spend the whole day weeping unless she could ease
her mind by speaking what was in it. Carlo sensed that, he
was driving slowly, sometimes touching her for a moment

tenderly; he must have felt the faint trembling which she could not conquer.

" What is it, my dearest? " he asked. " Don't be afraid to say it."

" I'm worried," she breathed. " Terribly worried that Pina may do something."

" So am I." His jaw moved nervously.

" Isn't this desperately rash? If I thought the thing about Modena was a lie, what will she——"

" *Cara mia*, I know. I am being rash—reckless possibly. But Oh! *Dio!* " he cried in a sort of roar. " I have never had this before—never—and I want it! I love you, I am in love with you, I want to be with you every possible moment until——" And he stopped at a traffic light, turning to look at her with agony in his dark eyes. She sat pressing her lips together while tears ran down her cheeks. There was nothing she could do about it. Their hands clung, the fingers weaving together; then the light went green and he had to drive on.

" You've thought of everything I have," said Harriet. " I'm so terrified she will telephone my flat this morning, or your garage to see if you took out the Ferrari. You would, to drive to Modena."

" The Ferrari is having its carburettors cleaned, and if she asked any man in that garage a question he would automatically answer with a lie, having seen me leave with you."

In spite of her misery Harriet had to laugh. Italians were wonderful. " Well, and if she should telephone me——"

" Has she ever? " asked Carlo sharply.

" Not in this way that we are worried about. But oh, darling, she will," Harriet wailed. " I know she will because——" She could not say because she had ever descended to doing the same thing herself. " Anyway, if she does, Angela will tell her I am lunching with some Americans at a hotel and I will be home by three o'clock. And if she calls again after that——"

"You will be right there in bed with me," said Carlo savagely, "and you can tell her not to be an *ignorante* for interrupting your afternoon rest."

Harriet shivered. "It will be better when I am gone."

"Let us not talk about it any more," he said. "Do you think I am a fool?" He ran his fingers through his hair and gave expression to his own despair with a burst of speed which almost lifted the little car off the road.

They found their trattoria so readily that Harriet assumed, with the vestiges of her earlier amusement, that he was no stranger there, which was corroborated by the welcoming smiles of the padrone. But also she believed that the man had no idea who Carlo was. They sat at a table in a corner behind a palm tree in a tub, and not for the first time Harriet felt the appreciation engendered by natural Italian ways. This was a humble place in an ugly street in the ugly part of Monza, a place for ordinary people without pretensions of any kind. But the tables were spread with clean white cloths, each one had a little vase of flowers, an abundant basket of good bread, well-polished coarse glasses and cutlery. On a side-table stood the big basket of fruit with a ribbon bow tied to its handle, a tray of cheeses, and the makings of half a dozen kinds of green salad. It was nothing, and it was everything, in its proffering of amenity and restful good appetite, which shone in its true light when one compared this with an eating-place of its class in some other place, in England for instance, or the United States.

They did not stay long and even before three o'clock they were back in her flat. Harriet smiled at Angela and heard with relief that only Lydia had telephoned; everybody else, she said to Carlo, has spent the morning sleeping. There was a list of errands for Angela to do, the final preparations for the cocktail party to-morrow, and Harriet told her she need not be back for the evening. I don't know how long he plans to stay, she told herself, but when he leaves I mean to take a great big sleeping capsule and knock myself out.

He laughed suddenly, a startling relief after their mood of the past hours, watching her face.

" Why? " she asked, as they sat on the edge of her bed, yielding to the languor and the feeling of peace, illusory though they knew it was, which for the moment they needed more than any expression of love.

" You are so tired," he said, having long since returned to his own lovely language, full of diminutives and little words which had their special meanings all apart from literal ones. Harriet called it the " bees and the flowers " language but when he asked why, she had always refused, laughing, to explain. " You are so tired. Here. Here. There. And here." He kissed these and other features which he loved to talk about as much as to see and to touch with his lips and his beautiful sensitive hands. " You were thinking how you will put yourself to sleep later with one of those ominous American capsules, those frightening yellow and red and green things you Americans love so."

" Everybody else loves them too," she murmured, tracing the planes of his face with her lips. " They all beg us to bring them by the hundreds whenever we come."

" I am better for you," he said. " I will make you sleep better than all the medicines you ever heard of."

" But later," she whispered.

" Ah. You are not quite ready to sleep now? "

" Not quite."

He gripped her bare shoulders, still smiling, delighted with her, eager, excited. But while she watched, his face changed, the light went out of it, his eyes and his lips tightened and narrowed, he wore the grimace of real pain. " My love, my dearest love," he sobbed. " I cannot bear to lose you."

" And I? " She was very pale, he saw the clear blue veins at her temples, her eyes wide and full of something she did not know how to conceal, the forbidden shadow of a different world where people who loved did not expect to lose each other.

Next evening at half-past seven Carlo came into Pina's small sitting-room beside her bedroom, where she had her Empire desk, her pretty tables laden with family photographs, and her French arm-chairs covered with exquisite pale brocade. She was seated in one of them, dressed in a negligee, reading a fashion magazine.

" Are you not ready? " asked Carlo. He had been at home for the past hour, sitting with the children while they ate their supper, and now he had put on fresh linen and a dark pin-striped suit. " It is about time to go to that cocktail."

Pina said, " I am not going."

He stood staring. " But Pina." She had not looked up from the magazine. " Are you ill? "

" Certainly not. I am simply not going."

" My dear, will you please put down that paper. What do you mean? "

Pina laid the magazine on the floor and looked at him. Her face was as expressionless as will-power could make it. He might have let his anger flare but this was no time for stupidities. " There is not anything to say about this," he said, " that you don't know. I think we have to go to that party as we had to go to the ball on Tuesday," He watched her, stiff, impassive. " It is for your own sake, Pina."

" It is an insolence to tell me what is best for my sake. I tell you I am not going to that woman's flat nor will I continue any other part of this travesty."

He thought for a moment. Then he drew a long breath to strengthen his patience and said, " It would be too irrational to pretend about this. The thing that matters is that she is leaving very soon, that all our friends and some who only act like friends, will be at this cocktail and that if you do not appear it will be a scandal."

" Let it."

" You cannot mean that. I tell you again, you have been wise and patient up to now, I have said it before and I mean it. Believe me. I appreciate you and in the end you always know I appreciate you. I know I try you, but you know that——"

" That's enough. You are gargling with words. I am not going."

" Then I shall have to go alone," he said, furious, " and say you are ill."

" If you do that I shall go to La Scala."

And show all Milano that he had lied; and be there when people came, gabbling, straight to the theatre from the cock-tail. Pina had deliberately chosen, of several alternatives sure to be a scandal, the one which meant that neither she nor he would go to Harriet Piers's party. This would be the most mortifying to Harriet, but its reverberations would be hateful for him and for Pina too.

" You are a fool," he said.

" So are you, to think I would put up with anything more. Now she can look a fool too."

" Oh? " He jerked the chair at her desk half-way round and sat in it, facing her. He dialled a number on the telephone. Pina watched him, perfectly rigid; he saw her pinched mouth, the rise and fall of her breast.

" Pronto," he said. " Let me speak to the Signora, Giorgio. Yes, Mamma? "

Pina's eyes were glassy, he saw her swallow.

" Mamma, will you do something for me? " He spoke with forced calm but he was very tense. " You know Mrs. Piers is giving a cocktail this evening."

" I know," said his mother. Her voice was cold. " I had a card, but of course I never go to such things, I am too old."

" I have to ask you to go there, Mamma. Just for a moment, just to appear. Will you? "

" Carlo, this is outrageous! I had reason to hope you would have come to your senses by now."

" Mamma, I know. I wish—but there is no time now. I implore you."

He knew that his mother understood what had happened. She was silent; then she said, " If there is no other way to keep you and Pina out of a scandal I will go there for a moment. But this is not excusing you, you will come here to-night and listen to what I have to say to you. We are all at the end of our patience—I more than anybody."

" Yes, Mamma. I am desperately sorry to involve you in this. But I have no choice. I will come to see you later."

He put down the telephone and they sat looking at each other. Once his hand moved to the dial again; then he glanced at the little crystal clock ticking on the desk, and he shrugged. He could not warn Harriet now, too many people would be arriving at her party.

"You will regret this bitterly," he said to Pina. He was pale with rage.

"And you, I suppose, expect to go unscathed? As usual?" She sat clutching the cushion of her chair, the veins like cords on the backs of her beautiful white hands, her long nails digging into the silk. "Or not so long as your precious mother is here to——"

"Pina!" He stood over her, horrified to find himself with one hand raised. He had almost struck her.

She did not move. She said, "That would not surprise me, nor anything else you did, after the spectacle you have made of yourself with that woman."

"Have you gone back to your childhood?" he said. "Have you gone stark mad with jealousy?"

"Not so mad as you. Are you stupid now, are you a clout, not to realise what you have done?" She did not raise her voice, she spoke in the same dark tone as always, but he had never seen her in such a state. She looked like a figure cut from stone. She went on speaking. She said, "I always know. I always take the same stand, play the same part, God help me. But I am past playing now. And so are you."

"What do you mean?" He still stood over her, his arms folded, his face contorted. Pina did not reply at once. She sat looking away, biting her lips, fighting, he saw, to keep control of her anger and say, if she spoke at all, cold brutal fact. After a time she drew a long breath and said, "Up to now I have always won. And bitter victories they were. But certain things I knew——" She paused. "Not any longer. This one I played like all the rest. I've known, I know,

M

everything. Where and when and how. You fool, I always know."

" Does anybody not? What do you think you are," he said, " the Delphic Sibyl? Do you think I did not know about René de Brissac two years ago at St. Jean? You, the exemplary wife and mother, the pillar of virtue——"

" I said, you are a fool. Why do you think I did it? Why do you think I do anything? Why do you think I went to Brussels a month ago? "

She paused to take advantage of his bewilderment. He stood silent, loathing this and waiting.

" There was nothing the matter with Zia Grazia," she said. " I went there to play out rope. I knew what you would do, I knew you would go to join that American somewhere. I thought to give you both rope enough to hang yourselves. That was a last resort. I had done all the other things," she said wearily, leaning back for a moment and closing her eyes as if overcome by weakness. Her fingers let go the cushion of the chair. She went on speaking, in a half-voice, with her eyes half-closed. " All the other things, the damned, damned comedy, the invitations, the graciousness, the friendship with that treacherous blonde bitch, that precious friend of hers. Always the play for time, always the smooth façade, until you should tire of her."

There was another silence.

" But it was no use! " Pina sprang from her chair, her voice came in a low, hoarse scream. " No use. I've fought with everything I had, everything I ever knew. It was no use," she cried, " because you are desperately in love with her." She clutched her face in her hands and broke into strangled sobs. He turned away and stood staring at the wall, staring at a panel of rosy silk, graceful with cupids and flowery garlands, beneath which he saw the writhing of furies. Pina's sobs were harrowing. He had almost never known her to shed a tear.

" Desperately in love with her," she cried again, " and you have never been in love in all your life before! "

He heard her with horror, with sweat running down his face, his hands clenched. She had said her last word, the rest was her terrible rasping sobs. There was nothing he could do. He would have sold his soul to give her comfort, but there was nothing he could do. He turned after a time and looked at her, still bent over with her face in her hands, and he said, " I cannot say a word which will not make this worse. I can only tell you that she will go away soon. If you can find the courage——" He stopped. " We have always been protected by your loyalty and your wisdom, Pina. And your pride."

Slowly she raised her head. " And you do not see the difference now? "

" I see the difference. But beyond that there is no difference, no change. We are speaking grave truths. You are suffering. So am I. So is she. I do not ask your mercy for her, but you are my wife. Only you can do as my wife should do until she goes."

" You mean you intend to see her until she leaves."

" I do. And I do not intend to lie to you. I have made you suffer enough in those ways. I wish to spare you ignominy and every kind of pain except the one I cannot help. But it will not be for long."

" You ask too much."

" I ask nothing. I tell you, you are my wife, I tell you what that means in a crisis like this."

" And suppose I will not be as you wish me to be? "

" Then you will be courting disaster."

" You threaten me? " She stood staring at him, her eyes enormous.

" Of course not. Up to now this is a tragedy, Pina, that is bad enough. But it is not a disaster. And the rest——" He paused with a look of real tenderness with which he tried to quench the anger burning in her eyes. " The rest is up to all three of us."

Most of the guests had come by eight o'clock and Harriet could turn her attention from greeting them to the state of the party itself. It was relaxed and gay. It was small, she had asked about thirty-five people, almost all members of the same intimate circle who had known one another always, amongst whom there played the currents of past involvements, amorous and otherwise; of intensities, jealousies, quarrels, peace-makings, lingering animosities and deep affections, as well as the sparks of present situations and future possibilities. Gossip was oxygen to them, they lived for it, and they dealt it out in a special virulent vernacular which would make the stranger suppose them to be cruel people, devoid of loyalty and taste, which was not the case at all. One simply had to understand them and know their capacities for warmth and friendship and hospitality and loyalty, usually tribal. They possessed all these and many other lovable qualities, beside their charm and their gaiety, their grace of manner and their looks. They had come to this cocktail primed and alert to the possibility that the thing between Carlino and the pretty American whom they had in their different ways come to like was at a point where something was likely to happen. And they were waiting to see; if not to-day, they shrugged, perhaps to-morrow.

Harriet was aware of this, for Lydia's warning had been concerned even more with this occasion than with Tia Ortolani's ball; but had Lydia never said a word, Harriet would have felt the crackle in the air, a spontaneous tenseness which leapt and darted between smiling faces, over the tops of handsome heads and the shimmering, fluttering creations of Ricci and her rivals of the Montenapoleone, all to the tune of bubbling laughter, rapid-fire chat softened by those gurgled R's, and a running strophe of " *Senti, tesoro* . . ."

But if Harriet let herself feel that certain of the women were more acute in their watchfulness than others, she did not require to seek the reason, she had long since realised it and even managed to surmount her initial revulsion at such stripping-away of her privacy. Now she felt, batting bright shuttlecocks of talk about, and thankful that the caterer's excellent barman and deft butler freed her of any material concern about her party, the new and terrifying degree in which these women were her enemies. She had a sudden white intimation, like a stripe down the centre of her brain, that if something should happen, that minatory, tremolant something which nobody could define, these women, despite their own reasons for hating Pina, would rush to concur in any public reassertion of her rights, the more so if this gave them the least advantage in beholding the discomfiture— possibly the mortification—of Harriet Piers. And then, while she was contemplating with even greater horror what would be their reaction to knowledge of the real truth about herself and Carlo, she chanced to look at the clock. It said twenty minutes past eight.

She widened her smile to something she feared was grotesque as a jack-o'-lantern and moved lightly to another group of people. Somebody would make a particular point of bringing her in on whatever it was that they were gabbling about. She knew now that she had been, since seven o'clock, in a state of quaking terror against the moment of Carlo's and Pina's appearance; and she knew too that she had been blanketed against that realisation by thankfulness for every minute that they were delayed. Finally in a flash of certainty that left her fighting dizziness, she knew that they were not coming; and in that moment she saw that everybody present knew it too.

I mustn't swallow, I mustn't take an extra breath, I mustn't look at the clock, I mustn't look at Lydia, I mustn't miss a word, I mustn't . . . mustn't . . . her mind was racing to the complete recognition of how horrible this was; she felt herself listening to every word that would be said in twenty, forty, a hundred places, spreading like plague from this pit of her mortification. Now she knew too what was the electric crackle that she had felt: the anticipation of this horror which these people had brought in with them and then stood waiting for it to happen.

Then the door bell rang. It rang in the kitchen and nobody else in the chatter-charged rooms could have heard it, but Harriet felt that she would have heard it had it rung in the Gobi Desert. The mid-point of the party was past, a few people had already left, and none more were to come. But the door bell had rung. Perhaps these past few minutes had been sheer hysteria on her part, probably Carlo and Pina were arriving now, tactfully late, with some murmured word about a delay which would never have existed except as a merciful way of cutting short their time here. Harriet turned towards the doorway, ready to greet them and join in carrying this off, for the last time surely. And all these people would have been mistaken.

It was Signora Nora who walked in, smiling, gracious, greeting those she passed as she went towards Harriet who came to welcome her.

" How nice to see you! This is such a pleasure, Signora Nora." Harriet's hands were trembling and something in her left ear beat like a metronome.

" I came so late," said Signora Nora, " because I stopped to see Lala." Pina and Carlo, she said, were kept at home because the child had been taken ill; " and one of us at least wanted to be here."

My God, thought Harriet, she is too wonderful. She can lie better than Carlo, and *she* isn't used to it. She said quickly that she hoped Lala was not seriously ill and Signora Nora said, " I hope not. One of those sudden fevers, you know, she will probably be much better in the morning, but, of course, parents——! " And they walked over to join Tia Ortolani and some people who were discussing the behaviour of a certain tempestuous singer.

Harriet stayed with them for a moment, drifted along, listened to compliments, smiled, returned compliments, moved to another group. She did not know what they were all thinking now, the armed clique of enemy women, the warm and kindly ones, the men so charming and easy of manner, every one of these people of whom five minutes ago she had been terrified. Perhaps she still was terrified, her agitation was so violent that her first concern was to keep it hidden. She turned to give an order to the butler and while she was speaking she heard behind her a muffled female voice say, " They must have renounced the telephone for Lent." Then laughter.

Oh, to be away from here, to be gone; her mind had sprung ahead to that, which had more urgency even than her wanting this party to end. She had the wit to look at Lydia, to say with a glance, " Go! Go early. Don't stay behind as if to stand by me when I need it." And in a little while they all began to go; the groups and pairs dissolved, the leave-takings were particularly cordial, some affectionate. Signora Nora was one of the first to go, followed by the Marchisi and the Ortolani. " *Ciao, tesoro,*" said Tia. " *Ci telefoniamo.*"

Smiling and wafting her guests away, Harriet nodded gaily.

Thirteen

In Signora Nora's drawing-room, alone with her next afternoon, Harriet said, " It was so good of you. So good—and I am a stranger."

There was no warmth in the face of Carlo's mother to-day. Her eyes were sombre and the necessarily false smile of yesterday had given place to an expression of profound concern.

" You must have no illusions, Signora Piers," she said. " You must understand why I came to you. It was for Pina's sake entirely, I could not let her make a scandal."

" I know that. But I have been the cause of it all and you protected me too. I feel terrible about it. It is so brutal and ungrateful after all your kindness, to have made such a mess. I never meant any such thing to happen."

Signora Nora sighed. A servant came and took away the coffee and when he had closed the door she said, " What I did was contrary to all my own feelings. I disapprove intensely. I told Carlo that and a good deal more, last night. And may God forgive me the lie I told!—a lie about my grandchild. There could not be a worse one. But I had not decided what I would say until I walked in there and saw some of those faces."

" I do not deserve it." Harriet bent her head. " I should never have let things come to this pass. I should have left weeks ago. I knew it—and I was so selfish as to stay." She looked up into the dark eyes where she still found the quality that she had long since noted, the power to convey reproach while clothing it in lenity and understanding. " At first," she said. " I thought——"

" I know what you thought, Signora Piers. That this was a game anyone might play, a game that Carlo always plays with somebody. It is a fact of life, like many other things— but it does not excuse either of you." Harriet stared at the fine face, cold with reproof as she had never seen it. She had not dreamt that there could be a person like this woman. But as she watched, the expression began to change; was it a softening, warmed by love of her son; or could it possibly be the residue of what Harriet had felt before, a genuine liking for her which must with a certain regret, be sacrificed to the exactions of responsibility? Harriet did not know; she felt like a girl face to face with severe rebuke and at the same time like a woman towards whom Signora Nora was reaching even against her own will, to continue an understanding that could not quite have existed with anyone else. It was very strange. The silence beat like waves of surf at her ears. There was nothing she could say, and nothing to do but wait. Finally, Signora Nora, weighing something against her own ominous silence, said slowly, " In one sense I have nothing but disapproval, nothing. My son has been a fool and you——"

" I know," Harriet whispered. " I know."

" And in another sense," said Carlo's mother, in a different tone, " I cannot help understanding both of you. I condemn this with all my soul—but I know my son, I was the first to see. You two are seriously in love."

Harriet fought down a break into tears. Carlo's mother sat silent, while a great clumsy clock across the room ticked and tocked, marking a sense of time as grave as the forces at work here now. When Harriet felt she could speak, she looked up and said with trembling lips, " You are extraordinary, Signora Nora. There is nothing I can say—except that I shall leave as soon as possible."

" I know that. It took me a time to realise it—but when I did, I saw that I could trust you, no matter how great a risk it seemed or how much you and Carlo might have to suffer. But I did know it—you remember the day you lunched here? "

" Yes. I knew it too. That was what you were telling me. I was and I am very deeply grateful to you for it."

" I also hope I told you——" She paused for a moment and Harriet saw that she was weighing something carefully. " I am going to speak very frankly. It is not right for me to say these things to you, but I think of Carlo——" She made a little shrug, with a sad smile. Harriet sat very still, her great pale grey eyes fixed on the wise, ageless face. " I cannot defend Carlo in many of his ways," said his mother. "People think I do, they think I indulge and excuse him for everything because I am such a doting mother." She shook her head slowly. " Who should know his faults better than I? "

Harriet did not move.

" Carlo has a very rich life," said his mother. " Perhaps he has too much, perhaps it comes too easily. Perhaps he is too charming for his own good. Perhaps he is selfish, I know he can be unkind. But he has not had everything that there can be in life. He has never really been in love—before."

Harriet felt impelled to glance towards the table where stood the photograph; she did not do so, but she had for an instant the unearthly feeling that a beam, as of light or warmth, was emanating from that corner. How strange, she thought, how mystical; but after all it was not strange, it was the reason why this woman could know whereof she spoke. She said, " And when I understood what Carlo felt for you, I knew that he must have the experience. He was bound to have it one day. I was distressed, yes. I saw the dangers. At first I was afraid. An American; it can be frightening. We suppose here that when Americans fall in love they break up families, they think nothing of divorce, remarriage—if it can be called marriage——"

" I know." Harriet spoke in a low tone. " I know, Signora. We——" She checked herself. " We are riddled with it. It is true. And I too will say something without reserve." She paused. " If this had happened to me at home, if I had fallen so much in love with a man there, I would have expected to marry him." She paused again. " Not here. I know that. Believe me, I know it."

Signora Nora nodded. " And so I felt you could be trusted. I felt you might give Carlo what he has never had, what he could not have in marriage, what marriage is not designed to give. I thought too that you "—the dark eyes kindled—" might give even more than you received. And if so—of course be richer in the end yourself."

" Oh," said Harriet. " Oh, Signora." Her face was very pale.

" Pina is a cold woman," said Signora Nora thoughtfully. Harriet felt that she was speaking as much to relieve her own mind as to inform Harriet's. " Cold and passionate. It is a difficult combination. And Carlo is the most difficult kind of husband. Her lot is not easy, but she makes it harder for herself by her arrogance and her jealousy."

" I have found her wise. Wise and disciplined."

" Disciplined, yes. And practised in fighting off other

women. I think it never occurs to her that she in no danger, as Carlo's wife. But she is madly in love with him, she always was; and that is no basis for marriage. Especially not to such a man."

Then Harriet looked at the picture. Carlo's mother nodded, with a sad smile. " I see what you are thinking. That was one of the very rare cases. But we never expected it. We were married—and then we fell in love. And such love, in or out of marriage——" She made a gentle, airy gesture, as of flying wings. " It is like the moth which flies away in due time—but leaves us the cocoon of the silkworm, to make the strongest filaments that there can be."

Harriet looked at her with wonder. Signora Nora thought for a moment, then she said, " Pina, poor woman, cannot know any of that. Her passion is one-sided and wilfully kept aflame. I thought the marriage would be different. Carlo entered into it with reason and at a suitable age. The basis of it is sound, a good alliance for both families." She made a balancing motion with her expressive hands. " We have more money, they have more race. Something solid from both sides."

Harriet thought of her own life and her mother's and those of most of the people she knew.

" The sad truth is, though," said Carlo's mother, and she paused. It was clear that she had said more than she intended and surely more than she could have thought correct or permissible. Yet, Harriet knew, this was a moment when a long-borne burden of discretion and restraint had to be relieved by honest communion; but how extraordinary that she has made me her confidante. Perhaps it is her way of laying upon me still greater responsibility; and at that point Signora Nora said again, "The sad truth is that I have not grown fond of Pina. She does not like me, nor our family—well, that does not matter. She is his wife."

" I know." They looked at each other with perfect understanding. Harriet said after a moment, " I shall plan to leave at once."

Signora Nora held up a finger. " Gently. Nothing has happened to drive you away as if you had to flee. Time it gently. Give yourself time to have a plausible reason for changing your plans. You had taken your flat until the first of April? "

Harriet nodded.

" Well—in due time. But gently," she said again.

It was the moment to go. Harriet started to rise, but she hesitated. Then she sank back into her chair and said, " Signora, may I ask you something? Would you prefer— shall I promise you——?" She could not speak.

Carlo's mother thought for a time. " I ought to make you promise me," she said slowly. " The sooner you two are parted the better, now. I ought to let you promise me not to see him again while you are here." She looked at Harriet gravely. " After you leave you will not see him again."

Harriet kept her eyes fixed on Signora Nora's solemn face.

" It would be beyond my courage," said Carlo's mother, " to ask you not to see him while you are still here. I could not bring myself to punish both of you so much."

If I weep now, Harriet knew, I shall not be able to stop for hours. She held herself stiff, crossing the room with Signora Nora to the door. Carlo's mother did not kiss her in farewell as a more sentimental woman might have done; they stood for a moment, their hands clasped; then Harriet started blindly down the stairs.

Carlo was there, pacing the floor, when she came in. He sprang across the room and seized her in his arms with a cry. " Oh, Harriet," he said hoarsely, " oh, my love. I am so desolated." He looked into her face, at the deep-set eyes ringed with dull hollows, the trembling of her lips. " Where have you been? " He held her tightly, her head buried in his shoulder. " I have been frantic. Where have you been? "

" With your mother." She drew away and pulled the hat from her head, dropping it with her purse and gloves on a chair.

" Ah." He sat down, looking up at her with tears in his eyes.

" She is the most wonderful person I have ever known in my life."

" She is too good to me," he said.

" Well, and to me."

She stood beside him for a moment, then he reached up and drew her into his arms. They were silent, too crushed for any expression beyond this, merely to be still. It was a long time before they moved or found anything to say. When they did, Carlo said, " I was desperate last night when you would not speak to me. And this morning."

" Darling, I couldn't. I couldn't have done it. Angela told you."

" Yes, she gave me the messages. I understood, but I wanted you to know that I——"

" Oh, I knew. One of the troubles with this is that we know everything without having to explain."

" And so you know what Pina did."

"And you know what your mother said to me to-day."

"And where are we, then?"

"We know that too, my dearest. I am going."

It was dreadful to watch the colour fade from his face, leaving it the tint of clay. The shaven tone of his cheeks looked ghastly against it. His eyes were strained, extremely dark, the pupils indistinguishable from the darkness surrounding them. He did not say anything. His wretchedness was beyond words and beyond anything she could ever have suspected he could feel. Like a ghost, passing through an epoch of ages ago, there drifted through her memory the bold, laughing creature of play and gasconade, wit, charm, and mischief. Where was he now? It is not possible, she thought, taking his face between her hands, letting her lips lie on his eyelids, one and then the other, with infinite tenderness; it is not possible I could have done this to such a man. How could that happen, and in almost no time at all?

She had suffered so much since yesterday that to some degree she was benumbed. Finding herself in the part of comforter, striving to console him, she felt his grief more poignantly than she could at this time feel her own. Her hour would come, and she hoped to be far away when it should strike. Looking over his bowed head at the silent sweep of drawn curtains across the room, she found the final knowledge which she now saw that his mother had possessed, but she herself not until this moment. Dearly as she loved him, surely as she was in love with him, he was even more in love with her. The realisation was dismaying, a terrifying responsibility.

After a long time he raised his head and said, " The only reason I must ask about it is because I cannot bear not to know. Every moment you are here is a reprieve for me. How soon must you go?"

She told him what his mother had said. He answered, shaking his head in a way which she had never noticed before, but which was Signora Nora herself, "She is so wise. God bless her."

"So—I don't know. Ten days, perhaps; something like that. I haven't thought it out. I don't want to see people meanwhile. And yet in a casual way, I shall have to."

"Of course. And listen, *cara mia*. You may hear this or that——" He paused.

"I think I know what you mean."

"The Verocchi." He stood up, beginning to pace the room again and hating what he was trying to say. Harriet sat and watched him. "You do not see them, of course. But others, friends of theirs—righteous prigs or busybodies or bootlickers or whatever they are—a certain part of those people will do their best to——"

My poor darling, she thought. I've got to find a way to help him. She found a reassuring smile in her heart's bag of tricks and quickly brought it out. "I know what you mean, my dearest," she said in English. "In America we call it ganging up. It won't bother me because you and your mother and I know the truth, and beyond that I don't care what anybody thinks."

His face lit up, his eyes began to glow, he looked himself for the first time.

"*Dio mio*, but you are marvellous! You have courage!"

"Well, why not? I come of tough Western stock, I'm a mean ornery American, and nobody ain't goin' to ride me out of town on a rail, honey."

His jaw dropped. He poked his head forward, his eyes

N

were as big as if she had performed a prodigious feat of magic. " Ah, come to bed," he cried, seizing her. " Come to bed."

They went to Bergamo to spend Saturday and Sunday, so much against Harriet's better judgment that she scarcely dared breathe what she felt. She could not and would not ask him about Pina. He said, when he was making the plan, " This is not a deception. We shall not act with bad taste or do anything flagrant, but believe me, the comedy is finished. This I want and this I will have—and you are so magnificent that there is no reason to renounce our last days together on your account."

" But my love," she murmured, with everything she knew about women stirring an ugly mess in her mind, " it could still be a mistake . . ."

" No," he said. " Nothing will happen. There is nothing left to happen."

He had her go alone in her little car to his garage, where they took the Ferrari. Once again he cut through a maze of back streets where nobody would be likely to recognise them but, he said, it does not really matter now. At the entrance to the Autostrada he stopped the car and said, " You drive."

" No, darling. Why? There's no reason to."

" Yes, there is. I love to see you do it. I love everything you do."

" Very well," she said, sliding across to the other seat. " You asked for it. Shall I let it out? "

He nodded eagerly. Their mood was good, the morning was fine, their grief was firmly in hand, and she had spoken lightly. Before the last word was out of her mouth she could have strangled on it. From the sealed vault inside her a thought so frightful had jumped out with his quick assent that she had to sit for a moment forcing it away. He couldn't have had it, never in a thousand years ... nobody of his religion. And she could not confess to the least such notion of her own. No. It was not a thought after all, it had no form, it was a wisp of horror, not meant to be recognised, only a figment of sleepless nights and anguish ...

It was as well that they had come. Here lay the deepest illusion of peace that they could find; and I have never before, she said, been so ruled by feeling which came to me through the sense of sight. In the afternoon they leaned together from a window, their elbows on the broad sill, gazing at the vista in the blurred fading light. Someone below was working in the garden, she heard the click and rattle of tools. She bent far out, to see where they had been that noon, when Carlo took her down through the cellars and the foundations of the house, each level perhaps a century, even two, older than the one above it; and finally when they could see daylight through a distant archway he switched off his electric torch and they came out at the bottom level of the garden, where the worn stones of a narrow footway led straight into the foundations of the house. This was the original path, the mule-track, Carlo told her, which had wound its way up from the empty plain to the city on the hill, the only means of access to it; this house and those beside it were built on top of the old road which had never been removed.

A hundred feet higher they leaned from the window, overlooking it all. The knobby dark tiles of the ancient roofs filled the foreground with the profound serenity that no other sight can give, the strange benison of refuge for the troubled eye which in turn calms the turbid mind and heart. " I wonder why it is," she said. " I wonder if other people feel this too. The peace that comes with the sight of very old roofs. Do you feel this, Carlo? Am I mistaken? "

" No. You are not mistaken. It is something you imagine, of course, it is a fantasy. You find peace in looking at them, someone else might be stirred to imagine all the life and suffering that they have covered in their time."

" That too. I think of that. But only old roofs are tender. And full of humour, look at them. Look at the chimneys with their little crooked hats. Think of chimneys anywhere, they are like the people of each country. And old roofs are so loving, they have sheltered their people, protected them. It is not the same with walls, they have to bear stress."

He laughed softly and caressed her cheek. " You would not make much of an engineer, *cara mia*."

" Oh, I know. I know this is an aberration of mine. But nothing else in the world gives me what I get from the sight of old roofs. And of course there are none in my country."

" Then how do you feel about all that? " He pointed to the modern city down on the plain. " It is growing so fast that it changes week by week. Look at the high buildings, high for Bergamo. Look at the mills and factories. They are not beautiful."

" From here they are not ugly either. They are simply reality—but seen in relation to loveliness and fantasy like my roofs, one accepts it for what it is. A matter of proportion, do you suppose, or perspective? "

" What else? " He was surprised at the allegorical turn of his thoughts, but he said nothing.

They lingered for a time but the light was fading fast and in the distant reaches of the plain they saw the vestigial fog, almost finished for the year, darkening the farthest spaces like smoke. The air was chilly. Harriet shivered as they turned to the room, shutting the window behind them. Domenico came to close the shutters and draw the curtains and at Carlo's order to touch a match to the logs and brushwood faggots in the great marble fireplace.

" They think such extravagances mad, of course, even the central heating, but I don't care." He sat in an arm-chair before the fire and Harriet sat on a cushion on the floor, curled up close to him with her cheek on his knee. They did not talk. After a long time, when Carlo suggested a drink before dinner, she sighed. " It is so difficult to realise that all lovers feel as though no others in all of time have ever had what they have. What we have."

" That is the least of their follies, poor devils. But since there is nothing new under the sun, what difference does it make? You are not anybody else, my dearest, nor am I; therefore this has never happened before."

How simple he makes it seem, she mused. That is one Italian way of seeing a thing; the other is so profound and so intricate that one must have had their two thousand years' saturation in reason and patience to see and feel as they do.

They came back to town late on Sunday night and he brought Harriet to her door. She had said that she would not linger to say good night in the car; he should drive away at once, even though the street appeared deserted. She did not want his car seen at her house.

" Don't be so nervous, my love," he said. " Be calm, there is nothing to fear—any more. I will see you inside the door and then I will go. The garage will bring your car round in the morning."

" I shall need it. I have a lot of things to do. Things I want to buy." Because I am never going to see Milano again? I should get used to the idea, it is probably the truth. She sat

silently eyeing the shuttered houses and shops as they swept
through the dark, clean streets. They would never believe,
in that mess that New York has become, how clean these
streets are. They would never believe a lot of things about
this city, and why somebody could come to love it—even
though my love is now completely enclosed in pain. I
wonder if I shall ever see it again. Perhaps if I should, only
the pain would remain.

Carlo stopped before her house and did as she had asked,
he was quick, he gave her one kiss, whisked her and her small
bag across the pavement, opened the night door with the big
extra key, and whispered, " To-morrow, after six, *amore
mio*. God bless you."

She was both sad and heavily relieved to go to bed without
him.

She was up and dressed early on Monday morning, finished
with the telephone—Carlo, Lydia, Tia, young Boninsegna
who asked her to go dancing, the dressmaker about some
fittings—and at her desk in the sitting-room, making a list
of the shopping she was going out to do, when Angela
appeared at the door. There was a strange expression on
her face.

" Signora," she said, " there is a lady to see you, the
Signora——"

Before she could name the caller, Pina Dalverio came from
behind her and walked into the room. Angela withdrew and
closed the door. Harriet rose slowly, saying, " Good morning,
Pina." For the first time she looked squarely into the golden-
brown eyes. They were heavy, and Harriet needed to restrain
rather than give rein to her imagination, to know what Pina
Dalverio had been going through. " Won't you sit down? "

Pina did not want to sit down, that would be too civil a

frame within which to pose whatever she had come to say. But she took a place stiffly on the edge of a chair, and Harriet watched her, appalled. Harriet was concealing a degree of shock and of disapproval so great that her thoughts tumbled about in a mêlée of fragments and jagged splinters, the memories of all the wreckage she had ever wrought in a time of unbridled jealousy and the mistakes to which it had prompted her. It now seemed many lifetimes ago. But she had never done this, and she did not see how this woman could have committed so monstrous a blunder. Harriet was wary and repelled by what was about to happen, but she held to the knowledge that she was without fear and that Pina had put herself at a disadvantage. She waited for Pina to speak, but Pina did not, so Harriet sat down and offered her a cigarette. Pina shook her head.

" May I give you a cup of coffee? "

" No, thank you."

There was another silence. Then Harriet said, " Of course I understand why you have come. Now that you are here, you may as well say it."

" It is not a matter of words." Pina's face was almost without expression, its smooth oval contour a prodigy of control. The warm blend of ivory and pale bronze tones of skin and hair, the lustre of her beauty, were all dulled; she looked half-alive and at the same time smouldering. One would be a savage, Harriet thought, not to feel sympathy for the suffering that had brought her to this pass. But one could not say so, one could say nothing; and unless Pina soon broke this silence Harriet would have to take some step. But Pina said after another moment, " May I ask you your intentions? "

" Why, I have no intentions, Pina, which could be of the

slightest interest to you. I hope you are not putting things in your mind in a light which has no relation to reality."

" I do not think you understand reality as we see it. I do not think you know what it is."

Harriet was surprised. She said, " I would not say that."

Pina, she saw, was growing angry, but she doubted if that would come to a breaking point. There must be some sense of amenity still alive beneath her agitation; yet she had come here, and so far had given no reason except to confront Harriet with the undeniable fact of her identity. Her silence was almost unbearable, and Harriet felt goaded to goading her to get this over with. " Have you really come here," she said, " to ask me not to see Carlo again? Or to find out when I am leaving? "

She saw that her use of Carlo's name was infuriating. Pina would have had her say " your husband."

" And are you leaving? "

" I always was, at the end of this month or sooner; and I still am. What else did you want me to say?—whatever it might be it would be sure to offend you and I ask you to believe that is not what I intend." She paused because the sound of her own voice, low and controlled, was drilling in her ears; and while she waited to surmount that, she was shaken by the irrelevancy of astonishment at the thought how lightly six months ago she had undertaken to learn Italian. Surely she had never dreamt that this, or her talk with Carlo's mother, would be her use of it, and she was surprised now as she had been then, that she could speak as she needed to, knowing that she did not phrase her thoughts as an Italian would. But she was at no loss for words.

Her attention came back with a jerk to Pina, who was saying, " It does not matter what I wanted to hear you say.

There is no reason in anything you say or do, you are without responsibility."

Harriet stared. " I thought I had just made clear to you——"

" You have. You are going—well. But why did you come? Not as a tourist, not as any person visits any foreign land. You came here and brought the thing you are into our midst——"

" Pina, exactly what are you trying to do? I think we can dispense with insults. You know better, you are a woman of the world."

" I am, but I am a woman, first. A wife and a mother, a daughter to my parents—the things that you are not. You are divorced, you belong to nobody, you have no children, you have no home. If you had, what would you be doing here all this time? You would be at home, taking care of your family. That is a woman. What are you? " Pina's voice shook on the edge of abandon. Her eyes were loaded with contempt.

Harriet clasped her hands, pressing them hard together as if to confine inside them the thing that might escape, and in escaping explode. She had nothing to say. Pina had. She added, " You have no life of your own—why come here and bring disorder into ours? "

" I suppose no such thing has ever touched you before? "

" Not this thing. Not this American thing, this disease of divorce which is sickening even if we do not succumb to it."

" It has nothing to do with you."

" You are wrong. I shall not be divorced, none of us will here—but you Americans spread your evil everywhere you go. You are like neglected children, uncared for and undis-

ciplined in moral things. Our life is for men and women—
it expects them to be what they are both in good and in bad
behaviour. But it is for men and women, for mature people.
It is maddening, then, to be intruded upon by immature
barbarians who do not——"

Harriet was struggling to keep her temper. Whatever she
might later feel about this, she was determined now only to
insure that the reaction should be a delayed one. She had
no wish to conciliate Pina but she did want to get her out
of here in some degree of dignity. She said, " I think you
have spoken more violently than you mean. I have not
maliciously caused you misery and of course you will not
believe me, but I have been extremely unhappy about you."

" Then why did you not prove this distress of yours by
leaving? "

Harriet looked again straight into Pina's eyes, staring
deeply and long enough to cause them to drop; then she
said, " You will not suppose that an immature barbarian
could have understood this; but precisely because Carlo is
not a boy. He is a man and he is your husband and nothing
has happened which changes that. Nothing will. For the
rest—you really cannot expect me to sit here and refute
what you have said by telling you things about him and
about life which you know better than I do."

" But he is—— "

" Pina," said Harriet quickly. " Let us not make the
mistake of talking about Carlo. Let us talk about you instead,
at least to the extent of saying that you have been extraordinary in your wisdom and your dignity. Can't you
manage to hold on to those, keep up your gallantry—without
seeing me, of course—until I leave? "

" And when are you leaving? "

" As soon as I can go without giving the impression that you did anything which precipitated my departure."

" And in the meantime——"

" That is the point at which we pretend you never came here this morning. It was a mistake, you know that. There is only one thing more, and you know that too and will be outraged at my saying it. Besides, I am not supposed to know about men and women," said Harriet bitterly. " But if Carlo should ever learn that you came here he would be furiously angry. Any man would." She paused. " I just want you to be sure he will never find out about it from me."

When the door had closed Harriet stood in the middle of the room, surrounded by the echo of every word that Pina Dalverio had said. Some of it was truth so entire that she had never looked it square in the face before, and some was passion spurred by fear, ugly and muddied, but still tinged by truth. And then the clamour in her mind was violently augmented into shattering sound, as though the brasses, the tympani, the heaviest voices of an orchestra had come up from the floor to batter the air with a massive fortissimo; the blare and crash of the words that Pina Dalverio had not spoken. Harriet stood with her teeth and her fists clenched, swallowing repeatedly to stave off tears or nausea, she did not know which. She was weak from this effort and that which she had made with Pina, and sick with shame. Carlo had now become so unreal that his identity at this moment was only the instrumentality of a hideous experience. The idea of him in any other light was unendurable, the thought of herself as Pina Dalverio saw her, more unendurable still. Those unspoken words were howling around her . . . ingrate, thief, betrayer of hospitality, false friend, double-dealer, traitress . . .

Where was the beauty she believed she had seen in any of this, where the consecrated moods in which she and Carlo had lingered, where the loveliness, where the wisdom and loftiness of Carlo's mother? All gone, in a convulsion of disgust and guilt. She burst into sobs so racking that Angela came running, crying " *Signora! Ma, Signora! Non soffrire così, non piangere! Oh, Dio! Madonna*! " and with a babble of comforting words and invocations to the Holy Family and various saints, she took Harriet to her room and got her into bed.

Fourteen

Lydia was sitting beside Harriet's bed at the end of the day when they heard Angela admit Carlo; in a moment he was in the room, full of anxious surprise.

"But what is it?" he said. "What has happened?" He dropped a kiss on Lydia's cheek, saying "*Ciao, bella!*" and sat on the edge of the bed, holding Harriet's hands. "What has happened?"

"Oh, it's nothing," said Harriet. "Just an upset. Probably something I ate, or a bug." I can look at him now, she thought, but this morning I'd have said I never wanted to see him again.

"But you look so white, really ill. Has the doctor been?"

"Of course," said Lydia. "I sent my doctor as soon as she telephoned——"

"I was to have lunched there."

"He's given her a shot of something to calm her stomach. She really is much better, but she was a sick puppy this morning."

"But one does not get this at this time of year," said Carlo, making a silly, uncomprehending gesture. "In the summer, sometimes . . ."

Lydia laughed, and Harriet too. How efficiently Italians settled everything! And for all his belief that one could not get food poisoning or summer gastritis in March, it had not crossed his mind that she had suffered a violent gastric attack from extreme nervous tension. Well, thank God, Harriet thought, if he suspected that he might try to find out what caused it.

" The doctor said she should stay in bed for a day or two," said Lydia. " It's a bore, but some of us will run in to keep her company."

Carlo still looked nonplussed. " Have you had such things before? " he asked. " Are you subject to this? "

Harriet made a face, wrinkling her nose. " Once in a while. Some stupid organ with an ugly name acts up. Now it's reminded me that I was supposed to have it peered at, so I've decided to go to New York on Saturday and see my own doctor. It's only a little sooner than I'd have gone anyway."

She had of course planned with Lydia that she would say this in just this way, by far the best way to tell him. He would be prevented by Lydia's presence from showing his distress; and later when they were alone he would have accepted the *fait accompli* no matter how hard it had hit him. He only said, and Harriet approved his calm, " What a pity! " She saw at once by his expression that he too, overriding his feelings, appreciated the sense of her using this as a suitable reason for leaving. Nobody would be in the least deluded about the situation, but an importance almost Oriental in its quality was still given here to the element of face.

" But I feel much better," said Harriet, stretching, and putting her arms behind her head. She lay there smiling at Carlo and Lydia and then she said, rolling her eyes, " Do you two seriously want me to believe that you never even flirted across a room? Carlino wasn't blind when you came here, darling."

He shook his head ruefully. " Not that I wouldn't have

been enchanted," he said. " But this blonde thing arrived, the bride of one of my best friends——"

" And pregnant from the first, make no mistake. Sandro's no fool, he knows his friends and brothers." Lydia chuckled. " And by the time the novelty had worn off and the baby was born, we were all old friends and it was too late."

" It is never too late," said Carlo, with mock ardour.

" I must go home," said Lydia. " You'll call me if you need anything, darling? I'll come by in the morning. And you've got the doctor's number right there? " She looked to make sure it was by the telephone. She bent over Harriet to kiss her, whispering, " You were wonderful," and Carlo saw her to the door. When he came back the urbanity was gone; he looked miserable, but resigned. He kicked off his shoes and lay down on the bed beside Harriet, putting one arm under her head and caressing her face with the other hand. They said nothing. Outside they heard the thrum and pop and roar of the traffic, it was the hour when everything was stirring, the hour when the crowds were strolling through the Galleria and the Montenapoleone, as they strolled through certain streets in every town in Italy, the hour of the *passeggiata*, when their work was done.

Harriet lay very still, grateful that Carlo in his concern about her wanted nothing more than to be with her quietly and comfort her if he could. It is curious, she thought; if I had got through that horror this morning without this upset, and had tried to play a comedy now and be full of gaiety and guile, I could not have endured it when he wanted to make love to me. I might have hurt his feelings terribly and I would hate myself even more in the end. She turned her head and smiled at him a little and knew of course how she loved him.

" You were wonderful when I said I am leaving on Saturday," she said quietly. " You are an angel, you are doing everything you can to help us through it."

" The agony is that there is nothing I can do. Oh, if you could only dream of all the things I want to do."

" But you are already——"

" No," he said. He turned her a little in his arms so that he could see her face while he talked, sometimes brushing her eyes with his lips. " No. I would like to do everything in the world for you. Take care of you——" He paused, with a funny grimace, teasing. " Of course you don't need it, such a clever, resourceful, wilful, independent American. You don't need it—or you only think you don't."

" I only think. Or never think."

" That's better. I would like to take care of you, and give you everything you could ever want, and make you need me in every way beside——" He sighed.

" Beside the way I do."

" I would like you never to be concerned or worried or troubled—or alone."

She raised a finger, as if to warn him away from forbidden ground.

" I know," he said. " I know these thoughts are dangerous, preposterous. I know that they are only thoughts, they will never be anything else. But I am so selfish as to tell you that I have them, because like everything else I feel for you, they are for you alone."

" Oh, Carlo——"

" I would like to be with you all the time. When you want me underfoot, and when you don't. When you are confident and beautiful and when you are tired and cross. When your hair is rumpled and your face is covered with grease. When you are nothing more than any woman is at times—and a man is there to bear the brunt of it."

" Oh, Carlo," she said again, and gave in to the comfort of silent tears. He took them away with his lips and said, " I have wanted to give you things, every kind of thing that is fine and beautiful enough for you, ever since I loved you. I have wanted to go with you when you order clothes and sit there and tell you what I think and make you have something much more beautiful than you would buy for yourself, and spoil you as though you were the only woman in the world, and could have nothing except you had it from me."

She looked at him with wonder.

" And I have given you nothing, ever," he said with bitterness, " except flowers."

" They have said what we must never forget," she said. " And you said it too at Lech."

" Yes. But to-morrow I am going to buy you a jewel. I tried to think of a way I could take you with me when I go to select it, but that would not do. What would you like, my love? Tell me, because it must be to your taste as well as mine."

" It is the same thing." She smiled a little, looking at him, and said, " Could you have guessed how long I have tried to think of a gift for you which you could——"

" Ah, *cara*." He kissed her. " There is nothing you can give me which I may carry or use or keep among my things without—you know."

" Yes, there is," she said. " I thought of it finally. It will be ready for you this week."

" Well, and I am going to Cusi to-morrow to choose something for you. What shall it be? "

" What you choose," she said. " Let it be a surprise."

o

They were quiet for a time. Carlo said, " This is Monday. You will not make any plans for this week except to be with me? "

" With good sense," she said. " I can't stay hidden after I've spent this day or two in bed." The memory of Pina this morning came over her like the regurgitation of a bitter medicine. She managed not to shiver, and buried her face in his chest.

" Do you feel ill again, dearest? Are you all right? " He had felt something trouble her.

" It is nothing," she said.

" Have you eaten to-day? "

She laughed. " No, thank you! "

" It is nearly eight o'clock. Surely the doctor ordered something you should eat."

" He told Angela."

" Well." Carlo moved to a chair and rang the bell. Angela came, saying it was time for the semolino which the Signora should have. She brought it and Carlo took the cup from her. He sat on the edge of the bed again and fed it to Harriet in small spoonfuls.

" This must be good for you," he said. " It is the *pappa* that we give to babies."

She ate it meekly, thinking, in one day I have been from heaven to hell and back again. And he will never know.

The week went fast. First she had to manage to block her mind to the thought of Pina, who would be watching the clock and the calendar, surely having heard from somebody when Harriet was to leave; listening and waiting, saturated in wretchedness. Beyond that Harriet managed to put one foot before the other and do the things that she still wanted or needed to do. It was important only to get through the

week, giving people the least possible cause to notice her, at
the same time being seen just enough to let them know that
her head was in the air. She was to go on Thursday to the
Scala with Lydia and Sandro, and on Friday to lunch with
the Ortolani. Carlo would not be present, but well-chosen
people would who would surround Harriet's leave-taking
with aplomb and grace. The rest of the time she spent with
Carlo at his insistence. At moments she was tempted to ask
him to temper this with prudence but that would be no
more suitable than it would have been to beg him to be with
her had he decided otherwise. She knew that he spent time
with his children every day and that this, in the long reckoning, would matter more to Pina than anything else. But
Harriet was impatient for Saturday to come. There is no
mercy, she thought, in prolonging the time until the axe is
to fall.

She found to her astonishment that it was less difficult to
keep in hand the great looming grief of parting from Carlo
than to suppress the minor pangs which sprang at her as she
went about Milano finishing her errands. Crossing the Piazza
del Duomo in the same quick-step as the Milanesi, while
strangers and tourists strolled, paused, and gazed, she overheard two English people exchanging the usual clichés about
the scene, deploring the cathedral, the hideousness of the
Piazza, the vulgarity of the advertising signs, the cars parked
along the cathedral walls. She wanted to snap at them,
" Why don't you go to Pisa? Why don't you go to Chartres?
This place is not a museum—it is *alive*! " Irrational, of
course, and sentimental, to her amazement; but there it was.
She whizzed through the traffic in her efficient little car,
loving the traffic cops who ran the show with the flamboyant
gestures of orchestra conductors; it had always been a

favourite game of hers to note how the traffic policemen in every country personified the essence of the national character. Think of the solemn, courteous bobby, the excitable gendarme with his cape and his flashing baton, the gruff military German, the slouching Austrian, the tough, cheerful, profane American . . . what was she doing, whipping round the Foro on her way to the Via Carducci with tears streaming down her face?

On Thursday afternoon she came out of Borghi's, the shop where she had bought some upholstery silks to take to her mother which, she hoped, would put out the eye of the decorator who had most recently done up Mrs. Murdoch's apartment ; and found herself in a drenching cloudburst. She ran along under the arcade of the Corso Matteotti, hoping that the rain would let up enough to let her get to her car which was parked not far away. But the water came down in sheets, and she ducked into the sweet-shop of Sant Ambroeus to sit it out. This place was effectively a jewel-box; there were no other such pastries on earth, they made nonsense of everything that had ever been said of Rumpel-mayer or Dehmel or Gerstl. Harriet did not care for sweets, but she had had to taste these as an experience; and she still remembered the look on the face of a child she had taken there, the daughter of an American friend who was passing through Milano last autumn, when the girl had her first spoonful of their chocolate ice cream. Harriet took a tiny table in a corner and sat there over a cup of tea, going through her long list which was almost finished.

Behind and to her right there were two women, heads together, gossiping as the women all came here in twos and threes to do, stuffing themselves with the pastries and with various sweet drinks. Why they were not all as fat as barrels, this being their habit on top of the bread and farinaceous food that they ate, Harriet had never understood; but they were not fat and many of them had very good figures. It must be the air here, she thought, it helps to burn up the calories; and she was so absorbed in minding her own business that she did not immediately know she had heard one of the two women say, " But flagrant, my dear, you have no idea. He is with her every moment."

" You mean there is nothing his wife can do? "

" Well, they say the woman is leaving, so I suppose the Verocchi . . ."

" Not soon enough to avoid a scandal, evidently."

" Oh, it's too late for that, *tesoro*. It's a rocking scandal, all their friends have taken sides, it's tremendous . . ."

Harriet had never heard either of the voices before. The women were total strangers. But beneath the waves of her rage and disgust she found herself thinking clearly. This was what she had expected all along. It was vile, but it was no shock. A startling thought swept into her head, cold and forceful as the stream from a fire-hose, to put out the flames of her own mortification, leaving her full of concern for all the Dalveri. They would be here, still facing this out, when she would be away from it in America. She stood up to go, turning a cold stare on the two women. Of course they had no idea who she was.

They sat in the passengers' lounge at Malpensa waiting for Harriet's flight to be called. " And when it is, my dearest, you promise you will leave? At once? "

" I promise."

" You won't kiss me there. No parting, no good-bye." This was last night, in bed, when they had talked for hours on end; a whole night without sleep, of voyages, as Carlo said, through starlit space, though the room was tightly shuttered, to worlds that they had never reached before. Then rest, profound, entire; but rest without sleep; and then they talked.

"It is not good-bye in that sense anyway," he said.

"But for a long time. Time enough . . ."

"To stop loving you? In a sense that time will never come. I have scoffed more than any man at vows of deathless love, the word ' forever ' is children's folly. But something that I have for you I know I shall have always. It is like the strongest friendship, which nothing can destroy—but it is more than friendship, too."

"I know. For me also."

"And I do come to New York, you know, every year or two. And you will be in Europe."

"But not in Milano."

"No. But somewhere—if fate wills us to be together. But I will say more, this will show you how I love you. You will marry, Harriet—and you should."

"Oh, Carlo." Right here in his arms? "Isn't this a strange time to tell me so? "

"No, it is because I love you. I love you enough to want your life to be a real one, not a thing of shadows and memories."

"My memories are divine."

"But not the stuff of daily life. You must live too, in the ways which are as necessary as this that we have had."

She thought again of what he had said in Austria, and told him so.

"Ah, I was never as wise as that," he said. "It is all very well to remind me of my own fine words, but——" his voice changed entirely, the urgent, plangent note came into it, he cried, " What am I to do without you? Oh, my love, my love . . ."

That time they were both in tears.

Now he looked at the watch on his wrist and the glance they exchanged was more eloquent than any words. Yesterday he had brought her his gift, smiling and determined to make their last evening gay. Angela, who by now adored them both, had prepared the best menu in her simple repertoire, and the flat was like a garden with his flowers. He had chosen for Harriet a bracelet that was a wonder of the goldsmith's art, wide and spectacular, but delicate as didiscus flowers, high and airy, spun and twisted of threads of gold and platinum, the diamonds like drops of rain trembling amidst flowers, petals of ruby and leaves of emerald. " Oh, darling," she wept. " it is so beautiful, so beautiful it hurts. It looks like something that grew in a garden, which was never made by any hands at all."

He put it on her arm and kissed the fine blue veins in her wrist, below the lacy clasp; and then because they were both too shaky, he cried, " Well? And what is this talk of a gift for me? I drive a hard bargain, I'd have you know—I give nothing for nothing! "

She gave him a box to open and watched the astonishment which she had anticipated, as it came into his face. She had got an identical duplicate of the beautiful gold wrist watch that he always wore, with exactly the same woven gold band. He held it in his hand for a moment, looking first at it and then at her. Then, with a secretive smile he opened the back of the watch. Inside her picture, laughing, had been photographed on the gold. And beneath it in her tiny handwriting, the forbidden word, Darling.

" Oh, you are wonderful! " he cried. " How could you think of such a thing? " He was like a child, so full of delight and excitement. " Aren't you proud of yourself? " he said. " The only way you could have given me a keepsake that I can wear all the time."

He was surprised that she seemed uneasy. " Are you sure it's all right? " she asked, with her head bent. " It isn't— it wasn't——"

" No," he said. " The old one was not given me by Pina, but by my mother." He kissed her. " And Mamma would approve—but I am not going to tell her."

He took off the old watch and gave it to Harriet. " Keep it," he said. " You can have no use for it—but I want you to keep it—a talisman. Ah, Harriet, why must I love you so? Why must you be this—and not just a pleasure? Why are you my only love? "

If there could have been, they murmured, sitting at Malpensa, a more perfect evening and a more exalted night, no two lovers had ever had words to tell of it. " And you will sleep," he said, having made sure that her berth would be made up as she had ordered. " You will be tired and you have been too efficient to-day, remembering not to forget anything . . ."

Her mouth fell open. " Oh, my God, darling, I did forget something! I'd never have thought if you hadn't said that."

" What? "

She was opening her purse. " I forgot to leave Angela the keys to lock the heavy luggage she is packing. It is going on Tuesday by Air Express."

" Well, I will take her the keys and then send them to you."

Harriet detached them from her key-case and gave them

to him. " Monday morning is soon enough," she said. " I told her to take this evening and all day to-morrow off. She's worked so hard all this week."

They sat for a few minutes more, minutes of agony when each was thinking of the desolate time to come, yet knowing it would be better to have this over quickly. They looked at each other; one thing that they had never discussed was whether they would write or not. It would be meaningless, he thought; and she, I could spend the rest of my life with him, but I don't see how I could write him a letter. " But you must give me your address," he said, as if they had spoken it all aloud, " on account of the keys."

She had made rather a fetish of the notion that she would not leave him an address, as a sign of the finality which had to stamp this parting. She had driven herself so hard in the effort to help him through his ordeal that she had not had the strength or the courage to contemplate her own. It was going to be hell beyond every imaginable definition of hell. And she had been childish of course about the address. Lydia would have given it to him, he had a hundred ways of finding it.

She wrote it on a leaf of his pocket memorandum book. He looked at it and read it aloud, while she said, " It's my apartment, I've had it opened, but I don't know how long I'll be there." (Or where I might go or what I would do instead, it will be the most frightful loose end at which anybody ever dangled. What in God's name shall I do?)

" You will not be with your mother? "

She shook her head, unwilling to explain her reasons, which would be incomprehensible to him; he had expected she would go to her mother, any Italian would expect it. Her flight was called. She rose, he helped her into her coat, she put her handbag on her left arm. They exchanged a con-suming look, their eyes open very wide to fend off tears. Around them people embraced, exclaimed, wept, said good-bye. The engines of an in-coming plane roared in their ears.

She held out her right hand, he bent and kissed it exactly as he had done at the time they met. She took her dressing-case and turned to the door, while he strode away as he had promised to do.

But he forgot his promise not to see her plane out of sight. He walked out of the terminal and across to his car in the parking-place; he might have been drugged for all the volition he was exerting. He got into the car and sat there stupefied. Once he looked up as if he expected to be able to see the plane, obstructed by the airport buildings. The boy came to take the parking ticket. Carlo without thinking gave him a thousand lire instead of a hundred. It was nearly dark, a clear evening with the last streaks of the sunset dyeing the sky.

He started the car and drove slowly out of the airport and turned right on the road that led to Gallarate. The road ran past the confines of the field, and he moved along it until he reached a place where he could see the plane. He pulled off on to the shoulder and stopped the car. He watched them shut the doors, he saw the propellers turn, one by one, the engines flash; he listened to their roar; he saw them remove the blocks, he saw the fire truck and the service truck scuttling away, the ground crew salute in the tradition of air etiquette, the big thing lumber off to its take-off place on the strip; he listened to them testing the engines. He might never have seen any part of all these commonplaces before, but he might have seen or known nothing of any kind before; he was lost.

The plane began to move, gunned fast, it was down the runway and off the ground in a lightning take-off; he watched it lift and dip, circle, level off. It was gone. He sat staring at the empty sky where it had been. He sat while the auto-pullmans and the cars from the airport passed, and the last bustle of the day scattered away. He sat staring at the empty sky, at the deepening darkness sliced by the beams of the airport beacon. He thought no more of time than of any other substantivity, he thought of nothing. He might have been an empty shell, reamed hollow by pain.

When he moved, stiff and chilled, to glance at the clock on the instrument panel he saw that he must have been there nearly two hours. He started the car and drove madly fast to town, passing every car on the Autostrada, but when he was in the Park he slowed down, confronted by the thought of Pina. He had already made his resolutions to start at once to reconstruct the parts of their life that he had shattered; he was not a man to go into hiding with his despair and feed upon it there until it poisoned him; he was, or he would be in a day or two, ready to take up life as it demanded to be lived. But he would need Pina's help. Bitter as she was, justifiably so, alas, he would ask of her the most that she could give. It would strengthen both of them. But he was not sure of Pina yet, she had it in her to punish him extremely before she would meet him in the effort that they must make together. He could face no punishment to-night, no cruelty from Pina. She might feel herself justified, but he could not stand up to it. He was balancing on a very thin line indeed. He did not want to see Pina to-night, and he drove to his mother's house. He told a servant to telephone his house, to say where he was and that he would be at home in the morning. He went almost immediately to bed.

That night was his only respite, for Pina on Sunday morning proved herself determined to do and to say everything he dreaded and everything his mother knew would be disastrous. He tried to tell her so, he did his utmost to bring her to her senses, he kept his own exacerbated nerves in hand while he sought to calm hers. Above all, he pled the futility of her attitude, but Pina was adamant. She did not know what she wanted; she had not lost her husband or even stood in danger of losing him: why could she not forgo her vindictiveness, and join with him in putting the derailed carriage back on the track? Derailed, he pointed out, but not wrecked; it needed only reason and effort to be in order again. She would have none of it.

In the end he was disgusted; he had no idea of staying shut up here all day with a virago. He took the children for the day to his farm at Trezzo d'Adda, to which he had not given any time this year. The administrator had been writing him about the crops, the cattle, and many things to be decided. They had a peaceful, restoring day, tramping through the fields, looking at the new lambs and calves, rejoicing in the fine stand of wheat, admiring the bags of American hybrid seed corn which Carlo had imported from Iowa, as a member of a national agricultural project for improving the yield and quality of Italian corn. The children were ecstatic. Neither of their parents had neglected them during the past weeks, but children know when tension exists whether or not they know why; and they are the happiest when it is past. He brought them home at seven o'clock and had supper with them, Pina having gone to her mother's; and before she returned he was locked in his dressing-room, asleep. He had got through the day without a break in his resolution to resist heartbroken thoughts of Harriet; he was an intelligent man, he knew the time would come when he could bear excursions into memory, but not until long after the raw wounds had healed. Only for a moment, going to bed, when he swallowed two of the capsules about which he had teased her—she had left some of them with him—did he waver; he buried his face in a handkerchief of hers, breathing her perfume; and he suffered very much before he fell asleep.

He avoided Pina next morning; he intended to telephone her before one o'clock, and tell her that he would come home for luncheon only if she had got control of herself and could assure him that there would be no more scenes. He left the house very early, telling Bruno to stop at Harriet's house for a moment. The chauffeur usually drove him to his office in Pina's car. Angelo opened the door at once when he rang at the flat, pathetically glad to see him; she too, he saw, felt like a lost soul. And she was relieved about the keys. He gave them to her and said he would come by again on Wednesday morning to pick them up and send them to the Signora.

" The Signora—she departed safely? " asked Angela.

" Oh, yes," he said. " She is in New York already—she has been there since yesterday."

" It seems impossible! " said Angela.

" In more ways than one," he said.

" She is a most lovely lady. I never knew such a lovely, gentle lady." He did not know whether the woman thought more to comfort him or to ease her own sadness. It was unusual for a servant to become so attached to a person in a few months. " I am very sorry that she had to suffer so much last week."

" We all suffer from time to time," he said. There was

nothing more to say, he wanted to leave now, why draw this out? He had money folded in his hand, he pressed it into Angela's and said, " Thank you again, Angela, for taking such good care of the Signora."

" But not good enough," said the woman, beginning to cry. Then her eyes opened wide with alarm, she put her hand over her mouth.

" What do you mean? " he said.

She shook her head; God help her, she had almost forgotten her promise to the Signora, now how could she keep it if the Signore pressed her? He did press her. He insisted.

" I only meant I wish I could have saved her from— from——" she stopped.

" From what, Angela? " His tone was sharp, he was a man, a Signore, a person that one obeyed. " From what? Tell me! "

She told him. He went out to the street, his face suffused, his lips bitten hard together, and got into the car. He sat rigid while the man pulled away from the kerb. Then he leaned forward and said, " Not to the office, Bruno. Take me home."

Fifteen

HARRIET WAS not on bad terms with her mother; it was merely that there were no terms upon which to be with Mrs. Murdoch unless one were exactly like her. Harriet was not like her and never had been. She would perhaps not have thought about her mother during the flight to New York had Carlo not mentioned her; since he had, the contrast between his mother and hers became one of the elements upon which she dwelt in the intervals between staring sleepless into the dark and breaking down altogether. Carlo had known perfectly why she had been so particular that her berth be made up before she boarded the plane. She had counted on her will-power to carry her into the aircraft and through the aisle as far as that pair of closed curtains. Inside them she did what she had not done all the past week, not in the intervals when she was alone, not even on the day when Pina Dalverio had ripped away the last of the illusions which had lain between Harriet and bare truths about herself. Sickness had been merciful compared with what she suffered in that plane, lying on her face miles above the earth, suspended in a nowhere far less navigable than the air through which the craft was flying. The plane, moreover, had a destination while she had none; no place, no person, no purpose.

That had spurred her to thinking of her mother. Carlo for instance would have been shocked to know that Harriet had not told her mother exactly when she was coming. She had scribbled a note saying that she would be in some time during this week-end, and would telephone. They were not in any case people who made a ritual of meeting and seeing off, which was good sense when one travelled as much as Harriet had done in recent years; one got through everything faster alone. But Italians would have been incapable of this. To them it would seem to lack feeling. But so would everything else, Harriet reflected, which defined her mother's life and her own relation to it. Mrs. Murdoch was a silly woman; in the light of Harriet's Milanese experience not necessarily sillier than many women there, yet even the silliest of those was essentially responsible to or for somebody, while Mrs. Murdoch had never lived by any such measure in her whole life. I only know this now, she saw, because of what I have been through. I am only afraid of it because it shows me not so much what I have lost—that was not mine to lose— as what I have never had. And whether I can ever hope to have it? She could not envisage the hope nor clothe it even in the most imaginary identity, for her heart and her reason were now pre-empted by Carlo Dalverio who was another woman's husband and certain to remain so, fixed in his own immutable world.

It would have been no reassurance at all to have been met at Idlewild by Mrs. Murdoch, gabbling questions about that glamorous, dreamy life in Italy, its accoutrements, its clothes, its ease, its fascinating people; or chirping out a run-down of what had happened in Harriet's absence, a catalogue of the only sort which interested Mrs. Murdoch: who was mad about whom, who had divorced, remarried, or was embroiled in the intermediate stages. Worst of all would have been the implied question as to what Harriet had

" proved " in the more than eight months that she had been away; weeks and weeks in England, six months in Italy; why, that was *ages*, she could hear her mother's high, rippling drawl; people settled *everything* in half that time! No; it was better to be alone while she tested the ground cautiously to find whether there might be any footing here, and she did not feel ready yet to venture the first of those steps.

She sat in the enormous hired car which had met her at Idlewild, staring at the monstrous vehicles which streamed along right and left, driven by deluded people who thought themselves the fortunate possessors of something worth having. Harriet shuddered. The excess of visual vulgarity in this symbol of the good life as most Americans defined it was to her horrifying; and her spirits sank lower as she was driven past hundreds of acres of newly erupted housing developments, stultifying and stratifying every aspect of their inhabitants' lives to a degree that was alarming the sociologists; they were writing books about it now.

The car swept on to the approaches to the Triborough Bridge. It was a sunny morning, the East River a spanking blue, the concrete white and the steel glittering, the towers of Manhattan sparkling in one fantastic panorama caught from this vantage point in an unbelievable whole, the flag on Rikers Island snapping high on its staff against the bright sky. Oh, God, she breathed, clutching the arm-rest, there is beauty here too, and this kind is part of me; I have to belong to something, I do belong to this; oh, my God, what is to become of me? For an instant she imagined Carlo's face should he be sitting here beside her, how thrilled it would be, how live with admiration; wonderful, they all said, and he too, New York is wonderful, they all adored it.

Perhaps I was wrong to come here, she thought, as she

P

stepped from the elevator with her latch-key in her hand; perhaps I should have gone to a hotel. " Thank you," she said, to the man in the lift, " just leave the luggage out here in the entrance-hall when you have brought it up," and gritting her teeth she opened the door and walked into what for some years she had called her home, what she might still call her home but for the memory of Pina Dalverio's voice: You have no home! It was true. She walked through the hall and across the drawing-room to the windows high over Central Park, noting with residual fastidiousness that they had been properly cleaned as, indeed, the whole place had been cleaned; it looked very nice. There were ways of having these things done here if one were prepared to pay excessively for the services, but they were as impersonal as those thousands of identical houses whose occupants cared more about being like their neighbours—or better—than they cared about being themselves. Perhaps they have no selves to be, she reflected, staring down at the Park which had as yet no tint of fresh spring green; and I suppose that is true of me. Or at this time it seems so. Whatever self I am, or was, I have left back there in Carlo; and who is this, standing alone in an empty apartment in Fifth Avenue, the owner of it and of everything it contains and of a good deal else in one way or another; but not the owner of a self.

She was very tired. She had not slept and the night she had passed was the distillation of wretchedness. She was too tired to be able to think, she realised only that while she had thought to wire the housekeeping services company to clean and open her apartment, she had forgotten to tell them to furnish her some kind of visiting maid. Even a total stranger opening the door and acting as if I lived here, whether I myself can act that way or not, would have been better than this, she saw. But what did it matter? The apartment house could provide a limited form of hotel service and to-morrow she would do something about a maid. The memory of Angela struck at her then, with such force that she stood on the threshold of her bedroom trembling with exhaustion and ready to weep again, for the loss of that simple grace and gentleness.

Hers was a lovely room, furnished like the whole apartment with French pieces that her grandmother had collected with taste and shrewdness; Harriet found herself rather comforted to see it. She took the damask coverlet off the bed, folded it and put it away, turning from the linen cupboard bewildered to see that she still had on her gloves and her hat. She ran a bath, left all her mussed-up clothing in a pile in a closet to be dealt with to-morrow, bathed, and went to bed. She lay still, thrusting aside each thought that trundled unwelcome into her mind, the hours she could count since she had last seen Carlo, his words and phrases which she never stopped hearing, his voice, day after day, every day, every morning. Her eyes fell on the telephone beside her; she looked for a moment, shrank down with her face buried in her hands; it was half-past nine in the morning, the hour when he always telephoned. Oh, God, she cried aloud, please, please, don't let me say it. Never. She was so afraid to face the word in mind or in sound that she dragged the bedclothes over her head and lay huddled with her hands pressed to her ears.

" Well, darling," said Mrs. Murdoch, " I'm dying to hear all about it. Was it too, too divine? "

" It was, pretty much. I loved it."

" That dress . . ." Mrs. Murdoch's bright blue eyes

expertly absorbed every line of Harriet's black wool dress, cut with devilry and finished with wit. " Did you get a lot of clothes? "

They were dining the same evening in Mrs. Murdoch's apartment, the hotel rooms whose decorations and furniture had been ecstatically photographed by the most expensive magazines. It looked exactly like a brilliant stage-set for a drawing-room comedy and Mrs. Murdoch was the right occupant for it, tiny, chic, with a fluff of wonderously tinted pale golden hair and a fifty-odd-year-old body on which she lavished enough time, money, will-power, and emotion to keep it outwardly what it had been when she was Harriet's age. She loved nothing better than her friends' envious exclamations that she and Harriet looked like sisters; if anything, that Harriet, who was taller, looked the elder.

" Quite a lot," said Harriet. " The hats are heaven." There was nothing in the world to talk about except what she did not want to hear or say, anything to do with anybody's life: men, love, marriage, any of it.

" I don't see why you stayed so long though. No, no, angel precious tweetums, down! Can't have chicken! Bones, bad for Tweetie! " The little poodle bitch, a quivering bundle of nerves, fur, and astronomically priced clipping topped off by a coral and rhinestone collar, yapped indignantly and jumped at her mistress's lap. Mrs. Murdoch lifted her up and fed her one or two titbits, saying, " I can't resist her. Isn't she precious? "

Thank God for the dog, thought Harriet, it's really the only thing her attention stays fixed upon. Harriet when dressing an hour ago had seen with horror her face in the glass; she looked like death and had done her best to paint it over. She knew how her eyes appeared and had dreaded her mother's concern when she should notice. But of course she hadn't noticed; Harriet had actually forgotten what she was like. She had hugged Harriet and kissed her, then started her scrutiny of Harriet's Italian clothes, missing nothing, not a button, a fraction of an inch, the pitch and shape of her heels.

" Is it true their hairdressers are so wonderful? " she asked.

" No, for a wonder, it's not. Ours are better."

" Then why does everybody say——?"

" It's their heads," said Harriet, thinking of Carlo and then of a dozen other people. " They've got the most beautiful heads and hair in the world. So of course they look well—besides, the women all stop in at their hairdresser's to have their hair combed whenever they're on their way somewhere."

" How divine! Without an appointment? "

Harriet shrugged. My God, how long would it be before her mother said something? Mrs. Murdoch then said it: " Well, darling, did you *meet* anybody there? Did you fall in love? "

" Oh—moderately." Harriet tried to look flippant.

" Was that why you stayed all that time? Is it *serious*? "

" Of course not, Mother. I wrote you, that flat fell into my lap and I liked everything so much I just decided I'd stay for the winter."

" But who is he? "

" He isn't—in that sense. Just a, you know—a thing. Skip it."

Mrs. Murdoch pouted. " I do think you're foolish, Harriet," she said. " You mean you've just drifted around all this time and nothing's *happened*? "

" Nothing's happened."

" Well, other people have more sense than you! I wrote you, Edie Starbuck's married to Johnnie Disston and *really*, you needn't have let *that* happen! "

Harriet looked dully across the table. " What in the world did it have to do with me? "

" Oh, you know what I mean. If he was going to the trouble of leaving that drear he was married to, he'd much rather have done it on account of you than Edie Starbuck."

The waiter came to remove the table and then there was a long thing about the dish he had brought with food for Tweetie. It was all wrong, Mrs. Murdoch had to telephone the *maître d'hôtel*, this was not what she had ordered— Harriet sat longing for time to elapse until she could plead exhaustion after her journey and get away. Tweetie settled the affair of her supper by refusing to eat at all, and Mrs. Murdoch's attention finally came back to Harriet. She dropped into a low chair, crossing her pretty legs below a skirt so short that the line from knee to toe was artfully unbroken, and lighting a cigarette, she said, " Do you really mean to tell me you've been gone the best part of a year and have nothing whatever to show for it? "

" I can speak Italian," said Harriet in a voice that would have alarmed a different mother. " Damned well, too."

" I simply can't understand you," said her mother with petulance. " What earthly use will that be to you—when you say you haven't even got anybody there? What are you going to do now? "

Harriet shrugged. There's the last quarter from which I need to have that question asked, she thought, I'll go mad if I don't stop asking it of myself. " I only got here this morning, Mother," she said. " I need a good night's sleep before I can take on anything like that. And a maid or a cook or a something.”

“ It's hell,” her mother agreed. “ Why don't you move to a hotel like this? And sell your apartment, you'd get a mint for it.”

“ I'd rather keep it.” I'd rather live in something which began with something real, even if it's only Grandmamma's furniture; that looks like somebody's home whether it is or not. It's not a mushroom like this, with a fly perched in it. She reviewed in mind her mother's progressions through three totally separate identities with all their appurtenances; name, address, furniture, ornaments, friends, servants, charge accounts, bank accounts. . . . There sat that pretty, vain, meaningless woman who had had a child and never thought to give it more of a hold on real life than she was giving Tweetie now. Harriet sat perfectly still, gripped by the memory of the dark, handsome house in Milano, the heavy furniture, the family impedimenta, the classical grey head and profound eyes of Carlo's mother. She had to rally every muscle to press this down, lock it hard away again, and give no sign.

“ I'm dead tired, Mother,” she said, with a smile. “ I've been terribly dull, I know, but those flights leave one so exhausted. Especially westbound, it's endless.”

“ Didn't you come in a jet? ” Mrs. Murdoch regarded the latest version of anything as the only imaginable one.

“ There are none directly from Milano yet and it's more trouble to change at Rome or Paris.” Harriet got up to go. “ It's lovely to see you again. I'll give you a ring in the morning.”

“ Do you want to meet Sylvia Lovejoy and me at the Colony for luncheon? ” Mrs. Murdoch lunched there, or at the Pavillon, every day of her life. Not to be seen at one or the other would be to leave the abode of the living, in her view.

" No thanks, Mother. I can't do things until I've made some kind of order, all the unpacking and everything. I'll see you in a day or two."

Tweetie woofed from her pink-cushioned basket as Harriet kissed her mother and the door closed behind her.

Harriet knew that as soon as she had telephoned half-a-dozen people and started word going round that she was back, her time would fall into the chronic checkerboard with its counters in the squares of luncheons, dinners, cocktails, theatres, this party and that week-end and some plan to go somewhere, with all the variants which gave the members of her set their reasons to say that they never had a minute free; and to make their engagements sufficiently far ahead of time to immure themselves in that certainty. Thus they felt assured and occupied and safe from the danger of having to be at home by themselves or with whatever families they had. This had never seemed grotesque to Harriet until now, when the natural thing before re-embarking on the carousel was to compare it with the life she had known in Milano, which was at once gayer, warmer, more impromptu, and lived around the core of the family at home; the relaxed midday meal, thoughtfully planned and carefully cooked and hand-somely served; and the evenings whose occupations were oftener than not the result of something delightfully un-expected. The first thing, then, she told herself on Monday morning, is to wait until my habits have stopped going round like a top nearing the end of its spin, in the pattern which has nothing to do with anything here, and then I will not be comparing this rat-race with something I like better. It will have to work itself out with time.

But the truth was that she could not yet bear the thought of a face that was not Carlo's, of a voice or a hand or an hour to be spent in company that was not his. And she knew at the same time that she must find the resolution to conquer this and come to terms with things as they were. I only need a little time, she felt; just a little time. After all, I have known since the first that I would come back here alone and have all this to go through; what is the difference because I have come a few days sooner? She remembered her best moments in the past three months, the times when she had seen most rationally what she was doing and where it would lead her; and she reminded herself that Carlo had given her this sense of reality even while he was living with her in a dream. She had been roused from that too brutally, that was the worst of the trouble now; she was stunned by the happenings of the past fortnight and by the blow of the parting which had come too soon and too suddenly. She knew better, but it was hard not to think with pitiful ineptitude that had she been able to stay with him until the date when they had always known they would have to part, she would not be so bereft and so unreconciled now.

Well, she sighed, sitting up in bed and preparing to deal with the things she must attend to in order to be able to live here at all, I am not going to torture myself. If I want to hole in here and lick my wounds I shall do it, and when a different time comes I will see about it then. She had never been moody and introspective, she had never before had reason to be depressed and she had sense enough to know that this despondency was contrary to her natural temper. Carlo, for one thing, would be the first to be bored by anything so woebegone as you, she told herself; buck up! Try to act as though he were here and you had to be everything he liked you for in the first place. That was a good idea until she remembered his grey, stricken face on the evening she had come from her talk with his mother. Oh, she said, putting her hand across her eyes, oh, he is going through this same torment too, he is suffering like me, why couldn't we somehow have been allowed to go through hell together? It was a moment before her better sense replied, because you were only destined to enter hell after you were apart.

So Monday and Tuesday were a dark passage of time broken only by concerns like arranging for a part-time maid to come every morning and a visiting cook to be summoned when she was needed for dinner; but my God! she said, when am I ever going to care whether I dine again or who is to dine with me? Meanwhile the apartment house had a restaurant which could send up meals if one were content to have them at fixed hours, and this was one of the reasons why Harriet had bought this apartment in the first place. Her life with Norton Piers had been so peripatetic that she had found it impossible to run a household permanently staffed, and such permanencies were becoming unrealistic in New York anyway. She thought with longing of Angela, smiling and willing and expecting to do everything necessary to keep the Signora comfortable and cared for and groomed and fed. Here one intended to achieve the same results; one was not going to throw up the sponge and surrender the last of one's taste and physical dignity to a tidal wave of drip-dry, push-carts, and frozen pre-cooked messes which went by the name of modern American food. But the battle cost a great deal of money and Harriet knew that most of the price was the penalty of refusing to give in and be like everybody else.

On Wednesday morning she was in bed with her breakfast tray across her knees, mechanically reading *The Times* but shaken to find as she had done each time she had tried to read something, that the print conveyed no information to her brain. A wall stood between it and almost everything to which it was supposed to react. It is a wall of grief, I suppose, and I do not need anybody to tell me that time will presently begin to chip at it, working faster and faster and taking down bigger pieces each day, until at last the wall will be gone. She knew this perfectly well, she was not a fool; but how does this help me now, she cried aloud. How am I to get through this now?

It was a dark morning, streaming with rain, a day to deaden anybody's spirits. She was so aware of this that she put down the newspaper and leaned back, staring across the room, limp and buffeted and far inside her deepest self, ashamed to have come to this. It feels like the very lowest possible ebb, she thought, and if that is true, then there is nowhere else to go except up? She could not supply much of an answer, for the tears came to her eyes and as some kind of check to them, she resumed her meaningless reading and picked up her cup of tea. It had taken her less than a day to find that she could no longer drink the American coffee that she had previously thought good. It swam in her stomach instead of sitting there and holding everything together like the powerful Italian coffee upon which she had come to depend.

There was a knock at the door and she said, " Come in," without looking up. The maid, however, said nothing, so Harriet lowered the newspaper to see what she wanted. The tea from the cup in her hand spilled over the tray, the cup clattered into the saucer, and she said, " Oh, no. *Oh— no——*"

Carlo strode across the room, lifted the breakfast tray to the floor, and flung himself on to the bed, seizing her in his arms. " My love, my love, my love," he cried, covering her face, her throat, her breast, her hands, with kisses. " Oh, Harriet, *amore mio*! "

She clung to him, fantastically solid and present in a sea of the wildest confusion; she was bewildered and shocked, she could make no sense of this, she thought only of what he must have left behind in Milano, she thought of his mother, and she cried, " Carlo! What have you done? "

" Done? I have come! I am here! Look—feel—me——"

" Yes." She looked at his drawn face, his eyes heavy and enormous. " Yes, I see—but I don't understand."

" Don't try. Don't think, don't ask me now. Oh, Harriet, my dearest, you have been suffering."

" So have you." She tried to learn something from his face, but now it came upon her, overriding all else, how she loved him, how she could not see and feel him without responding helplessly, that her passion for him was real and that she could no more quench it summarily than she had been able to overcome her lonely misery ten minutes ago. They had to embrace, drawing apart to look at each other, then clinging together again. Finally they were calmer. He looked at her, pushing the dark hair from her forehead and touching her eyelids as he loved to do, and her lashes with his lips, tracing the heavy straight brows, the wide cheek-bones, the short span of her nose, the curve of her mouth. His fine brown fingers touched her with wonder as though he had never done this before.

She gave up the effort to ask him anything; what was there to say in the face of this? They stayed quiet, rediscovering each other after a lapse of three days which might, she felt, have been as many months. It was more than the surprise, the shock of his appearance, it was something else. Here was Carlo with all his warmth and eagerness and his beautiful head and hands, the man she adored; but something was strange. She cried, " Carlo! My love, my beloved. How did it happen? What has happened? "

He saw the bewilderment in her eyes; she was afraid to hear, afraid to believe either the worst or the best. And she waited for his answer, beginning to see that it was going to be an equivocal one. What in the world had he done? " But tell me," she said, finding the perplexity unbearable.

" I came to bring your keys! " He sat back, looking at her with brilliance again in his eyes and restored colour in his face. He had the look of appearing delighted with himself, the look she had always loved.

" Oh, no," she said again faintly. This was too much.

" We will talk later, we will talk when it is the time for that. I suppose we shall have to talk. But now I am here, my dearest love, never mind all the rest. . . . I am here! "

" Yes, I know it. Oh, Carlo, what have you done? " She had his face between her hands, searching his eyes which were no more disposed to answer questions than his tongue was.

" Not now. Only one thing matters now, something that requires no questions—except may I have a bath? "

" Oh, I love you." She laughed but she felt more inclined to weep. " There was never anybody in the world like you. You are terrible and dreadful and beautiful. There—I've said it—you are beautiful—in English, by God. I've always wanted to say it and I never have, do you know that? "

" *Per l'amore di Dio!* How can you talk so much? I tell you, I want you, have I flown four thousand miles just to hear all this language? If you don't stop talking I will have you, dirty as I am. Where is that bath? "

She waved at the closed door of the room which had been her husband's. After his departure she had turned it into a sitting-room, useful as an occasional guest-room and full of things for which there was no other place—television, gramophone records, random books and magazines, photographs—many of ski-ing scenes—and the trophies that she had won at ski-ing and tennis. " You'll find everything there," she said, kissing him again. " Wickedness."

" *Benone*. But listen to me, my love. The minute I disappear inside that door it is your intention to jump up, rush to your dressing-table, and begin to paint out the ravages to your poor little face. You will please do nothing of the sort. You will stay exactly as you are."

" Why? "

" You know why. I want to do all the repairing myself. I want to see my own handiwork and feel proud of myself."

She lay still while he was gone, too flabbergasted to make sense of this and afraid to try. Her helpless joy at seeing him and the anticipatory rapture of her body were so keen that her mind, with its wish to think this through, annoyed her; yet she had to give it play while she waited for him. Of course it was not literally possible that he had flown the Atlantic on an urge no more considered than to bring her her keys instead of mailing them. Any such thing would have been sheer insanity and a denial of the courage that they had built up to sustain them through the parting last Saturday. Unless some new factor had entered in after her departure, unless something had happened to make him do this for a reason other than irrational impulse. He does not do things in that way, she answered her own question, twisting a lock of her hair in a way she had had as a child when something puzzled her; he does not and Italians do not. He has had another motive. He has not found he could not stay apart from me. He might want to think so, but that is not realistic. What is?

One by one she drew the possible or the plausible answers from the recesses of her intelligence, cool despite her excited nerves and her racing pulse; cool because she found herself possessed of a sense of reason to which she felt unobstructed access for the first time in her life. Presently she saw. He had done it to punish Pina. Perhaps it was her own heart, roused by a stab of pity, which told her so; but she was sure that that had been his reason for coming and she needed to ponder very little more before she understood the sequence of what had happened. Poor Angela! There could have been no other way he could have found out, and for no other reason could he have been provoked to such a rashness as to rush here in this way. It had been wildly unconsidered and she could not think of his ever having done such a thing in his life. Then she imagined him, faced with all the hours of the flight in which to see what he had done, to reconsider it in perspective and be confronted with the decision how to present it to Harriet. He could never have been in such a situation before, it was of all things that which every iota of his heritage and his habit ruled out. My God, she said aloud, what is he going to do, what am I to do?—because this is an element of confusion which does not belong to what we have had and what we are. She was lying with her hand across her mouth, her eyes round as marbles, when he came back wrapped in a bath sheet and stood looking down at her.

" But my dearest! " he exclaimed, surprised at her expression. " What has come over you? "

She put up her arms in the way he loved, and he lay down bringing bliss with his ardour and his beauty. It is heaven, she thought, to know each other so well that coming together again is a return to a whole private world which we have created and perfected, a world which only an hour ago she had supposed she was never to revisit. But now she was here, sweeping through its spaces with Carlo, lost yet not lost, for she remained aware that her mind for the first time since the earliest ventures, had stayed apart. It had no wish, evidently, to ruin the pleasure of her body, but it had at the same time work of its own to do. This was a strange, baffling experience; she heard herself cry out with ecstasy, but in the later silence she found herself sad, not with the certain sadness familiar to this moment, but with something that she had not known before. The sadness was recognition, not a sadness of the heart or a sadness allied to the actual or the tangible. It was the sadness of the mind which has done its work well and come to the threshold of wisdom.

Sixteen

THERE WAS no use in letting him make plans for his time here, whatever that time was intended to be; if, indeed, he knew himself. She was not going to ask him. He was intuitive and in thinking of the past months she saw that she had seldom asked him any question at all. The best thing now was to leave this to his subtle, sapient wits. The first result of her decision was his acquiescence in her preference for staying quietly in the house. He must have been surprised, he must have weighed her motives, for this was unnatural to both of them. Like most Italians Carlo adored New York and he knew better how to enjoy it than many of its inhabitants. Of course he had expected to take her out, to dine, to go to the theatre, to go shopping; he had mentioned this. He loved to spend money and believe me, he said, there is no better place to do it.

" Oh, nonsense, darling, Milano is twice the fun."

" The side of it that you saw." He tipped his chin sarcastically.

" Anyway the weather is vile and we are much cosier here." She heard her own words with a twinge of disquiet, they were out of character and who knew that better than he? Could bad weather deter them from anything that they really wanted to do? There was even a glance of veiled agreement to table the memory of the weather on the drive from Austria down the Maloja. So it was equally un-characteristic of Carlo to conquer his restlessness and remain here in the house, which he had left only long enough to check in at the hotel where he always stopped, not ten minutes' walk from Harriet's.

On the next afternoon they were sitting by the fire in her drawing-room, full of the sense of paradise regained. But I know it is a false paradise, she reflected, smiling at him, and I have not known anything concerning us since the very first which he did not know I knew. So of course he knows this too. Perhaps we shall somehow get through this without ever talking it all out. Or perhaps we will talk when he is ready, and that is as soon as anything will be said. He lay back in a softly upholstered *bergère*, looking at her as she sat on a low stool before the fire, with her legs curled round under her skirt and her chin propped on her clasped hands, a way that she had. Her face was turned towards him and she had to trust to the joy that his presence gave her to keep her expression as untroubled as she meant it to be. She had never succeeded in dissembling, she remembered her early efforts to hide her growing love for him and the ease with which he had seen through them and through every-thing about her. But I am different now, she knew, and the changes are all due to him; so perhaps this will not be quite so plain. She sighed.

" What is it, *cara mia*? " he asked. " Why did you sigh? "

" Contentment. "

" Eh—I wonder. "

" No, truly. I was thinking about this accident, which is what it is, that we are alone here in this way. "

" Naturally I have thought about it too. Does nobody know that you have returned here? "

She shook her head. " I hadn't been in touch with anyone —so it is like a desert island. At the moment it is exactly what I want, but "—she raised her eyebrows—" I don't want to force it on you."

He reached down to touch her cheek and to draw her to him for one of the caresses which, he said, her eyes and her nose demanded for their own sakes, not because they were to lead him on to anything more portentous. " You force nothing on me, except the ways in which I find you irre- sistible. And since none of your friends know that you are here, the better for me. I have you to myself. But what about your mother? " Yesterday morning and to-day he had heard the telephone conversations in which Harriet had murmured vague excuses and vaguer promises about a meeting in a day or two. " You must see her the next time she asks you to, and I should like to meet her too."

" You would? " This time the strong dark brows were not arched, they were level, and she looked at him keenly from beneath them. " You would? Have you thought whether that would really be a good idea? "

" But in heaven's name, why not? Your mother——"

She said nothing. He quite misunderstood and his face showed it. He said slowly, " Do you mean she would be, what can I say, shocked at seeing me? Surely people here are not so——"

Her laughter, a little shrill and uneasy, made him pause. " Oh, darling! I don't quite know how to explain, but I only wish that were the case. No, she is like a lot of people I know, they would be anything but shocked, they would be worse, they would—how can I say it? "

" Say what? "

Surely this must be a feint, surely he could not be so

obtuse by intention? She wondered why he should take this attitude.

"Carlo, my love, you know as well as I do what I am trying to say."

"That New York in any way resembles Milano?"

"Of course not." She took his right hand and brushed its silky skin across her lips, rubbing her cheek on his wrist. "It is altogether different and all I am trying to say is that you would hate the view that they take here of people in our situation, they are——" she thought with a retrospective start of Pina. Immature barbarians were her words. A smacking insult. And not, of course, the truth. But those words held just sufficient thrust to remind Harriet why Pina and people like her, Carlo too, would be outraged at the flippant conclusion to which some of Harriet's friends would leap and the revolting publicity which would attend it.

"Do you mean my presence here would cause a scandal?" He looked disagreeably surprised, even a bit sullen, with his heavy lower lip set in the way which Harriet had never before caused it to do.

"Darling, there is not really such a thing here as scandal. The place is too big and nobody cares. But there is an attitude, the attitude that——" She paused; a look of relief came into her troubled eyes. "I am so stupid." She spoke quietly. "Perhaps I am only trying to say that all these people are the way I used to be."

He jumped from his chair and pulled her to her feet, standing with her clasped in his arms. He kissed her eyes and the corners of her mouth and ran his lips along her throat under her chin. "Let us not talk about it now. You are not stupid, *amore mio*, but I am a giraffe."

"Oh, darling." She looked at him, no longer trying to

hide anything. "Of course you understand. You are right, this is not the time to talk about it——"

The bell rang at the front door. She was annoyed, the maid had gone, her work was finished, and there was nobody to open the door. "Just a moment," she said, "it must be letters or something," and went to the door.

"Well!" cried her mother, sailing in with Tweetie prancing on a coral-coloured leash. "At least you're not dead! I've never heard of such a thing . . . if you aren't rested by now . . . don't believe a word you say any more . . . decided I'd come and find out for myself . . ."

All the while she was advancing through the hall and towards the drawing-room. Harriet walked helplessly beside her. Carlo, looking spectacular, was standing before the fire, one arm on the chimneypiece, smoking a cigarette. Mrs. Murdoch was too mondaine to show surprise and perhaps she was not surprised at all. She smiled and twittered; Harriet gravely presented Signor Dalverio; they sat down. Tweetie was sufficiently well trained to poise herself at her mistress's feet but she was quivering with female curiosity and the desire to rush about, sniff, and fawn on the exciting strange man. Harriet could have killed the beast. She had heard Carlo on the subject of the poodle cult which was just as bad in Milano as here, in Paris, or anywhere that women were rich and silly.

"Of course you are one of Harriet's friends from Milan," said Mrs. Murdoch. "Everybody seems to have been so kind to her there."

"We were all enchanted by her," said Carlo gallantly.

"They were angelically kind to me," said Harriet. "Carlo and his wife practically adopted me, they are Lydia's best friends there, you know."

" Oh," said Mrs. Murdoch. " Is Mrs. Dalverio here with you? "

" No, she is at home. I flew in to-day on business."

" Mother, wouldn't you like some tea? " said Harriet. " Or a drink? " She looked at both of them.

" Why not just a little drinkie," said her mother. " I gather you haven't anyone who will come if you ring for tea."

That could be a loaded remark; so could anything. It was the merest accident that Harriet and Carlo were up and dressed; they had done that in time for the maid to do up Harriet's room before she left. Harriet was tempted either to shudder or to giggle. How many afternoons had there been, like yesterday, when they had spent the hours blissfully in bed! And Mrs. Murdoch was aware of this. Her knowledge was revealed in the way she looked at Carlo, with an expression that was a mixture of appraisal, inquisitiveness, and a suggestion of archness which Harriet found shocking. She went to pour them whisky and soda; her hands were unsteady and she gripped the decanter convulsively lest it tinkle against the glasses and betray her nervousness. Her mother was babbling her appreciation of the Milanese hospitality to Harriet, and Carlo was spared the necessity to answer except with an occasional pleasant word; you are too kind, he said; and from the grave correctness of his tone Harriet knew exactly the impression that her mother was making upon him.

She brought two drinks for them, placing each on a small table, and went to bring one for herself. Suddenly her agitation was displaced by a sharp, clear thought. This is going to show him better what I was trying to say than any words in which I could have put it. This is dreadful, but it

is going to prove something. The inevitable corollary then
ran through her mind, straight, balanced as precisely as the
second of a pair of rails. He would see her mother not only
as the pretty, vain, superficial woman she was; he would
see her in a frame brought intact from the house of his own
identity, a frame dark and heavy and old and unwieldy, a
frame from the walls of the house in Bergamo or his mother's
house in Milano. A frame built of ancient feelings, habits,
and instincts, in which his own mother's image belonged,
and from which her dark, wise eyes could at this moment
be looking at him and at Harriet with their extraordinary
mingling of sympathy and censure. That was his frame for
the image of a mother; and what could he be feeling when
he had placed in it the painted doll's face of Mrs. Murdoch,
with the bright blue eyes which said, " Aha? Indeed? So
this is who it is! And where do we go from here? "

Once she realised this Harriet sat back and made no effort
to steer the chat towards or away from any subject. One
could not steer Mrs. Murdoch anyway, she flitted about in
her own mindless manner, leaping from this to that, pausing
to purse her lips and coo and rhapsodise over Tweetie. I
wonder, thought Harriet, whether he knows that Mother has
been married three times. I have certainly never said so,
but if he could realise that she has been, and a great many
other women like her, I am not going to have to explain a
thing.

" Now of course you must let us reciprocate while you are
here," said Mrs. Murdoch when Tweetie was growing bored
and the time had come to leave. " When you can dine?
Harriet, we might get Malcolm Osgood and go to the
theatre . . . how about Saturday, Mr. Dalverio? "

Oh, God, Harriet asked herself, what is he going to say?

She had no misgivings about Carlo's quickness, but was he going to make this harder for her or easier; what had she still to face?

" Thank you so much," he said. " It is charming of you. But I shall not be here on Saturday, I am going to Chicago and then to California. Perhaps when I return——"

" Of course. Harriet will know . . ." She rose, her heavy bracelets jangling, and clipped on Tweetie's leash. " It's been charming," she said, putting her tiny hand into Carlo's, approving when he bowed and kissed it. " We must see more of you here, such good friends of Harriet's . . . Darling, why don't you dine with me anyway? " she said, leaving the room. Harriet went with her.

" I'd love to, Mother, but I'm going to Bernardsville for the week-end. I'll give you a ring on Monday." She did not care whether her mother believed her or not. Putting on her furs, Mrs. Murdoch brushed Harriet's cheek with her own and hissed into her ear, " He's divine. He's a dream. My *dear* . . ."

" Lovely to see you, dear," said Harriet, seeing them out. She returned to Carlo, still standing beside his chair as he had risen to salute Mrs. Murdoch. His hand was gripping the back of the chair and his face was the most serious that she had ever seen it. I have seen this face, she thought, in every imaginable phase of expression; I have seen it fired with passion and melting with love, I have seen it good and bad, calculating, playful, tricky; illumined with tenderness for his children and his mother, I have seen it—and she remembered acutely the moment when Pina had asked her to Cortina—I have seen it inspired with pride in his wife. But I have never seen this, the reflection of one look into a world which repudiates everything that he believes in and lives by. She stood silent while he remained, his mouth tightly closed, his eyebrows stitched in a straight black line, his eyes condemnatory and sombre. He had not at all forgotten her presence but he looked as though he had. She stood for a moment with her hands clasped tight to stop their trembling, then she burst into sobs and he swept her into his arms.

"*Piangi*," he said, in the extraordinary way that Italians do when grief is there and has to be expressed, and everybody else implores one not to cry, and they say "Weep!" He held her as he had never quite done before, tightly, but with the tenderness that holds a child; tightly for reassurance, but without passion. He put his cheek against her hair, he held her but he did not kiss her. When she felt she could speak she moved her head and looked at him.

"You see what I was trying to say," she said. She took the handkerchief from his breast pocket and wiped her eyes.

"I see. I am a stupid, blundering brute not to have seen from the first instant. Harriet, my dearest love, can you forgive me? For everything—for coming here——"

She put her fingers on his lips and said, "I do love you. You know that. I love you and I love what I have learnt from you."

"Only you have learnt, my dearest? Only you?"

"It was I who had the learning to do. But I have so much, oh, I have so much to be grateful to you for."

"*Taci*," he whispered. "You make me ashamed."

"No, I want to talk about it now. I want you to know what you have done for me. And if you should stay here——"

"I would spoil it. I know."

"I feel very bad about Pina."

" So do I. And you are right, this is where I feel bad. At home she has to deal with her own world, some of it is difficult but——"

" But there is not confusion." Harriet spoke quickly. " That is what I've been trying to say about all this."

" I see now."

" You always have seen. You have never made confusion, with me or with Pina, even though you can be unkind to her. But she knows where she stands, the thing you've always said —or she did, until you rushed off here."

" She had done something very wrong." He frowned.

" Need you tell me? But she has suffered enough, every-body has. So it would be terrible to make confusion here when we made none there. We made none because we were there, in your world, your mother's."

" Oh, all those words of mine. Sometimes I wish I had never said them."

" They were the best words I have ever heard, why do you think I never forget them? I have lived in your world where each of these elements has its place. If you were to stay here and we went about together, you and I would not confuse the elements. But other people would be heaping confusion upon us."

" Beginning with your mother."

Harriet put her face against his and whispered, " I am ashamed to tell you how true that is."

He sat down again, holding her in his arms. The fire crackled, the room was quiet and glowing with lamplight, the colours soft and faded, pale apricot, dim robin's egg blue, the patina of old fruitwood, the gleam of ormolu. " I never expected to find you in a setting like this," he said.

" I've always loved it." She told him about her grandmother and her passion for collecting French furniture. " We aren't entirely barbarian, you see." What would he say if he could know why she used the word! They treasured the quiet for a time.

" Where is your—the man you were married to? " asked Carlo.

" Married again." She shrugged. " That was a mess, Carlo, and quite as much my fault as his."

" And do you also remember something else I said? Once when I was loving you even more than I wanted you? "

She nodded. " It is still much too soon to think about that."

" But it will come. And oh, Harriet, when it does——" He looked at her eyes. She returned his gaze steadily.

" I shan't make a mistake. I never knew what marriage was before—but now I can never have a reason to make a mess of it again."

" Are you really sure? "

" Really sure. I cannot imagine who it might be that I might marry, but I can tell you what kind of marriage it would be. No matter what happens," she said slowly, " no matter what anybody does, for any provocation, I will never be divorced again. Never."

There was a silence.

" From you," he said, " not like us, not bound by our religion, and also not like these people here, that means something extraordinary."

She thought of his mother. Once he is home again, Signora Nora will not hold this against me. I want to be as she believed me to be. I want to feel as she said I would feel.

" What are you remembering? " he asked, watching her face.

"Something your mother said to me, my dearest."

"And I am remembering certain things too. Once I said that you had been afraid to live."

"And I was, and I did not know it."

"Well, now I do not think you are afraid of anything. You have courage, you are not afraid of love and you are not going to be afraid of life. You are going to live it as it really is and you will do that better than I have done, for you are not cruel or selfish or unkind."

"I don't feel quite ready to try it yet," she said, using his handkerchief again.

"But it is true. And I have made it harder for you with this wild impulse of coming here. As usual I was selfish."

"No. I was upset when you came, but you see, you were right after all. You always are."

"How was I right, my love? It seems to me I have done nothing but harm."

"No. That parting at Malpensa was unbearable, wasn't it?" They agreed. "We had been torn apart, we were not ready for it. But now we are. Don't you feel it?"

He was reluctant but he agreed again.

"We will be sad," she said, "but I am not going to be afraid. When I left Malpensa I hadn't the courage to say good-bye. I thought I was practising some fine old Anglo-Saxon gallantry, but of course it wasn't. I was only flinching from reality."

"*Dio mio!*" he said. "Must you punish yourself? Must you talk so much?"

"Well, yes." The musing look in her eyes reminded him of the earliest passages when he had scarcely known her, and had wondered what she was really feeling, or whether she felt anything at all. Now he knew. "Yes. Sometimes one needs to talk and this seems to be one of the times. I was only going to say that when you leave to-morrow——"

" Am I going to-morrow? "

" Aren't you? "

He put his face in her breast and held her tightly. After a time he looked up and said, resigned, " Well? I am not used to this, you understand, I do not think a woman has decided anything for me since I was a boy."

" But I am not deciding." She kissed him. " You are."

" Very well, it is decided. And what is it you were saying —when I leave? "

" You will see. You are right, I ought to stop talking now. But I still want to remind you," she said, hoping to lift their spirits and bring back light into the dark pools of his eyes, " how much I love my teacher." The word as she had used it before to please him had its own effect.

" Ah, *cara mia*! " he said. " After so much sorrow and tribulation can you possibly be inviting me to make love to you? "

" I can be, but you can be too stupid to understand."

" Eh! " he said, springing up and carrying her across the room. " I will show you some prime stupidity! And to-morrow——"

" To-morrow will not be like to-day."

The plane stood at the far end of the air-strip, waiting its turn to take off. Harriet stood on the observation deck of the airport, a straight figure pencilled sharp by the wind. The weather had cleared, it had been a beautiful day, gusty and blue, and they had spent it as Carlo wished, filling a few hours with the follies he liked best. They went shopping, to buy a gift for her which he insisted must be a fur, while she insisted that there was nothing she needed less. He had his way, she had a sable stole, but there was also a wrap of honey-coloured mink for Pina which Harriet had had brought out and shown him. He looked from the lovely thing on the model to Harriet, who smiled at him and turned away when she saw that his eyes were moist. He bought it without a word of remark. Then they crossed Fifth Avenue to the toy shop on the opposite corner and Carlo went harmlessly mad, buying for Tonino and Lala everything that they could want which he had never seen before.

" But how will you get it all through the Dogana? " Harriet looked at the pile of boxes which were to be sent out ahead to the airport in the car that they had taken for the day.

" *Me ne frega*," he shrugged. " The hell with the Dogana. A man from my office will be there to deal with them."

And so would Pina and the children, to meet him. Because he knew that it would give her peace he told Harriet that he had cabled. They walked down Fifth Avenue, Carlo window-shopping as avidly as the idlest woman; why, she wondered, have Italians got such a passion for doing this in New York?

" Where would you like to lunch? " he asked her.

" What would you like to eat? "

" A cold lobster, a beefsteak, a grapefruit. Those are your country's claims to gastronomic honour, and not so bad, not so bad."

" Frozen, especially. Let's not go to any of the obvious places."

" That is for you to decide."

They went to an excellent steak house full of business men from advertising and newspaper circles. Everything was just as Harriet had hoped; nobody she knew, very good food, a secluded table where they sat for nearly three hours, sometimes talking, sometimes silent, until the time came to leave for the airport. " You have been wonderful, my love," she said. " I think you have never been so wonderful. I love you very much."

" I love those words in your language now. They used to horrify me—until I found out what they can mean. I had never known before."

In the car on the way to Idlewild they sat hand in hand and Carlo gazed at the skyline of New York with the very expression which Harriet had imagined when she was coming in, less than a week ago. She told him about it. " It doesn't seem possible that all this has happened so fast. Do you realise it is only a week ago to-morrow that I left Malpensa?"

" Do you realise that three months ago we scarcely knew each other? "

" How could that be possible! "

" I know. It not only seems like always, but in some sense I feel it really must have been. Do you know when I first felt that; where? "

She nodded slowly, with her eyes on his face. She tried to remember a time when she had not known him, but all she could find in a past before his time was a woman who was wholly a stranger. She has left a few things for me, furniture and some other possessions, and a few memories that are worth keeping; but she was a stranger just the same.

" Do you know where it was? " he asked again.

" In Bergamo," she said. " Of course I felt it too. Something happened there." The recognition of which he had spoken, the difference between this and everything else he had ever known. " I would have loved you very much if we had never gone there. But I might not have remained linked to you in some way that I am, that I shall always be." She saw the hands of his mother, their vivid gesture of fluttering wings. " The extraordinary thing is that this link is not the love that we share, it is something different."

" I know." He lifted her hand to his lips and held it there. He does know, she thought, and it does not matter that he is going because the time for that has come. A sense of vision, broad and clear, had taken possession of her mind, as though a closed portal had slowly opened, to let her pass through, to see beyond a vista complete in time and scope like the ancient roofs and the modern plain spread before the windows of the house in Bergamo.